Critical acclaim for Alan Furst

'For anyone who understands that the best history is both drama and romance, Alan Furst is an addiction'
Peter Millar, *The Times*

'His exquisitely wrought spy thrillers, set in the Thirties and Forties, have set new standards for the genre . . . It is in the characterisation, allied to a sure sense of time and place, that the power of the story resides. The novel captures the extraordinary febrility of the pre-war years, with all Europe holding its breath, waiting for Hitler to make his next move . . . as in other Furst novels, it is the sense of ordinary people having to summon extraordinary courage that gives the writing its power . . . Furst catches that end-of-an-era mood with virtuoso skill'
David Robson, *Sunday Telegraph*

'Alan Furst has produced an espionage thriller which is haunting, elegiac and seductive. It is suffused with forlorn hopes, risktaking and heartbreak. I wanted it to go on and on . . . a masterwork'
Philip Oakes, *Literary Review*

'Readers of Furst's earlier work will understand how admirably the subject suits his particular strengths. The novel is saturated with the topography of Paris, the atmosphere of its restaurants and the mood of its people as they react to the gathering stormclouds of European politics . . . Such fluency with historical detail is rare, and to be prized'
Ian Ousby, *TLS*

'No one can better him at the underplayed, the scaled-down, the descriptive phrase that nails a feeling or an emotion into one's consciousness ... And he does it so effortlessly; like all great writers, he makes his work look easy ... in my estimation, Kingdom of Shadows is a masterpiece. Furst is here writing at the height of his powers, confident in his style, tone and content. And his evocation of that dark time of the soul, before and during the Second World War, reverberates in the mind just as that famous Beethoven symphony call-sign echoed in the airwaves over Europe all those years ago'

Vincent Banville, *Irish Times*

'If you haven't been there, go. In the space of six novels, Alan Furst has recreated in jewelled detail a crepuscular world of romance, intrigue, and melancholy choices. It represents the 1930s spy thriller tradition of Eric Ambler, overlaid with the rueful wisdom of the great story-tellers of Mittel Europa'

Patrick Bishop, *Daily Telegraph*

'Furst's fictional odysseys illuminate the moral ambiguities of shifting allegiances with the clarity of truth. Reading his novels is like unearthing a family secret, known about, but not admitted; shedding light on a rich, if terrifying, landscape that finally makes sense of everything else' Penelope Dening, *Irish Times*

A sophisticated, well written, highly atmospheric tale of adventure and espionage in wartime Europe from one of the best in this genre' *Bookseller*

Alan Furst is widely recognised as the master of the historical spy novel. Born in New York, he has lived for long periods in France, especially Paris. He now lives on Long Island, New York.

By Alan Furst

BLOOD OF
VICTORY

ALAN FURST

PHOENIX

A PHOENIX PAPERBACK

First published in Great Britain in 2002
by Weidenfeld & Nicolson
This paperback edition published in 2003
by Phoenix,
an imprint of Orion Books Ltd,
Orion House, 5 Upper St Martin's Lane,
London WC2H 9EA

A CIP catalogue record for this book
is available from the British Library.

ISBN 0 75284 872 0

Printed and bound in Great Britain by
Clays Ltd, St Ives plc

In 1939, as the armies of Europe mobilized for war, the British secret services undertook operations to impede the exportation of Roumanian oil to Germany. They failed.

Then, in the autumn of 1940, they tried again.

UKRAINIAN
S.S.R.

Kishinev

Odessa

ROMANIA

Brasov

Danube R.

Ploesti

Black
Sea

◎ Bucharest

Constanta

Giurgiu

Danube R.

Ruse

BULGARIA

Southeastern
EUROPE
1940~1941

Edirne

Miles
0 ——————— 100

0 ——————— 100
Km.

TURKEY

Istanbul

© A.Karl/J.Kemp, 2002

A
CALL
TO ARMS

On 24 November, 1940, the first light of dawn found the Bulgarian ore freighter *Svistov* pounding through the Black Sea swells, a long night's journey from Odessa and bound for Istanbul. The writer I. A. Serebin, sleepless as always, left his cabin and stood at the rail, searched the horizon for a sign of the Turkish coast, found only a blood red streak in the eastern sky. Like the old saying, he realized – red sky at morning, sailor take warning. But, a private smile for that. *So many ways,* he thought, *to drown in autumn.* The *Svistov* creaked and groaned, spray burst over the bow as she fought the sea. With cupped hands, Serebin lit a Sobranie cigarette, then watched the dark water churning past the hull until the wind drove him back to the cabin.

As he pulled the door shut, a soft shape stirred beneath the blanket. '*Ah, mon ours,*' she said. *My bear.* A muffled voice, tender, half asleep. 'Are we there?'

'No, not for a long time.'

'Well then . . .' One side of the blanket rose in the air.

Serebin took off his shirt and trousers, then his glasses, slid in beside her and ran an idle finger down the length of her back, over the curve, and beyond. *Smooth as silk,* he thought, *sleek as a seal.* Bad poetry in bed, maybe, but she was, she was.

Marie-Galante. A fancy name. Nobility? It wouldn't shock him if she were. Or not. A slumflower, perhaps. No matter, she was stunning, *glamorous.* Exceptionally plucked, buffed and smoothed. She had come to his cabin, sable coat and bare feet, as she'd promised at dinner. A glance, a low purr of a voice in lovely French,

3

just enough, as her husband, a Vichy diplomat, worked at conversation with the Bulgarian captain and his first officer. So, no surprise, a few minutes after midnight: three taps, pearlescent fingernail on iron door and, when it opened, an eloquent *Bonsoir*.

Serebin stared when the coat came off. The cabin had only a kerosene lantern, hung on a hook in one corner, but the tiny flame was enough. Hair the color of almonds, skin a tone lighter, eyes a shade darker – *caramel*. She acknowledged the stare with a smile – *yes, I am* – turned slowly once around for him, then, for a moment, posed. Serebin was a man who had love affairs, one followed another. It was his fate, he believed, that life smacked him in the head every chance it got, then paid him back in women. Even so, he couldn't stop looking at her. 'It is,' she'd said gently, 'a little cold for this.'

The engines hammered and strained, the overloaded steamship – Ukrainian manganese for Turkish mills – was slow as a snail. A good idea, they thought, lying on their sides, front to back, his hand on her breast, the sea rising and falling beneath them.

Serebin had boarded the *Svistov* at the Roumanian port of Constanta, where it called briefly to take on cargo – a few crates of agricultural machinery cranked slowly up the rusty side of the ship – and a single passenger. The docks were almost deserted, Serebin stood alone, a small valise at his side, waiting patiently in the soft, southern dusk as the gangway was lowered.

Earlier that day there'd been fighting on the waterfront, a band of fascist Iron Guards pursued by an army unit loyal to Antonescu. So said the barman at the dockside tavern. Intense volleys of small arms fire, a few hand grenades, machine guns, then silence. Serebin listened carefully, calculated the distance, ordered a glass of beer, stayed where he was. Safe enough. Serebin was forty-two, this was his fifth war, he considered himself expert in the matter of running, hiding, or not caring.

Later, on his way to the pier, he'd come upon a telegraph office with its windows shattered, a man in uniform flung dead across the threshold of the open door, which bumped against his boot as the evening wind tried to blow it shut. Roumania had just signed the Tripartite Pact with Germany, political assassinations were daily events, civil war on the way, one poor soul had simply got an early start.

Dinner, in the freighter's wardroom, had gone on forever. The diplomat, Labonniere, a dry man with a fair mustache, labored away in university Russian – *the weather, quite changeable in fall.* Or *the tasty Black Sea carp, often baked, but sometimes broiled.* The Bulgarian captain did not make life easy for him. *Yes, very tasty.*

It had been left to Serebin to converse with Madame. Was this on purpose? He wondered. The wife was amusing, had that particular ability, found in Parisian women, to make table talk out of thin air. Serebin listened, spoke when he had to, picked at a plate of boiled food. Still, what could any of them say? Half of France was occupied by Germany, Poland enslaved, London in flames. So, all that aside, the carp. Madame Labonniere wore a cameo on a velvet ribbon at her throat, from time to time she touched it with her fingers.

On a shelf in the wardroom was a green steel radio with a wire mesh speaker at the center shaped like a daisy. It produced the transmissions of a dozen stations, which wandered on and off the air like restless cats. Sometimes a few minutes of news on Soviet dairy production, now and then a string quartet, from somewhere on the continent. Once a shouting politician, in Serbo-Croatian, who disappeared into crackling static, then a station in Turkey, whining string instruments and a throbbing drum. To Serebin, a pleasant anarchy. Nobody owned the air above the sea. Suddenly, the Turkish music vanished, replaced by an American swing band with a woman singer. For a long moment, nobody at the dinner table spoke, then, ghostlike, it faded away into the night.

'Now where did *that* come from?' Marie-Galante said to Serebin.

He had no idea.

'London? Is it possible?'

'A mystery,' Serebin said.

'In Odessa, one never hears such things.'

'In Odessa, one plays records. Do you live there?'

'For the moment, at the French consulate. And you, monsieur? Where do you live?'

'In Paris, since '38.'

'*Quelle chance.*' What luck. For him? Them? 'And before that?'

'I am Russian by birth. From Odessa, as it happens.'

'Really!' She was delighted. 'Then you must know its secrets.'

'A few, maybe. Nobody knows them all.'

She laughed, in a way that meant she liked him. 'Now tell me,' she said, leaning forward, confidential. 'Do you find your present hosts, congenial?'

What was this? Serebin shrugged. 'An occupied city.' He left the rest to her.

7:20. Serebin lay on his back, Marie-Galante dozed beside him. The world winked at the *cinq-à-sept amour,* the twilight love affair, but there was another five-to-seven, the *ante meridiem* version, which Serebin found equally to his taste. In this life, he thought, there is only

6

one thing worth waking up for in the morning, and it isn't getting out of bed and facing the world.

From Marie-Galante a sigh, then a stretch. *Fragrant as melon, warm as toast.* She rolled over, slid a leg across his waist, then sat up, shook her hair back, and wriggled to get comfortable. For a time she gazed down at him, put a hand under his chin, tilted his head one way, then the other. 'You are quite pretty, you know.'

He laughed, made a face.

'No, it's true. What are you?'

'Mixed breed.'

'Oh? Spaniel and hound, perhaps. Is that it?'

'Half Russian aristocrat, half Bolshevik Jew. A dog of our times, apparently. And you?'

'Burgundian, *mon ours,* dark and passionate. We love money and cook everything in butter.' She leaned down and kissed him softly on the forehead, then got out of bed. 'And go home in the morning.'

She gathered up her coat, put it on, held the front closed. 'Are you staying in the city?'

'A week. Maybe ten days. At the Beyoglu, on Istiklal Caddesi.'

She rested her hand on the doorknob. '*Au revoir,* then,' she said. Said it beautifully, sweet, and a little melancholy.

Istanbul. Three-thirty in the afternoon, the violet hour. Serebin stared out the window of a taxi as it rattled along the wharves of the Golden Horn. *The Castle of Indolence.* He'd always thought of it that way – melon rinds with clouds of flies, a thousand cats, rust stains on porphyry columns, strange light, strange shadows in a haze of smoke and dust, a street where blind men sold nightingales.

The *Svistov* had docked an hour earlier, the three passengers stood at the gate of the customs shed and said good-bye. For Serebin, a firm handshake and warm farewell from Labonniere. Sometime in the night he'd asked Marie-Galante if her husband cared what she did. 'An arrangement,' she'd told him. 'We are seen everywhere together, but our private lives are our own affair.' So the world.

So the world – two bulky men in suits lounging against a wall on the pier. Emniyet, he supposed, Turkish secret police. A welcoming committee, of a sort, for the diplomat and his wife, for the Bulgarian captain, and likely for him as well. The Sûreté no doubt having bade him good-bye at the Gare du Nord in Paris, with the SD – Sicherheitsdienst – and the NKVD, the Hungarian VK-VI, and the Roumanian Siguranza observing his progress as he worked his way to the Black Sea.

He was, after all, I. A. Serebin, formerly a decorated Hero of the Soviet Union, Second Class, currently the executive secretary of the International Russian Union, a Paris-based organization for émigrés. The IRU offered meetings, and resolutions – mostly to do with its own bylaws – as much charity as it could manage, a club near the Russian cathedral on the rue Daru, with newspapers on wooden dowels, a chess tournament and a Christmas play, and a small literary magazine, *The Harvest*. In the political spectrum of émigré societies, as mild as anything Russian could ever be. Czarist officers of the White armies had their own organizations, nostalgic Bolsheviks had theirs, the IRU held tight to the mythical center, an ideology of Tolstoy, compassion, and memories of sunsets, and accepted the dues of the inevitable police informers with a sigh and a shrug. Foreigners! God only knew what they might be up to. But it could not, apparently, be only God who knew.

★

8

The Hotel Beyoglu, named for the ancient quarter in which it stood, more or less, was on a busy street, just far enough from the tumultuous Taksim square. Serebin could have easily afforded the Pera Palace but that would have meant people he knew, so he took one of the chill tombs on the top floor of the musty old Beyoglu. Home to commercial travelers and midday lovers, with twelve-foot ceilings, blue walls, the requisite oleograph of Mustafa Kemal, oil-printed in lurid colors, hung high above the bed, and, in the bathroom, a huge zinc tub on three claw feet and a brick.

Serebin undressed, shaved, then ran a bath and lay back in the tepid green water.

There are leaves blowing on the road now,
there are people you don't see now.

Late October in Paris when he'd written that. He'd waited patiently for the rest to appear but it never showed up. Why? Autumn had always been kind to him, but not this year. *It's the city.* Paris had died under the German occupation, the French heartbroken, grieving, silent. In a way, he hated them. What right did they have to it, this soft, twilit despair? Like some rainy image floating up from Verlaine. In Russia they'd gone through nine kinds of hell, got drunk on it and sang their hearts out. Famine, civil war, bandits, purges, the thirty-nine horsemen of the Apocalypse and then you stopped counting.

So, he'd come to Istanbul. Couldn't breathe in Paris, fled to Bucharest, that was worse. Got drunk, wandered into a steamship office. Oh, he had *reasons.* You had to have those. Some IRU business, and a letter from Tamara Petrovna. *Of course I want to see you. One last time, my love. So you can tell me not to think such things.* They'd had two love affairs; at age fifteen, and again at thirty-five. Then Russia had taken her, the way it took people. The letter mentioned money, but he didn't have to come all the way to Istanbul for that, the bank in Geneva would have taken care of that.

The life of Istiklal Caddesi drifted in the open window – braying donkey, twittering birds, a car horn, a street musician playing some kind of reedy clarinet. *Go back to Odessa.* Oh, a fine idea, Ilya Aleksandrovich. *That* would finish his poem. Some of the émigrés tried it, more often than anyone would believe. Off they'd go, deluded, fatalistic, hoping against hope. Their friends would wait for a letter. But, nothing. Always, nothing.

Serebin dried himself off, put on his other shirt, fresh underwear, and socks, then peered at himself in the steel mirror. Lean and dark, average height – maybe a little less, black hair, thick enough so that he could wear it hacked off short by whoever had a scissors – Serebin hated barbers – a muscle in the jaw that sometimes ticked. Tense, restless eyes. Pretty? Maybe to her. 'Clearly,' a lover in Moscow once told him, 'there is something on fire inside you, Ilya. Women know this, dear, they "smell something burning," and they want to put it out. Though there will be one, now and again, who will want to throw oil on it.'

Carefully, he tied his tie, took it off, threw it on the bed. Left the top button closed, looked like a Greek communist, undid the button, let it go at that. *Poetic license.* Put on his brown tweed jacket. Made in London, it endured, withstood restaurant adventures and nights in railway stations, would surely, he thought, outlive him.

His other side was not to be seen in the mirror. His grandfather, the Count Alexander Serebin, had died in a duel in a St. Petersburg park in 1881. Over a ballerina, the story went. Serebin unbuttoned a second button and spread the vee of his shirt. *Now you look like a Lebanese raisin salesman.* That made him laugh – a different man!

He fixed the shirt, left his hat and trench coat in the armoire, and went downstairs to find a taxi.

In front of the hotel, the same driver who'd brought him to the Beyoglu was busy with a rag, polishing the dents and gashes in his old Fiat taxi. 'Effendi!' he cried out, delighted at the coincidence, and opened the rear door with a flourish. Obviously he'd waited at the hotel for Serebin to reappear; a commercial instinct, or something he'd been paid to do. Or told to do. *So the world.* Serebin showed him an address on a piece of paper and climbed in.

The house he'd bought for Tamara was in Besiktas, a summer resort just north of the city. It was after five when Serebin's taxi crawled through the old village, the muezzin's call to evening prayer sharp in the chill air, long red streaks in the sky above the domes and minarets, as though the sun were dying instead of setting.

The driver found the address easily enough, an ancient wooden summer house, a *yali,* painted yellow, with green shutters, on a cliff above the Bosphorus. Tamara was waiting for him in the little garden that looked out over the water. Instinctively he moved to embrace her, but she caught his hands and held him away. 'Oh I am so happy to see you,' she said, eyes shining with tears of sorrow and pleasure.

His first love, maybe the love of his life – sometimes he believed that. She was very pale now, which made her jade eyes bright in a hard face, the face of the bad girl in an American gangster movie. Her straw-colored hair looked thin, and she wore it shorter than he remembered, pinned back with a pink barrette. *To give her color.* She had dressed so carefully for him. There was a vase stuffed with anemones on the garden table, and the stone terrace had been swept clean.

'I stopped at the Russian store,' he said, handing her a box wrapped in colored paper.

She opened it carefully, taking a long time, then lifted the lid to reveal rows of sugared plums. 'From Balabukhi,' he said. The famous candy maker of Kiev.

'You will share,' she said firmly.

He pretended to hunt for one that especially appealed to him, found it, and took a bite. 'Also this,' he said. A bag of dry cookies with almonds. 'And these.' Two bracelets of ribbon gold, from a jewelry store near the hotel. She put them on and turned her wrist one way, then the other, so that the gold caught the light.

'You like them? Do they fit?'

'Yes, of course, they're beautiful.' She smiled and shook her head in feigned exasperation – *what is to be done with you?*

They sat together on a bench and looked out over the water. 'Forgive me,' he said, 'but I must ask you how you are.'

'Better.'

'All better.'

'Much better. Good, really. But, you know, the *chahotka*.' Wasting away, it meant, the Russian word for tuberculosis.

In 1919, during the fighting between Bolshevik and Czarist forces, she had served as a nurse in a Red Army medical unit and treated the sick and dying villagers in the shtetls of Byelorussia. She had not been ordered to do this, she had done it on her own. There was no medicine for the illness, all she had was a pail of heated water and a cloth. But, cold and wet, exhausted from advancing, retreating, working day and night, she persisted, did what others feared to do, and the *chahotka* came for her. She spent eight months in bed, thought the illness was gone, and went on with her life. But in the bad winter of 1938, it returned, and Serebin had arranged her departure from Russia and installed her in the house in Besiktas.

'You see the doctors,' he said.

'Oh yes. Spending money like water.'

'I have money, Tamara.'

'Well, I spend it. I rest till I can't stand it anymore, eat cream like a cat – your ladies don't leave me alone for a minute.' He had found two sisters, Ukrainian émigrés, to live in the house and care for her. 'Are you happy in Paris?' she said. 'Very adored, I suspect.'

He laughed. 'Tolerated, anyhow.'

'Oh yes. Tolerated every night – I *know* you, Ilya.'

'Well, it's different now. And Paris isn't the same.'

'The Germans leave you alone?'

'So far. I am their ally, according to the present arrangements, the Hitler–Stalin treaty, and a literary celebrity, in a small way. For the moment, they don't bother me.'

'You know them?'

'Two or three. Officers, simply military men assigned to a foreign posting, that's how they see it. We have the city in common, and they are very cultured. So, we can have conversation. Always careful, of course, correct, no politics.'

She pretended to shiver. 'You won't stay.'

He nodded, she was probably right.

'But then, perhaps you are in love.'

'With you.'

Her face lit up, even though she knew it wasn't true. Or, maybe, only a little true. 'Forgive him, God, he tells lies.'

Fifteen years old, in empty apartments, on deserted beaches, they had fucked and fucked and slept tangled up together. Long summer evenings in Odessa, warm and humid, dry lightning over the sea.

'And do you walk?' he said.

She sighed. 'Yes, yes, I do what I must. Every day for an hour.'

'To the museum? To see our friend?'

She laughed at that, a loud, raucous caw. When she'd first come to Istanbul they had visited the neighborhood attraction, a naval museum. Exquisitely boring, but home to a twenty-three-ton cannon built for an Ottoman sultan called Selim the Grim. A painting of him hung above the monster gun. His name, and the way he looked in the painting, had tickled her wildly, though the laughing fit had produced a bright fleck of blood on her lip.

One of the Ukrainian ladies stood at the door to the terrace and cleared her throat. 'It is five-thirty, Tamara Petrovna.'

Serebin rose and greeted her formally – he knew both sisters' names but wasn't sure which was which. She responded to the greeting, calling him *gospodin,* sir, the genteel form of address that had preceded *comrade,* and set a tray down on the table, two bowls and a pair of soup spoons. Then she lit an oil lamp.

The bowls were heaped with trembling rice pudding, a magnificent treat for Serebin when he was a child. But not now. Tamara ate hers dutifully and slowly, and so did Serebin. Out on the Bosphorus, an oil tanker flying the swastika flag worked its way north, smoke rising from its funnel.

When they finished the pudding, she showed him where the roof tiles had cracked and come loose, though he could barely see them in the failing light. 'That's why I wrote to you,' she said. 'They must be repaired, or water will come in the house. So we asked in the market, and a man came and climbed up there. He will fix it, but he says the whole roof must be replaced. The tiles are very old.'

Is that why you wrote? But he didn't say it. Instead,

standing at the dark corner of the house, waves breaking at the foot of the bluff, he asked her why she'd said *one last time*.

'I wanted to see you again,' she said. 'That day I feared, I don't know what. Something. Maybe I would die. Or you.'

He put a hand on her shoulder and, just for a moment, she leaned against him. 'Well,' he said. 'As we seem to be alive, today anyhow, we might as well replace the roof.'

'Perhaps it is the salt in the air.' Her voice was soft.

'Yes. Bad for the tile.'

'It's getting cold, maybe we should go inside.'

They talked for an hour, then he left. The taxi was waiting in front of the house, as Serebin knew it would be, and on the way back to the hotel he had the driver wait while he bought a bottle of Turkish vodka at a café.

A practical man, the driver, who had contrived to learn a few crucial words for his foreign passengers. When Serebin returned from the café he said, 'Bordello, effendi?'

Serebin shook his head. The man had watched him, in the rearview mirror, as he'd rubbed his eyes with the sleeve of his jacket. Well, the driver thought, I know the cure for that.

No, no cure. She had that damn photograph on her dresser, cut from a newspaper and framed, amid sepia portraits of her mother and grandmother, and snapshots of her Polish lieutenant, who'd disappeared in '39, and her dog Blunka, descendant of every hound that roamed the alleys of Odessa. She showed Serebin the small room where she slept, and there was the famous photograph.

Taken at a railway station captured from Denikin's cossacks on a grainy April morning. A gray photograph; the station building pocked with gunfire, one side of the roof reduced to blackened timbers. The young officer Serebin, looking very concentrated, with two days' growth of beard, wears a leather jacket and a uniform cap, the open jacket revealing a Nagant revolver in a shoulder holster. One hand holds a submachine gun, its leather sling hanging down, the other, bandaged with a rag, points as he deploys his company. *Bolshevik intellectual at war.* You could smell the cordite. The photograph had been taken by the renowned Kalkevich, who'd chronicled young dancers, backstage at the Bolshoi, for *Life* magazine. So it was very good, 'Bryansk Railway Station: 1920.' Was reproduced in French and British newspapers, appeared in Kalkevich's New York retrospective.

'We remember your photograph, Ilya Aleksandrovich.' Stalin said that, in the summer of 1938, when Serebin, certain that he was headed to the Lubyanka, was picked up by two chekists in a black Zil and whisked off to the Kremlin at midnight.

To be praised, it turned out, for the publication of *Ulskaya Street,* and to eat salted herring and drink Armenian champagne. He could barely get it down, could still taste it, warm and sweet. Beria was in the room, and, worse, General Poskrebyshev, the chief of Stalin's secretariat, who had the eyes of a reptile. The movie that night – he'd heard they watched one every night – was Laurel and Hardy in *Babes in Toyland*. Stalin laughed so hard that tears ran down his face. As the torch-bearing hobgoblins marched, singing, out of Bo-Peep's shoe.

Serebin went home at dawn, and left Russia a month later.

And when the writer Babel was taken away, in May of '39, knew in his heart that his name had been on the same list. Knew it because, at a certain point in the evening, Poskrebyshev looked at him.

★

Back at the hotel, the night clerk handed him an envelope. He took it up to his room, had a taste of the vodka, then another, before he opened it. On cream-colored paper, a note. A scented note, he discovered. And not only did he recognize the scent, he even knew its name, Shalimar. He knew this because he'd asked, the night before, and he'd asked because, everywhere he went, there it was, waiting for him. *'Mon ours,'* she wrote. Friends for drinks, at the yacht club, slip twenty-one, seven-thirty. She would be so pleased, so delighted, if he could join them.

A cloudy morning in Istanbul. From Serebin's window, the Bosphorus was gray as the sky. The room service waiter was long departed, and Serebin had become aware that Turkish coffee was only a partial ameliorant for Turkish vodka – a minor lapse in the national chemistry – and had to be supplemented with German aspirin. The fat slice of pink watermelon was an affront and he ignored it.

In Constanta, waiting eight days for the Bulgarian steamship to make port, he'd wired the IRU office in Istanbul and let them know he was coming. Life as an executive secretary had its particular demands; Serebin had learned this the hard way, which was pretty much the way he learned everything. As a writer, he'd been a free spirit, showed up where and when he liked, or didn't show up at all. *A visit from the muse* – or so people wanted to believe, a permanent excuse. But, as an administrator, you had to announce yourself, because a surprise visit implied inspection, you were trying to catch them at it, whatever *it* was. The last thing Serebin ever wanted, to catch anybody at anything.

10:20 – time to go. He made sure to take his briefcase – emblem of office – though there was hardly anything in it. No matter, they were sure to give him paper enough to fill it up. He only then realized, too late, that he had no paper to give them. He went downstairs to the lobby, started toward the main entrance, then changed his mind and left by the back door. Hurried down a side street and out onto the avenue, then put ten minutes of distance between himself and the Beyoglu. *Forgive me, my friend, I do not mean to cause you difficulties.* Truly, he didn't know why he'd evaded the driver. Nameless instinct, he told himself, let it go at that, stepped into the street and hailed a taxi.

In heavy traffic, they crept across the Golden Horn on the Galata Bridge to the old Jewish district of Haskoy. This was only the most recent address of the IRU office. It had moved here and there since its founding, in 1931, as had the offices in Belgrade, Berlin, and Prague, finding its way to Rasim street a year earlier, across from the loading yard of a tannery.

They were now in two comfortably large rooms on the second floor, at one time the office of the émigré Goldbark, who'd become rich as an exporter of tobacco and hazelnuts and was now one of the directors, and chief financial supporter, of the International Russian Union: Istanbul chapter. The building itself was ancient and swelled alarmingly as it rose, leaning out over a cobblestone lane.

At the top of the staircase, a sign on the door in Cyrillic, and one in Roman letters. Inside, magnificent chaos, Russian chaos. A steamy room with a radio playing and two women seated at clacketing typewriters. Two old men with long white beards were working at a bridge table, addressing envelopes with nib pens and inkwells. On one wall, drawings from the Russian kindergarten, mostly trains. Flanked by Pushkin in profile, and Chekhov in a wicker chair in the yard of a country house. A dense oil painting of the Grand

18

Bazaar, in vibrant colors. A brown and black daguerreotype of a steppe.

On the adjacent wall, a mimeographed schedule for the month of November, which Serebin, for the moment left alone, felt he might as well read. A lecture about wool, a meeting of the stamp club, Turkish lessons, English lessons, meeting for new members – please sign up, memorial service for Shulsky, and a film, *Surprising Ottawa,* to be shown in the basement of the Saint Stanislaus church. Tacked up beside the schedule, underlined clippings, news of the Russian community cut from the IRU Istanbul's weekly newspaper.

'Serebin!' Kubalsky, the office manager, hugged him and laughed. 'Don't tell anybody you're here!'

Kubalsky took him around the office, introduced him to a bewildering assortment of people, sat him down at a table, pushed aside stacks of newspapers and files, and poured him a glass of tea from an ornate copper samovar.

'Life's being good to you?' Serebin said, offering Kubalsky a Sobranie.

'Not too bad.' Kubalsky had a long, narrow face and deep-set eyes that glittered like black diamonds. Twice, in Berlin, he'd been beaten up as a Jew, which made him laugh, through split lips, because his grandfather had been a Russian Orthodox priest.

Serebin blew on his tea. Kubalsky, prepared for the worst, drummed his fingers on the table. 'So, what brings you to Istanbul?'

'Truth?'

'Why not?'

'I had to get away from Paris.'

'Oh. Claustrophobia.'

Serebin nodded.

'Have you seen Goldbark?'

'Not yet. How is he?'

19

'Crazy as a bedbug. Says he lies awake all night, worrying about money.'

'Him?'

'"I make a fortune," he says. "Where is it? Where is it?"'

'Where is it?'

Kubalsky shrugged. 'Thank God for the wife, otherwise he'd make us all crazy.' He tapped cigarette ash into a cracked cup used as an ashtray. 'The real problem here, of course, is the politics.'

Serebin agreed.

'It's a zoo. The city's crawling with spies – Nazis, Hungarians, Zionists, Greeks. The German ambassador, von Papen, is in the papers every day, but so are the British. The Turks are scared. Hitler went through the Balkans like shit through an eel. Now he's got Bulgaria – maybe he stops there, maybe he doesn't. The Turks are neutral, officially, but, so far, they're neutral on our side. Still it's difficult to navigate. That old business about the Middle East – to walk across a square you have to make three moves.'

'What if they sign on with Germany?'

'We run. Again.'

Serge Kubalsky knew all about that. In 1917, he'd been a successful 'boulevard journalist' for one of the St. Petersburg newspapers that lived on gossip and innuendo. Then came revolution, and the husband of the woman he was sleeping with that week rose, overnight, from clerk to commissar. Kubalsky got away with eighty roubles and a canary. Settled in Berlin but couldn't tolerate the Nazis, so he went to Madrid in 1933. The Republican secret service booted him out in '36, he went to Lisbon, was hounded by Salazar's thugs and left in '37. Tried Switzerland – sorry, no residence card. Sofia the following autumn, wrote the wrong thing about the king, so off to Amsterdam, sneaking in the back door just about the time the Wehrmacht was breaking down the front. 'I no longer,' he once told Serebin, 'speak any language whatsoever.'

An old woman with a cane came over to the table, kissed Kubalsky on both cheeks, then disappeared into the other room. Kubalsky finished his cigarette and stood up. 'Well,' he said, 'you'd better take a look at the finances.' He went to a file cabinet and returned carrying a ledger filled with spidery bookkeeping.

Serebin ran his finger down the expense column. *Ah, Sanskrit.* But he worked at it, found the stamps, the ink and paper and envelopes, the lifeblood, then came upon an entry for *rent.* 'What's this?' he said.

'Rental of office space.'

'I thought Goldbark gave us this place.'

'He does. But we pay the rent and he donates the money. It helps him with his taxes, he says. Turks are old-fashioned about taxes. The strangling cord may be out of style, but the point of view hasn't changed.'

The following pages were given over to loans and gifts, it went on and on, small amounts, the names not only Russian but Ukrainian and Jewish, Greek and Tatar, many others, a history of migration, a history of flight.

'So many,' Serebin said, subdued.

'People wounded in the war. Sick. Drunk. Or just broken. We come from a brutal place, Ilya. The list would double, if we had the money.'

Serebin knew. In Paris, he gave more than he could afford.

'What we try to do,' Kubalsky said, 'is to help the Russian community as a whole. The Turks are basically fair-minded people, cosmopolitan. Hospitality to strangers is a religion with them. That's what Kemal was all about. He outlawed the fez, changed the alphabet, kept Islam out of government. Everybody had to have a last name – they had lists of suggestions nailed up in the public squares. Still, foreigners are foreigners, and Russia and Turkey have always fought wars. So, the community is suspected of harboring Stalinist agents, the NKVD is active here, and every time some plot blows up and hits the newspapers, we all get blamed. Old story, right?'

Kubalsky sighed. Why did life have to go like this? 'Christ,' he said, 'you have to live somewhere.'

The yacht club was in the village of Bebek, just north of the city, where Istanbul's wealthiest citizens had summer homes. Serebin, with Marie-Galante's note in his pocket, visited a bar by the ferry dock in Eminonu, thought about not going, then decided he might as well. It had been a long, long day in the world of the International Russian Union. He had left Kubalsky to have lunch with Goldbark, followed by a visit to the eighty-five-year-old General de Kossevoy, in a tiny room so hot it made him sweat, and by the end of the afternoon he'd had all the émigré business he could bear. He stood at the rail of the crowded ferry, watching the caiques and the feluccas sliding through the water, the oil lamps on their sterns like fireflies in the darkness.

He found the yacht at slip twenty-one. Sixty feet of teak and polished brass. *La Néréide – Tangier* was painted in gold script on the stern and two crewmen, in green uniforms with the yacht's name on the bands of their sailor hats, waited at the gangplank. He wondered about the nationality of the *Néréide,* sea nymph, but Tangier, in the Vichy French colony of Morocco, could have meant anything, and he knew, from talk on the docks of Odessa, that some yachts never called at their home ports. *A flag of convenience* – the legal words better, for a change, than poetry.

One of the sailors led him onboard, down a corridor, and into the salon. *The 16th Arrondissement.* At least that, Serebin thought. Black lacquer tables, white rattan furniture. The cushions had red tulips on a pale red background, there was lemon-colored Chinese paper on the walls. People everywhere, a mob, chattering and yammering in a dense fog of cigarette smoke and perfume.

The aristocrat who hurried toward him – he could be nothing else – wore blazer and slacks. Trim body, sleek good looks, ears tight to the head, graying hair combed back and shining with brilliantine. The Duke of Windsor, as played by Fred Astaire. 'Welcome, welcome.' An iron grip. 'We're honored, really, to have you here. It must be Serebin, no? The writer? God I thought you'd be, older.' The language French, the voice low and completely at ease. 'I am Della Corvo,' he said. 'But Cosimo to you, of course, right?'

Serebin nodded and tried to look amiable, was a little more impressed by the whole thing than he wanted to be. His life drifted high and low, but up here he found the air a trifle thin.

'Marie-Galante!' Della Corvo called out. Then, to Serebin: 'A Bulgarian freighter. Extraordinary.'

Marie-Galante broke through the edge of the crowd, a drink in each hand, a cigarette held between her lips. 'You're here!' His stunning caramel. Little black dress and pearls. She raised her face for *bisoux* and Serebin kissed each cheek in a cloud of Shalimar.

'We're having Negronis,' she said, handing Serebin a glass.

Campari and gin, Serebin knew, and lethal.

'You'll take him around?' Della Corvo said.

Marie-Galante slipped a hand under his arm and held him lightly.

'We must talk,' Della Corvo said to Serebin. 'All this . . .' A charming shrug and a smile – he'd invited all these *people,* now, here they were. Then he disappeared into the crowd.

'Shall we?' she said.

The *beau monde* of émigré Istanbul. Like a giant broom, the war had swept them all to the far edge of Europe.

'Do you know Stanislaus Mut? The Polish sculptor?'

Mut was tall and gray and irritated. 'So nice to see you.' *How about I choke you to death with my bare hands?*

Why?

Marie-Galante introduced him to the woman at Mut's side. *Oh, now I see.* Mut had found himself a Russian countess. Anemic, a blue vein prominent at her temple, but sparkling with diamonds. She extended a damp hand, which Serebin brushed with his lips while waiting to be throttled.

As they escaped, Marie-Galante laughed and squeezed his arm. 'Does romance blossom?'

'I think it's glass.'

A short, dark man spread his arms in welcome.

'Aristophanes!'

'My goddess!'

'Allow me to introduce Ilya Serebin.'

'Kharros. Pleased to make your gububble.'

'I often read about your ships, monsieur. In the news-papers.'

'All lies, monsieur.'

A tall woman with white hair backed into Serebin, a red wave of Negroni burst over the rim of his glass and splashed on his shoe.

'Oh pardon!'

'It's nothing.'

'Better drink that, *ours.*'

'What in God's name did that man say?'

'Poor Kharros. He's taking French lessons.'

'From *who?*'

She laughed. 'A mad language teacher!' Laughed again. 'How would you know?'

Monsieur Palatny, the Ukrainian timber merchant.

Madame Carenne, the French fashion designer.

Mademoiselle Stevic, the Czech coal heiress.

Monsieur Hooryckx, the Belgian soap manufacturer.

Madame Voyschinkowsky, wife of the Lion of the Bourse.

Doktor Rheinhardt, the professor of Germanic language and literature. Here there was conversation. Rheinhardt had come to Istanbul, Marie-Galante explained, in the mid-'30s migration of German intellectuals – doctors, lawyers, artists, and professors, many of whom, like Doktor Rheinhardt, now taught at Istanbul University.

'Serebin, Serebin,' Rheinhardt said. 'Have you perhaps written about Odessa?'

'A few years ago, yes.'

'The truth is, I haven't read your work, but a friend of mine has spoken of you.'

'What subject do you teach?'

'Well, German language, for undergraduates. And some of the early literatures – Old Norse, Old Frisian – when they offer them. But my real work is in Gothic.'

'He is the leading authority,' Marie-Galante said.

'You are too kind. By the way, Monsieur Serebin, did you know that the last time anyone actually heard spoken Gothic it was not far from Odessa?'

'Really?'

'Yes, in 1854, during the Crimean War. A young officer in the British army – a graduate of Cambridge, I believe – led a patrol deep into the countryside. It was late at night, and very deserted. They heard the sound of chanting, and approached a group of men seated around a campfire. The officer, who'd taken his degree in philology, happened to recognize what he'd heard – the war chant of the Goths. It went something like this . . .'

In a singsong voice, in the deepest bass register he could manage, he intoned what sounded like epic poetry, slicing the air with his hand at the end of each line. A woman with an ivory cigarette holder turned and glanced at him over her shoulder.

'Oh, *formidable!*' Marie-Galante said.

From Doktor Rheinhardt, a brief, graceful bow.

Serebin finished his drink, went to the bar for another. Where he met Marrano, a courtly Spaniard from Barcelona, and a nameless woman who smiled.

> *Then there was a man, who was wearing a sash,*
> *and a woman in a black feather hat.*

Finally, at last and inevitably, he thought, an old friend. The poet Levich, from Moscow, who'd gotten out of Russia just as the *Yezhovshchina* purge of '38 was gathering momentum. The two men stared at each other for a moment, then embraced, astonished to discover a lost friend at the Istanbul yacht club.

'You know Babel was taken,' Levich said.

'Yes, I heard that, in Paris.'

'You're still there?'

'For the moment.'

'We may go to Brazil.'

'You all got out?'

'Thank God.'

'Why Brazil?'

'Who knows. Another place, maybe better than here.'

'You think so?'

'Only one way to find out.'

All around them, people began to say good night. 'We have to meet, Ilya Aleksandrovich.' Levich wrote an address on a slip of paper and went off to find his coat. Serebin turned to Marie-Galante and thanked her for inviting him.

'No, no,' she told him, clearly alarmed. 'There is dinner to come. Just a few of us. You can't possibly leave.'

'I'm expected elsewhere,' he lied.

'Have a headache. *Please.* We are looking forward to it.'

'Well . . .'

She put a hand on his arm, her eyes were wide. '*Mon ours,* don't leave. Please.'

Eight for dinner. In the small salon. Apricot-colored wallpaper here, a celadon bowl with dried flowers as the centerpiece. There was mullet with olive oil, lamb with yoghurt, braised endive, red wine. 'You sit next to me,' Madame Della Corvo said.

Serebin liked her immediately; serious, very stylish and *chic,* with a short, dramatic haircut, fine features, no makeup. She dressed simply, a loose, cherry red shirt, and wore only a wedding ring for jewelry. 'My friends call me Anna,' she told him. Della Corvo sat at the head of the table, flanked by Labonniere and Marie-Galante. Then Marrano and his companion, a Danish woman called Enid, lean and weathered, as though she'd spent her life on sailboats. And, across from Serebin, a man he didn't remember seeing at the cocktail party.

Introduced as André Bastien but, from his accent, not French by birth. He'd probably grown up, Serebin guessed, somewhere in central Europe. He was a large, heavy man with thick, white hair, courtly, reserved, with a certain gravity about him, a cold intelligence, that told in his eyes and in the way he carried himself. You would want to know who he was, but you would not find out – so Serebin put it to himself.

Social conversation, at first. The complex marital situation of the Bebek shoemaker. A woman character in classical Turkish theatre whose name turned out to mean *stupefied with desire.* Then Marie-Galante mentioned that Serebin had found a long-lost friend and Serebin had to tell Levich stories. How they worked together, in their twenties, for *Gudok,* Train Whistle, the official organ of the Railway Administration, then for *Na Vakhtie* – On Watch – Odessa's maritime journal, where they took letters to the editor, particularly the ones that quivered with righteous indignation, and turned them into short stories, which they ran on the back page. And how, a few years later, Levich was thrown out a second story window in the House of Writers – he'd been feuding with the Association of Proletarian Authors. 'It took three of them to do it,' Serebin said, 'and they were big writers.'

'Good God!' and 'How dreadful!' and 'Was he injured?' Nobody at the table thought it was funny.

'He landed in the snow,' Serebin said.

'Russia is really like that,' Marie-Galante said.

'Even so,' Enid said, 'they've taught the peasant children to read.'

'That's true,' Serebin said. 'And they have also taught them to inform on their parents.'

'There is a last piece of fish,' Madame Della Corvo said. 'André, give me your plate.'

'Stalin is a beast,' Marrano said. 'And he's turned the country into a prison. But they are the only counterweight to Hitler.'

'Were, you mean,' Della Corvo said. 'Until the pact.'

'That won't last,' Marrano said. Serebin, watching him in candlelight, thought he looked like a Renaissance assassin. A thin line of beard traced the edge of his jaw from one sideburn to the other, rising to a sharp point at the chin.

'Is that your view, Ilya?' Della Corvo asked.

Serebin shrugged. 'Two gangsters, one neighborhood, they fight.'

Anna Della Corvo met his eyes. 'The end of Europe, then.'

'And where,' Marrano said, 'will you be when it comes to that?'

'Wherever the war isn't.'

'Oh yes?' Marie-Galante said.

Serebin persisted. 'I've seen too many people shot.'

'In battle?' Marrano said.

'Afterwards.'

Across from him, the man called Bastien smiled. *So have I. So what?*

Serebin started to tell him, but Enid said, 'There *is* no place to go, monsieur.' She set a small beaded evening bag on the table and hunted through it until she found a cigarette. Marrano took a lighter from his pocket and lit it for her. She exhaled smoke and said, 'Nowhere.'

Della Corvo laughed as he picked up the wine bottle and walked around the table, refilling everyone's glass, touching each of them, his manner affectionate and teasing. 'Oh, have a little more. 'Live today,' you know, et cetera, et cetera.'

Anna Della Corvo leaned toward Serebin and said, for him and not for the others, 'Please understand, we are all exiles here.'

'Do you know,' Della Corvo said as he returned to his chair, 'that I am a great admirer of *La Torre Argèntea?*'

What the hell was that?

'You're surprised. Not your personal favorite, perhaps.'

Oh Jesus he meant *The Silver Tower*. Serebin's first book, which he'd obviously read in the Italian edition. 'Well,' Serebin said, pretending that he'd been thinking it over. He then realized that given the pause for speculation, he was obliged to say something meaningful. 'I was twenty-eight.'

'Should that matter?' Della Corvo raised an eyebrow as he said it, would, in a minute, have the whole pack of them howling at his heels. *In a midnight blizzard, wolves chase the troika.*

'It's only that I might have done those stories better, ten years later.'

'What would be different? You don't mind my asking, do you?'

'No, no, it's fine. I suppose, now, I might call it *Kovalevsky's Tower*. Silver was how it looked in the heat of summer, but a man named Kovalevsky built it.' He paused a moment, then explained. 'A stone tower on a cliff above the Black Sea, near Odessa.'

'Why?'

'Did he build it?'

'Yes.'

'He had no reason. Or, his reason was, *I want to build a stone tower*. And we used to say, "It's a landmark for people lost at sea." Which it was, for sailors, but we meant a little more than that. Maybe. I don't know.'

Anna Della Corvo laughed. 'My love,' she said to her husband, and at that moment she utterly adored him, 'people don't know why they do things.'

'Sometimes in books,' Serebin said, laughing along with her.

Madame Della Corvo rang a crystal bell and a waiter appeared with bowls of fruit on a silver tray. There was another bottle of wine, and another.

Green bottles with no label. 'It's Médoc,' she explained, 'from a *cru classé* estate. We buy it from a ship's chandler in Sète.'

Were they often in France?

'Oh, now and then. Not recently.'

Obliquity – the base element of life in a police state, learn it or die. Serebin had learned it in the Russian school. 'So then, are you going back to Italy?'

'Well, we could.'

Was the *Néréide,* he wondered, a kind of Flying Dutchman, doomed to wander the seas, from neutral port to neutral port, for a fascist eternity?

Meanwhile, at the other end of the table, more of the same. 'I certainly considered resigning,' Labonniere said. 'But then, what?'

'A life in opposition,' Enid said. A silence, rather a long one. Then she said, 'In London, with de Gaulle.'

It was Marie-Galante who answered, choked-back tears of anger in her voice. 'De Gaulle hates him,' she said. '*Hates* him.'

Labonniere cleared his throat. 'We do what we can.'

'What can any of us do?' Della Corvo defended his friend.

Enid retreated. 'I don't know,' she said quietly. 'I finally heard from my sister, in Copenhagen. It's the first time since the occupation – just the fact of a postcard getting through felt like a great victory.'

'What did she say?' Madame Della Corvo asked.

'On the card, she wrote that I need not worry about her, the Danes are treated with respect by their German allies. Between the lines she's miserable, but Denmark will never die.'

'Between the lines?'

'Yes. Someone told me to check, and there it was. Invisible writing.'

'Secret ink?' Della Corvo asked. At least three people at the table glanced at Bastien.

Enid hesitated, then answered. 'Weewee.'

Hilarity. 'How did you . . . ?'

'Well, with a hot iron, there was a certain, oh, you know.'

Marrano didn't think it was funny. 'You could use plain water,' he said.

Marie-Galante started to laugh. 'Oh but really, why *would* you?'

Two in the morning. Serebin waited on the pier at the foot of the gangway. It was immensely quiet, the water shining like metal in the light of a quarter moon. Serebin had mentioned going back on a ferry, but Anna Della Corvo wouldn't hear of it. 'You mustn't. André

31

came in a motor launch, he'll have you dropped off at a dock near your hotel.'

Serebin heard the rumble of an engine, the launch appeared a moment later. He sat in the stern next to Bastien. A million stars above, the air cool and damp, to be out in the night the only cure for a dinner party.

Bastien lit a cigar. 'Will you stay in Istanbul?'

'Forever, you mean.'

'Yes.'

'No, I'll go back.'

'And stay out of trouble?'

'So far, the French do nothing.'

'It will come.'

'Perhaps.'

'Difficult, that sort of decision.'

'For you also, no?'

'Oh yes, like everybody else.'

They were silent, after that. Sometime later the launch slowed, and pulled in to a dock in the Beyoglu district. Bastien took a card from his wallet. Serebin read it in the moonlight, a trading company, with offices in Istanbul, then put it in his pocket.

'When you're ready,' Bastien said.

In Haskoy, 3:20 on a rainy afternoon. Serebin watched the drops run down the grimy windows of the IRU office, a glass of pink lemonade in his hand. The larger of the two rooms was set up like a theatre – desks shoved against the wall, chairs side by side. On stage: Goldbark, General de Kossevoy, and the guest of honor, I. A. Serebin.

So far, nothing had gone right. Goldbark, hair standing out from the sides of his head, ran around like a harassed waiter. Kubalsky had not returned from wherever he'd gone, nobody could find the *Welcome!* banner, there was a commotion out on Rasim street that began with a beaten donkey and ended with shouted insults, and poor old Madame Ivanova dropped a tray of glasses and had to be consoled.

'My God' – Goldbark shook his head in slow anguish – 'why are we like this?'

'Just enjoy it,' Serebin said. 'It's a *party*.'

True enough: frosted cake, lemonade, loud talk, laughter, two or three arguments, a hot, smoky room, a sad autumn day. 'Like home, Chaim Davidovich. What can be so bad?'

General de Kossevoy clapped his hands, pleaded for their kind attention, and eventually got everybody to shut up and sit down. He then introduced Goldbark, who rose graciously to speak just as a Turkish porter pounded on the door and hauled in a donation from Mahmoudov's grocery – a crate of fat, shiny aubergines. Goldbark closed his eyes, took a deep breath – at some point this afternoon the imps of misfortune were going to leave him alone. 'Very well, then. Today it is my pleasure to welcome . . .' Applause. 'And now, Lidia Markova, one of our many prize-winning students, will read a selection from the work of our dear guest.'

She was twelve, Lidia Markova, and very plain, wearing a white blouse starched within an inch of its life and a navy skirt that hung below her knees. She stood with shoes precisely together, adjusted her red-framed eyeglasses, and patted her hair into place. Serebin could only offer a silent prayer – *please God let nothing embarrassing happen to her.* In a tiny voice, she announced the name of the story, then began to read. '"In Odessa . . ."'

'What?'

'Speak up, child.'

'Sorry. "*In Odessa* . . ."'

'That's better.'

'Not too fast, now.'

Goldbark turned pink.

'"In Odessa, even the alleys are crooked. They are very narrow, you can touch the walls of the houses by spreading your arms, and they never go east and west. In Odessa, all the alleys run to the sea."'

A good choice, he thought. The first story from the collection *Ulskaya Street,* called 'The Cats and the Dogs.' Who had, in the alleys of the city, somehow contrived a truce, an *entente,* going about canine and feline business and essentially ignoring each other. Until, one summer day, a Dutch sea captain had rented a small house near the port and introduced a pampered and mean-spirited cocker spaniel into the neighborhood. It was a good story, people said, about tribes and war and peace, gingerly political, a fable to offend nobody, which was pretty much what you could write in Russia that year.

'"Well, the devil take them all, that's what I say!"' Lidia Markova did the voice of Futterman the umbrella salesman in a gruff baritone. '"They kept me up half the night!"'

Oh how she'd worked at this. Serebin felt it in the heart and, when Tamara Petrovna's tattered old hound wandered through the story, felt it even more. At the end – it turns out the captain's dog had belonged to his wife, who had died suddenly. 'What could I do?' he says, then sails off to Batumi, never to be heard of again – at the end there was enthusiastic applause and somebody said 'Bravo.' Serebin was very gracious as he thanked the girl, taking off his glasses as he did it. For a moment, when he'd finished, Goldbark rested a hand on his shoulder. It couldn't be put in words, but they had in common this army of the lost and forgotten, had somehow become its officers, and led as best they could.

The crowd flowed around him, compliments and questions, a misspelled word in a long-forgotten article called to his attention, a question about a book someone else had written, a question about the screenplay for the sequel to *Chapayev*, the famous machine gunner in the tower who fought the White army.

'A telephone call, Ilya Aleksandrovich.'

As he worked his way over to the desk with the telephone on it, he saw that the cake was gone, some of it no doubt into people's pockets. He picked up the receiver and said, 'Yes?'

'Can you meet me outside? Right away?'

'Who is this?'

'Kubalsky. Very urgent, Ilya.'

'All right.'

'See you in one minute.'

It was cold outside. Serebin shivered in his jacket and tried to stay dry by standing next to the wall of the tannery. The smell of the place was heavy in the wet air, the smell of a century of hides and carcasses and offal. Growing impatient, he looked at his watch. *Politics. Why in God's name* . . . He was staring at the front of the building when the windows blew out. A cloud of dirty smoke, glass and wood and pieces of the IRU office, the sound of it hitting the street lost in the echoes of the explosion which rolled away into silence as the screams began.

There were two Serebins at that moment. One sat down. The other, the real one, ran as far as the foot of the stairs, where he was forced back by the crowd. He saw the girl, she had blood on her and her eyes were vacant, but she was there, stumbling down the stairs between a man and a woman. The woman had one hand pressed over her eyes while the other gripped the shoulder of the girl's blouse. She was either pulling the girl away from what had happened in the office or holding on to her because she couldn't see. Or, perhaps, both. To Serebin, it wasn't clear.

He waited, it seemed to take a long time, people were coughing, their faces stained with black soot. Eventually, the stairway cleared and Serebin climbed up to the office. The air was thick with smoke and dust – it was dark as night and hard to breathe – but the building wasn't on fire. He didn't think it was. There were three or four people walking around in what had been the office, one of them knelt by a shape beneath a table. Serebin stepped on a shoe, heard a siren in the distance. Goldbark always wore a silver tie, and so did what he saw on the floor by a cast-iron radiator, now bent in a vee aimed at the ceiling.

'She's alive, I think.' A voice in the darkness.

'Don't move her.'

'What did she say?'

'I couldn't hear.'

He went up to Besiktas, to the yellow house on the Bosphorus. Tamara wore a heavy coat and a sweater, and, knotted under her chin, one of those head scarves that all Ukrainian women had, red roses on a black background. She'd bundled up so they could sit on the terrace, where the wind made the lantern flicker on the garden table, because she knew he was one of those people who don't like to be indoors.

'It's too cold for you,' he said.

'No. I'll be fine.'

'I'm going in.'

'Go ahead. I'll be right here.'

Stubborn. Like all of them. The word Ukraine meant borderland.

One of the sisters appeared with a pot of steaming tea – Tamara had asked for that because she thought it might settle him – and a bottle of vodka, which would.

When he told her the story she was silent for a long time, then shook her head slowly. She'd seen such things, been told such things, too often. Finally she said, 'Was it Russians, Ilya? Special services?'

'Maybe.'

'Why would they do this?'

He shrugged. 'Espionage, of some sort, maybe somebody running a network out of the IRU office. It's a convenient setting, if you think about it. And nothing new – every spy service in the world tries to recruit émigrés, and every counterintelligence office tries to stop it. So, what happens next, is the local people see something they don't like, and then . . .'

'But they spared you.'

Serebin nodded.

'That didn't just, happen.'

'No.'

She poured two cups of tea, took one for herself, held the vodka bottle over the other. 'You want?'

'A little.'

He moved his chair back from the table and lit a cigarette.

'You have family in it, no?'

'My mother's sister.' She had never been an *aunt*.

Tamara thought it over for a moment, then said, 'Ah, the Mikhelson girls.' She smiled – it was strange to remember a time when the world just went along, one day to the next.

A well-known story in Odessa, the life and courtship of the Mikhelson girls. Frieda and Malya. Zaftig, smart, they smoked cigarettes, wore black, read French novels, went to Polish spas. Frieda got Serebin's father, a son of the nobility – the real thing: handsome, brilliant, certainly a little crazy but who cared. So, now Frieda had a husband, Malya had to have one too, but it didn't last a year. She wore him out, going off to screw her lovers whenever the mood took her. A dancer, a baron, a colonel. The husband shot himself in the front parlor and they couldn't find the cat for days. And it was Serebin's grandfather who wept, *poor soul*. He'd

37

worked his heart out, selling agricultural machinery, for his darling girls, who gave him nothing but grief. In 1917, Malya joined her friends in the Cheka – the most stylish job in town that winter. 'God forgive me,' Serebin's grandfather whispered to him just before he died, 'I should've gone to America with everybody else.'

Serebin walked to the edge of the terrace and stared out at the lights on the Asian shore of the city. *A ferry, then a train across the Anatolian steppe to Persia* – he knew what was waiting for him in the lobby of his hotel. When he returned to the table Tamara said, 'Hard to believe that your aunt is still alive, after the purges. Most of them disappeared.'

'They did, but she climbed.'

'Took part in it, probably.'

'Probably.'

'*Had* to.'

'I would think.'

The sea mist was clouding Serebin's glasses. He took them off, pulled a handful of shirt out of his belt, and began to clean the lenses. 'Of course, all that who and why business is a *bubbemeisah.*' A story made up for children. 'Nobody knows what happened except the people who did it, and if they're a halfway professional organization, nobody ever will.' He finished his tea, and poured some vodka into the cup.

'Before you go, Ilya, I want you to see something.'

The interior of the house had grown in complicated ways over time. Tamara led him to the back, then opened a door to reveal a stairway so narrow he had to turn his shoulders as he climbed. At the top, another door, and a room beneath the eaves, the ceiling slanting sharply down to a single, small window. *A secret room.* At first, Serebin thought he'd never seen it before, then realized it had been worked on. The piles of dusty shutters with broken slats were gone, replaced by a cot covered with a blanket. A battered table and chair had been set below the window, and every board, ceiling, walls, and floor, had been freshly whitewashed. All it lacked, he thought, was the tablet of writing paper and sharpened pencils on the table.

'Of course you understand,' she said.

'Yes. Thank you.' It had gotten to him.

'Perhaps it's not to be, right away, but who knows, Ilya, the day may come.'

He couldn't really answer her. That somebody should want to do this for him, that in itself was refuge. And what more, in this life, could anyone offer?

He started to speak, but she pounded him gently on the shoulder with the side of her fist. *Oh shut up.*

When Serebin was fourteen, he would swim with his friends off a jetty north of the Odessa docks. The whole crowd, naked and skinny, from the Nicholas I Commercial School of Odessa. Joined, one sweltering August afternoon, by Tamara Petrovna and her friend Rivka. Fearless, they stripped down and dove in and swam way out. Later, lazing on the rocks, Tamara caught Serebin staring at her backside. She picked up a clamshell and heaved it at him – a lucky shot on the nose – Serebin's eyes ran tears and he got red in the face. 'What the hell's wrong with you?' he shouted, hand pressed to his nose. 'I'm not even wearing my glasses.'

The taxi was slow, returning to Beyoglu, the melancholy driver sighed and dawdled in the back streets, lost in a world of his own. Meanwhile, in Serebin's imagination, the Emniyet agents sitting in the lobby grew angrier and angrier when he didn't show up, but there was nothing he could do about that.

In the event, they weren't there. He reached the hotel after midnight, to find that a note had been slipped under his door. A Russian note, typed on a Cyrillic typewriter, asking if he would be good enough to drop by the office – an address in Osmanli street – in the morning and see Major Iskandar in Room 412. So, for a long night, he was to have the pleasure of thinking about it.

The desk of Major Iskandar. Born as conqueror's furniture in the days of the Ottoman Empire, a vast mahogany affair with legs like Corinthian columns and ball feet. But time passed, empires drifted into ruin, coffee cups made rings, neglected cigarettes left burn scars, stacks of dossiers appeared and established a small colony, then grew higher and higher as a hostile world hammered on the national door. Or picked the lock.

Major Iskandar, not very military in a rumpled uniform, had spectacles and a black mustache, with hair and patience thinning as he moved through his forties. He was chinless, with something waxy and unhealthy in his complexion, and reminded Serebin of an Armenian poet he'd once known, a great sensualist who died of drinking valerian drops in a sailors' brothel in Rotterdam.

Iskandar hunted through his dossiers until he found what he was after. 'Well,' he said, 'we'd planned to have a, a chat, with you when we saw the shipping manifest.' Suddenly annoyed, he snapped his fingers twice at the doorway to an outer office. That produced, a moment later, an orderly carrying two cups of black, sandy coffee. 'But then, yesterday's bombing on Rasim street . . .' He opened a dossier and turned pages. 'Any theories? Who? Why?'

'No, not really.'

'Was Goldbark a friend of yours?'

'An associate. I knew him as one of the directors of the IRU office.'

'Been to his house?'

'No.'

'Met his wife?'

'Maybe once. At some kind of event.'

'The crate of aubergines was sent to him, specifically. Three other people died, there are five or six in various hospitals.' He offered Serebin a pack of cigarettes, then lit one for himself. 'You got out, it would seem, just at the right moment.'

'A telephone call.'

'A warning?'

'No.' Serebin's voice was very cold.

'Then what?'

'"Please meet me outside. It's urgent."'

'And who was it?'

'I don't know.'

'Really don't?'

'No.'

'An unknown stranger calls, and you go charging off in the middle of a party held in your honor.'

'"An old friend" is what he called himself. I thought that was possible, and the tone of the voice was serious, so I thought I'd better go.'

The major tilted his head to one side, like a listening dog. *What do I hear?* Then decided that, for the moment, it didn't matter. He leaned back in his chair and said, 'This comes at a bad time for us, do you understand? There is a war going on in Europe, and we are under pressure from both sides. And in this country, and particularly in this office, we feel it. The more so because we know the thing is heading south. I could drive you up into Thrace, to the Bulgarian frontier, and there, in the border villages, you would see a new sort of tourism. Vacationing Germans, all men, in overcoats and alpine hats, with cameras or binoculars around their necks. It must be the birds, don't you think? That makes them so passionate to be in the Bulgarian countryside in November?

'And these days, where such tourists go, tanks follow. It isn't far from here, maybe six hours. And much faster by aeroplane. It's sad to see a city like London being bombed, night after night, terrible, a nice brick city like that. But here, of course, it wouldn't be night after night. Because one night would be enough. A few hours' work for the bomber pilots, and the whole thing would just, burn.'

Serebin knew. Dense neighborhoods of old, dry, wooden houses.

'So, we stay neutral, and treat every act of political violence as a potential provocation. A shooting, a stabbing, a bombing – what does it mean? Is it an *incident?* What comes next? Well, maybe nothing, in this case. It's England and Germany we worry about these days. Russia maybe not so much – we've spent three hundred years worrying about them, so we're used to it. Still, we have to be concerned, an attack of this sort, and our concern is, ah, concentrated by the fact that Goldbark was no virgin. There is at least some possibility that he asked for it.'

Serebin said 'Oh?' He meant *fuck you*.

But Iskandar was ready for him. Slid a photograph from the dossier and laid it on the desk, like a playing card. A clandestine photograph, a gray man on a gray street on a gray afternoon. Hands thrust deep in overcoat pockets, brooding as he walked. Perhaps a Slav, grave lines in the face, the corners of the mouth pulled down, a sensitive man who had long ago chosen the wrong life, one where the Emniyet took his photograph.

'Know him?'

Serebin shook his head.

'This woman?'

She was buying oranges from a market stall.

'No.'

'Sure?'

'Yes.'

'Goldbark knew them.'

Did he?

Iskandar laid down a photograph of Goldbark and the woman, leaning side by side on the railing of a ferry.

'Who are these people?' Serebin asked.

'Professionals – from the way they behave. Was Goldbark a Zionist?'

'I have no idea.'

'Communist?'

'Unlikely. He left the country, after all.'

'All kinds of people leave all kinds of countries. How much pressure would it have taken to force him to work for Germany?'

Serebin stared.

'It is not unheard of. I am sorry, but it is not.'

'He was too strong for that,' Serebin said. What remained of Goldbark was the memory of him.

Major Iskandar raised an eyebrow. He drank down the last of his coffee and snapped his fingers. Perhaps a comment on Serebin's answer, or maybe he just wanted more coffee.

'Do you plan to remain in Istanbul?'

Serebin thought it over. 'For a week or two, maybe.'

The major paged through an appointment book. 'That would make it the twelfth. Of December.' He made a note by the date.

They drank a second cup of coffee. The major said that it often rained, this time of year. Still, they hardly ever had snow. Spring, on the other hand, was pleasant, with wildflowers in the countryside. When Serebin left, a man he recalled, vaguely, from the IRU party, was sitting in the outer office. Their eyes met, for a moment, then the man looked away.

My God, who is she? She was radiant, strange, had the face of an uncomfortably beautiful child. Twenty minutes from Major Iskandar's office, in a tiny square with a fish market, Serebin sat at a table outside a lokanta, a neighborhood restaurant, and she came and sat on the edge of the other chair. When she pushed the hair back from her eyes he could see that her hand was shaking. She wet her lips, then spoke a few words – memorized, he thought – in guttural French: his friend, Monsieur Serge, wanted very much to see him. Then she waited, unsure of the language, to see if he'd understood her. *She is Kubalsky's lover,* he thought.

He nodded, tried to look encouraging. 'In Tatavla,' she said.

The Greek district.

'At Luxe cinema, tomorrow night.'

Her hands clutched the top of a purse, tight enough so that her knuckles were white and sharp. He said he understood and thanked her for the message, which earned him a sudden, luminous smile, on and off, then she stood and walked away, striding around the corner and out of sight.

After that, he walked and walked. Writing sometimes, staring at faces, adrift in unknown streets, far away on his own private planet. The world gnawed at you, he thought, better to be, now and then, *elsewhere* – it would all still be there when you got back. He would send flowers to the hospitals, would call on Goldbark's wife. Later, when Iskandar was done talking with her. She would lie to them, of course, as he had. One did.

For the moment, he studied a handsome chestnut tree, spidery winter branches trimmed back to the pollard shape, circled by an iron fence. A pair of girls in school uniforms, kohl darkening their eyes – after-school *femmes fatales*. A sidewalk vendor, tending skewers of lamb and onions that sizzled and dripped onto hot coals. This made him violently hungry, but he couldn't bear to stop walking. The neighborhood changed. To rows of elaborate stone buildings, five stories high, with brass plaques announcing important companies and banks. Standing restlessly in front, scowling doormen, Turkish wrestlers with brass buttons on their uniforms. Deutsche Orientbank. Banque de la Seine. At the end of the street: Société Ottoman des Docks et Ateliers du Haut Bosphore. *Title! 'On a certain cloudy morning in springtime, the bookkeeper Drazunov folded his newspaper under his arm and stepped off the Number Six trolley . . .'*

Yes, one lied to them. Always. 'Today a man talks freely only with his wife' – Babel had said that, the last time Serebin ever saw him – 'at night, with the blankets pulled over his head.'

He stopped at a Karagoz show, puppets made of camel hide, and stood at the edge of the crowd. Serebin was a man who truly hated puppets – hated the way they leaped and skittered about, the way they shrieked – but he was also a man who could no more pass by theatre in the street than he could fly. The Karagoz companies (Karagoz was Punch) wrote contemporary characters into their skits, so Serebin, in past trips to the city, had seen Mickey Mouse, Tarzan of the Apes, Marlene Dietrich, Greta Garbo. *Greta Garbo? I'll write you a puppet play about Greta Garbo – a love story. 'Ow! Oh! Don't punish me so, madame, I'm only the script girl!'*

He saw a bar he liked and sat at an outdoor table. They didn't have vodka, so he drank instead some kind of delicious brandy. Made of apricots, probably, the waiter drew one on a napkin for him. Then, walking again, he came to a boulevard with a fragrant breeze. A certain scent he recognized: rotting seaweed, salt, coal smoke. His heart rose. A harbor. A view of the sea. Down this hill? He would go and see.

7:20. A warm night for the season, cloudy and soft. No stars, when Serebin looked for them, *maybe later.* He always took émigré officials out for a good dinner, something most of them never got, so he scouted General de Kossevoy's neighborhood on his way to the old man's room and found a place with a basket of cucumbers in the window. When he peered inside he saw that it was crowded and noisy, steamy and smoky, the way he liked it, with harassed waiters on the run.

But, wrong again. 'If it's all the same to you,' de Kossevoy said, 'I've been meaning to look in at The Samovar, do you know it? The owner was one of my officers in the Urals and he's always asking me to drop by.'

Sodden kasha pierogi with suspiciously sour sour cream was the result of that, but de Kossevoy had smiled beatifically as they entered, his iron foot ringing out on the tile floor of the restaurant. The general's foot had been blown off by a mortar round in Smolensk and, when the wound healed, a local blacksmith had forged a substitute. De Kossevoy seemed to get along with it all right. He walked with a stick, and you had to watch out for him at parties – Serebin recalled a bearded luminary at an official reception, his eyes squeezed shut with agony as de Kossevoy trod on his toes, while a supernatural effort at courtesy kept him from crying out.

'Your excellency!' A humble shuffle and bow from the owner, hurrying past his empty tables.

'Champagne,' Serebin said.

'An attractive place.' That was the general's verdict.

Red velvet, red linen, tired from the years. 'Oh yes,' Serebin said. 'I think he does rather well.'

'Later at night, probably.'

'Mmm.'

Serebin ordered everything. *Zakuski* of smoked fish with toasts, sorrel soup, veal patties, and the kasha pierogi. 'You can fight a war on these,' the general said, a twinkle in his eye.

'Stalin was always recommending rusks.'

'Rusks!'

'Tukhachevsky told me that.'

'Your commander?'

'Twice. Outside Moscow in the revolution, then in Poland in '21.'

'And, for his trouble, shot.'

'Yes. You were with the Whites?'

'Damn my soul. Under Yudenich.'

'Not the worst.'

'Pretty close. I was sixty-two years old when they dragged me back into it, believed in order, in Christ our Lord, in life being as life had always been. I feared the rabble. I feared that, once the yoke came off, they would burn and murder. And then, in 1917, the yoke came off, and they burned and murdered. I was wrong on the *scale* of the thing, much grander than I ever imagined, but that's an old man's error.'

'Let me fill that up for you.'

'Thank you.'

'So, what do we do now?'

'With the Union?'

'Yes.'

'Damned if I know. I expected that Kubalsky would be in touch with me, but, not a word. Heard from him?'

'Not yet.'

'Well, Konev is in the hospital. Lost the sight in one eye, I'm told, but he's got another. I expect he'll take command, I'll do what I can, we'll survive, somehow, we always do. Will you stay on?'

'I'll probably go back to Paris.'

The general hesitated, didn't say what came to mind, then nodded slowly. 'Of course,' he said. 'I understand. You have to do what's best for you.'

Kubalsky's messenger had not mentioned a time, only 'tomorrow night,' so the idea was simply to be there, Kubalsky would do the rest. Serebin took a taxi to the docks, then another – Major Iskandar very much in his thoughts – to the edge of the Tatavla district, and wandered through the autumn twilight. He asked, now and then, for the Luxe cinema, which produced long bursts of Turkish, sometimes Greek, a variety of emphatic gestures – *down there, around to the left, big something, you can't miss it* – and an even greater variety of encouraging nods and smiles. Going to the cinema? Yes! Good! A fine thing to do tonight!

A poor neighborhood, crowded, with narrow, winding streets that sometimes ended suddenly, washing strung on lines above his head, small groups of men in workers' clothing and peaked caps, talking and gesturing, silent as he went past. Then, around a corner, next to an Orthodox church, the Luxe. Serebin watched the street for a few minutes before he went in but it wasn't much of a precaution. Perhaps he was followed, perhaps not, people everywhere, anybody could be anybody.

Serebin paid and went inside. The theatre was half full, almost all men, maybe twenty rows of wooden seats with an aisle down each wall. The projector whirred, cigarette smoke drifted slowly through the beam. On screen, along with a few excited moths, was Krishna Lal, *The Tiger of Rajasthan*. A champion, Serebin guessed, of his sorely oppressed people, somewhere in vast India. Pursued by the rajah's guards, in steel helmets and red silk pantaloons, the Tiger ran through a bazaar, angering merchants as he tipped over stalls of fruits and cooking pots. Cornered at last, he looked desperately for escape.

A pretty Tiger, with dark, liquid eyes and a sulky mouth, he slew a pair of guards with his curved dagger, climbed to a balcony, leapt to another, held a finger to his lips to quiet an old woman slicing onions into a bowl. Serebin lit a Sobranie, searched the pale faces in the audience for a sign of Kubalsky, found no likely candidates. The music changed, a single sitar now, giggling maids attending a princess in her milky bath. Poor Tiger – maybe, just maybe, lurking outside the window where a suggestive curtain stirred in the wind. The princess leaned forward to let a maid wash her back, then dismissed the girl with a flick of her hand and straightened up. Up, up – were they going to see something? A certain silence in the audience but no, not quite. She stared at the window, alerted by a noise, then gave an order and the maids appeared with a sort of royal towel, holding it stretched wide between a hundred Turkish men and the rising silhouette of a wet actress.

Kubalsky, where are you?

Somebody was snoring. A very fat man came down the aisle, footsteps heavy on the wooden floor. He peered down Serebin's row, looking for – a seat? A friend? Kubalsky? Serebin? Moved away slowly, one row at a time, gave up, and walked back up the aisle. On screen, the rajah, with the drooping black mustache that always meant villainy, scolded the leader of his hapless guard. *Fool! Jackass! Bring me the head of the Tiger!* Reached inside his silver-embossed black vest and brought forth a vial of amber liquid. From somewhere in back, a whispered exclamation.

Now, coming down the far aisle, *encore le* fat man. But here, Serebin corrected a writer's error. He wasn't a very fat man, he was a very heavy man. With a big face, the chin still square across the bottom despite years of baklava. *Or chicken Kiev, or Sachertorte.* Maybe he was just the manager. *I have a right to do this.* Somebody spoke a few words, snide, mocking. Whatever the line meant it sparked a ripple of laughter. Was it 'she's not here'? Something like that, Serebin guessed. The chief of the rajah's guard hurried through the lanes of a bazaar.

Serebin looked at his watch. The maid tried to refuse the vial of poison, but the rajah's guard insisted. The princess, wiping away a tear, wrote a letter with a quill pen. Serebin decided that Kubalsky was waiting for him outside, where, at the end of the film, the crowd would come streaming out a single exit. Despite himself, he tried to imagine what Kubalsky might want, what he'd done, what he knew about. Twenty-three years of exile, adrift in the shadows of Europe, what arrangements had he been forced to make? The Tiger and the princess met secretly, in a moonlit rose garden, eyes alive with longing, throbbing sitar and tabla suggesting the embrace that the director could not show.

But the lovers were not alone. The scene darkened, a spy crouched behind a hedge, and someone in the audience took advantage of this darkness to make a spontaneous exit. Serebin never quite saw him. He heard a few pounding footsteps, then turned in time to see a running shadow disappear through a side door into a black square of night. Two men followed. Amid shouts of irritation they forced their way to the aisle, threw open the door, and vanished. *Just stay where you are.* Outside, the flat popping noise made by a small-calibre pistol. Three or four shots, then silence. Serebin leapt to his feet and ran around the back of the theatre, arriving at the door with several men from the nearby seats. One of them tried the door, which opened an inch or two, then was slammed shut by somebody on the other side. The man was offended, tried again, harder this time, but whoever was out there was very strong and the door wouldn't open. Serebin heard voices, indistinct, muffled, then footsteps. The lights came on in the theatre and a man who seemed to be in authority came striding down the aisle, the others made way for him. He grasped the knob firmly and opened the door.

Serebin and the others stepped out into a long alley, lit by a streetlamp at the far end. There was a high wall three feet in front of them, the noise of the streets, nothing else. In the faint light, Serebin could see a stain on the cobblestones. Old? New? Somebody laughed. The theatre manager shrugged, then opened the door and waved his customers back inside. What oddities in this grand city, who could know, from one minute to the next, what people might do. Serebin changed seats, moving along the far aisle to a row toward the front of the theatre. There was a belted raincoat folded carefully on one of the empty seats. He waited until the end of the movie, the crowd shuffled out, but nobody claimed the raincoat.

He stopped at a lokanta on the way back to the Beyoglu, he wanted to drink something, maybe eat, and bought a French newspaper to keep him company at the table. A woeful dinner companion, it did nothing but talk about the war, in varying shades of the Vichy point of view, Churchill called 'that Shakespearian drunkard' and all the rest of it. The Italian divisions in the Pindus mountains of Greece failing nobly, poor boys, and the Italian fleet attacked – in fact destroyed, Serebin and everybody else knew that – at Taranto by Royal Navy Swordfish torpedo planes. However – an implicit *however,* the deftly made sneer a felicity of French diction – the industrial city of Coventry had been successfully assaulted by the Luftwaffe. Set ablaze by thirty thousand incendiary bombs. Serebin recalled the look on Major Iskandar's face when he spoke of wooden Istanbul.

The newspaper's correspondent in Bucharest reported on damage to the Roumanian oil fields caused by the recent earthquake. Then, following Hungary on the 22nd of November, Roumania had signed the Tri-partite Pact with the fascist powers, though Bulgaria had refused. Civil war continued in Roumania, sixty-four officials of the former King Carol government had been executed by the Iron Guard, who were also fighting units of the Antonescu regime in the city and some of the towns.

Bon appétit, monsieur.

But the paper didn't lie, not so much that you couldn't read the truth if you wanted to. Endgame in southern Europe. Mopping up in the Balkans to create a harmonious German continent. No, they hadn't gotten across the Channel to finish off the nation of shopkeep-ers, but the shopkeepers weren't going to cross either. So, they bombed each other and fired caustic epithets over the airwaves. Churchill noble and stoic, Goebbels sarcastic and sly. A stalemate, clearly enough, that could easily enough wind down over time to a brutal peace, punctuated by the oppression of the Jews and the unending political warfare that flowed from Moscow.

Poor Kubalsky. Poor Kubalsky – maybe. And wasn't *that* what they excelled at, the Bolsheviks. Not sure, don't know, too bad, life goes on. 'Molotov in Berlin for Important Talks,' said the newspaper. A fine alliance, teaching the world, if nothing else, what the term *realpolitik* actually meant.

Serebin's long day wasn't over. At the desk of the Beyoglu, a note for effendi. A sentence, painfully carved onto a sheet of paper with a blunt pencil, every letter wavering and hesitant. From one of the Ukrainian sisters: 'Please, sir, we beg you with all respect not to leave the city without saying good-bye to Tamara Petro-vna.'

He was there an hour later. Not quite midnight yet, but close to it.

She was in bed, wearing two sweaters and a wool cap, eating licorice drops and reading Bulgakov's *White Guard*.

'Ilya! What's wrong?'

'Why should anything be wrong?' He sat on the edge of the bed.

She shrugged, used a scrap of paper to mark her place in the book. 'It's late.' She stared at him for a moment, face flushed and pink. 'Are you all right?'

'I was supposed to meet Kubalsky, earlier, but something happened.'

'What?'

'He didn't appear, that's the short version. What about you?'

'A little fever. It comes and goes.'

'And of course you don't tell the doctors.'

'I do! There was one here this morning.'

'What did he say?'

'Humpf, harumpf.'

'Just that?'

'Drink liquids.'

'Do you?'

'What else to do with them? You can have a cigarette if you like, clearly you want one.'

'In a while. I'll go outside.'

'No, have one here and now. And give me one.'

'Oh sure.'

'I'm serious.'

'Tamara, behave.'

'Tired of behaving. And, anyhow, it doesn't matter. Now give me a cigarette or I'll send my ladies out to get them the minute you leave.'

'Who says I'm leaving?'

'Don't torment me, Ilya. Please.'

'You are impossible.' He lit a cigarette and handed it to her. She inhaled cautiously, suppressed a cough, lips tight together, then closed her eyes and blew the smoke out, a blissful smile on her face.

'Very well, you've had your way, now give it back.'

Slowly, she shook her head. She was, he knew, afraid of infecting him.

'So,' he said, 'it's only you who gets to say the hell with everything.'

'Only me.' She tapped the Sobranie on the edge of an empty glass on her bedside table. 'Why did God make us love so much what we mustn't do?'

He didn't know.

She sighed. 'Do you leave soon?'

'In a while. The police don't really want me here.'

'They told you?'

'Yes.'

She inhaled once more, then put the cigarette out in the glass. 'Did they mean it?'

'A suggestion, for the moment.'

'So you could stay, if you wanted to.'

'Maybe, yes. It would take, some work, but I probably could.'

'You can't do what you're doing now, Ilya.'

'I can't?'

'No.'

He was tempted to ask her what she meant by that but he knew what she meant.

'It's, *there*,' she said, 'this terrible war. It will come for you.'

After a moment he nodded – he didn't like it, but she wasn't wrong.

'So,' she said.

They were silent for a time, the wind rattling the windows, the sea in the distance. 'When France fell,' he said, 'that day, that day I was Parisian, more than I'd ever been. We all were. Exiles or born in the 5th Arrondissement it didn't matter. Everyone said *merde* – it was bad luck, bad weather, we would just have to learn to live with it. But we would all stay the same, so we told each other, because, if we changed, then the fascists would win. Maybe I knew better, in my heart, but I wanted to believe that that was enough: hold fast to life as it *should* be, the daily ritual, work, love, and then it *will* be.'

'That is sweet, Ilya. Charming, almost.'

He laughed. 'Such a hard soul, my love.'

'Oh? Well, please to remember who we are and where we've been. First you say you'll pretend to do what they want, then you do what they want, then you're one of them. Oldest story in the world: if you don't stand up to evil it eats you first and kills you later, but not soon enough.'

'Yes, I know.'

'So now, tomorrow, next day, you'll find a way to fight.'

'Is that what you want?'

'No, never. I fear for you.'

He stood up and walked to the window. Tamara yawned, covered her mouth with her hand. 'We weren't meant to live long lives, Ilya.'

'I guess not.'

'I don't care so much. And, as for you, you will die inside if you try to hide from it.'

'It?'

She gave him a look. 'You're the writer, go find a name.' She was silent for a time, he came back to her and sat on the end of the bed, she turned on her side and rested her head on her arm. 'Do you know what matters, these days?'

He spread his hands.

'You did love me, Ilya. I wasn't wrong about that, was I?'

'With all my heart.'

She smiled and closed her eyes. 'Women like to hear those things. Always, I think. It always makes them happy, God only knows why.'

SYSTÈME Z

REPUBLIC OF TURKEY
MINISTRY OF THE INTERIOR
BUREAU OF STATE SECURITY

<u>Special Investigation Service</u>
DATE: <u>2 December, 1940</u>
TO: <u>Major H.Y. Iskandar</u>
FROM: <u>M. Ayaz – Unit IX</u>

Subject: I. A. Serebin

At 10:35 on 30 November, Subject left Hotel Beyoglu and proceeded by taxi to the Beyazit district, exiting in front of the Hotel Phellos and proceeding on foot to 34 Akdeniz street, taking the stairway to the second floor where he entered the office of the Helikon Trading Company. He remained at that office until 11:25. Subject returned to the Hotel Phellos where he took a Number Six tram to the Beyoglu district and checked out of the Hotel Beyoglu. Subject proceeded by taxi to Sirkeci station, purchasing a first-class ticket to Izmir on the Taurus Express, Istanbul–Damascus. Subject boarded at 13:08, sharing a compartment with two unrelated travelers. Subject got off the train at Alsancak station, Izmir, at 23:40 and took a taxi to the Club Xalaphia, a brothel, in Hesmet street off Cumhuriyet square.

Subject remained at Club Xalaphia until 01:55, when he checked into Room 405 in the Palas Hotel. Six other clients were on the premises during the time that Subject was there:

R. Bey and H. Felim – Cotton brokers, from Alexandria

Name Unknown – Reputedly a trader in pearls, from Beirut

Z. Karaglu – Mayor of Izmir

Y. Karaglu – His nephew, director of Municipal Tax Authority

W. Aynsworth – British subject resident in Izmir

At 00:42, a taxi entered the courtyard of the club, but no passenger was observed. The taxi left at 01:38, without passengers. The driver, known only as Hasim, is to be interrogated by Unit IX personnel from the Izmir station. The proprietor of Club Xalaphia, Mme. Yvette Loesch, states that Subject visited the room used by S. Marcopian, where he remained for thirty minutes.

Respectfully submitted,
M. Ayaz
K. Hamid
Unit IX

The ceilings in the Club Xalaphia were lost in darkness, so high that the lamplight never reached them. The walls, a color like terra cotta, were covered in frescoes, painted a century ago, he guessed, when the city was still Smyrna. The dreamer's classical Greece: broken columns, waterfalls, distant mountains, shepherdesses weaving garlands. The madam liked him – he felt himself subtly adopted, lost soul in the whorehouse. 'I am French,' she explained, speaking the language, 'and German, but born in Smyrna.' Then, for a moment, melancholy. 'This was a grand restaurant, owned by an Armenian family, but then, the massacre in 1915. They disappeared.'

So, now, it was what it was. In the still air, heavy perfume and sweat, soap, jasmine, tobacco, garlic, disinfectant. 'You are welcome here,' she told him. 'And, whatever you can think up, of course . . .'

Serebin knew that.

She rested a hand on his arm. 'Don't worry so,' she said. 'She'll come back.'

The girls liked him too. Lithe and merry, veiled and barefoot, they teased him from a cloud of musky scent, wobbling about in gauze balloon pants. The *harem*. With a trio of musicians, in costume, sitting cross-legged behind a lattice screen. Two Eastern string instruments and a sort of Turkish clarinet with a bulbous end, like the horn played by a snake charmer in a cartoon.

A strange way to go to war. He'd returned to his hotel after three, tired and sad, certain that morning sun would burn off the midnight heroism but it didn't. So he stood at the window. In the light that covered the sea, the white gulls wheeled and climbed. *You can talk to Bastien,* he'd thought. Talk is cheap. See what he has to say. Thus, later that morning, Helikon Trading, a young Lebanese in a dark suit, a phone call in another room, an address in Izmir.

'Sophia,' the girl said, pointing to herself. 'Sophia.' She sat on his lap. *Soft.* Across the room, seated in a grandiose leather chair, a man wearing a tarboosh gave him a knowing smile and a raised eyebrow. *You won't be sorry!* Perhaps a Syrian, Serebin thought, Kemal had outlawed the hat for Turkish men.

'He will find you there, or along the way,' the Lebanese had told him. Excellent French, conservative tie. And what did Helikon Trading trade? That wasn't evident, and Serebin didn't ask. No trumpets, no drums, an office on Akdeniz street. But it had never been dramatic, this moment. Never. In 1915, age seventeen, a newly commissioned sublieutenant in the Russian artillery, his father had simply shrugged and said, 'We always go.' Next, the revolution, his regimental commander requisitioned a passenger train and took the regiment to Kiev. Then, inevitably, civil war, and he joined the Red Army, setting off drunk with two friends from the Odessa railway station. He was twenty years old, what else? 1922, the war with Poland, ordered to serve as a war correspondent by the office of the commissar. And, finally, Spain. A spring afternoon in 1936, the editor of *Izvestia* taking him to a *valuta* – foreign currency – restaurant in Moscow. 'Have whatever you want,' he'd said. Then, 'Ilya Aleksandrovich, I have to send you to Spain, and you have to go. How's your Spanish?'

'Nonexistent.'

'Fine. This will give you objectivity.'

Gone, two years later. Worked to death in a gold mine.

The girl snuggled up to him and whispered Turkish words in his ear. Ran a finger, slow and gentle, back and forth across his lips. 'Mmm?' Then she slid from his lap, pale and succulent beneath the gauze, and walked, if that was the word for it, toward the staircase, looking back at him over her shoulder. But his smile of regret told her what she needed to know, and she went off to another room.

Serebin closed his eyes. Where Tamara was waiting for him. He was never going to write stories in the white room. Eight years earlier, it was she who had left him. She'd become involved with somebody else but that wasn't the whole story and maybe he was, at the time, not all that sorry when it happened. But she was still in the world, somewhere, and that was different. That was different. He heard the sound of an automobile, the engine stuttering and grumbling, somewhere nearby. It idled for a moment, then died.

A few minutes later, the madam appeared at his side.

'Your friend is waiting for you,' she said. 'Upstairs. The door is marked number four.' No more the lost soul. Business now.

At the top of the stairs, a long, crooked corridor, like a passageway in a dream. Serebin peered at the numbers in the darkness – behind one of the doors somebody, from the sound of it, was having the time of his life – and found Room 4 at the very end. He waited for a moment, then entered. The room was heavily draped and carpeted, with mirrors on the walls alongside colorful drawings, lavishly obscene, of the house specialties. There was a large bed, a divan, and an ottoman covered in green velvet. Bastien was sitting on the ottoman, in the process of lighting a cigar.

Serebin sat on the divan. He could hear music below, the horn mournful and plaintive. From Bastien, a sigh. 'You shouldn't do this, you know.'

'Yes, I know.'

'It always ends badly, one way or another.'

Serebin nodded.

'Not money, is it?'

'No.'

'I didn't think so. What then?'

'Somebody told me what I already knew, that I had to get in or get out.'

' "Get out" means what?'

'Oh, Geneva, perhaps. Somewhere safe.'

Bastien spread his hands, cigar between two fingers. 'What's wrong with Geneva? Courteous people, the food is good. Quite a stylish crowd there, now, they'd be glad to have you. I'm sure you hate fascism, as only a poet can. A place like Geneva, you could hate it from dawn to dusk and never get your door smashed in.'

'Not to be.' Serebin smiled. 'And you're not in Geneva.'

Bastien laughed, a low rumble. 'Not yet.'

'Well . . .'

For a few moments Bastien let the silence gather, then leaned forward and said, in a different sort of voice, 'Why now, Monsieur Serebin?'

That he could not answer.

'Surely they've recruited you.'

'Oh yes.'

Bastien waited.

'It goes on all the time. Six months after I settled in Paris, I was approached by a French lawyer – would I consider going back to Russia? Then, after the occupation, a German officer, an intellectual who'd published a biography of Rilke. 'The Nazis are vulgar, but Germany wants to save the world from Bolshevism.' On and on, one after the other. Of course, you aren't always sure, it can be very oblique.' Serebin paused a moment. 'Or not. There was a British woman – this was in Paris, in the spring of '39 – some sort of aristocrat. *She* was direct – dinner in a private room at Fouquet, came right out and asked. And it didn't stop there, she said she could be 'very naughty,' if I liked that sort of thing.'

'Lady Angela Hope.'

'You know.'

'Everybody knows. She'd recruit God.'

'Well, I declined.'

Bastien was amused, some irony afoot that Serebin didn't understand, at first, but then, a moment later, he realized precisely what the smile meant: *that was Britain, so is this.* 'Sometimes it doesn't happen right away,' Bastien said. 'Takes – a few turns of the world.'

Serebin wondered if he meant time or politics. Maybe both.

'People who trust you will get hurt,' Bastien said. 'Is a dead Hitler worth it?'

'Probably.'

They were silent for a time. Somebody was singing,

downstairs, somebody drunk, who knew the words to the song the musicians were playing.

'I don't worry about your heart, Ilya. I worry about your stomach.'

Holding a cupped hand beneath the gray ash on the cigar, Bastien walked over to a table beside the bed and took an ashtray from the drawer. Then he settled back down on the ottoman and leaned forward, elbows on knees. 'So now,' he said, 'we will put you to work.'

The train rattled along through the brown hills, the sky vast and blue and, to his eyes, ancient. They had talked for a long time, in Room 4, the life of the Club Xalaphia all around them; banging doors, a woman's laughter, a heavy tread in the corridor. 'I will tell you some truth,' the man on the ottoman said. 'My real name is Janos Polanyi, actually von Polanyi de Nemeszvar – very old Magyar nobility. I was formerly Count Polanyi, formerly a diplomat at the Hungarian legation in Paris. I got into difficulties, couldn't get out, and came here. A fugitive, more or less. Now, for you to know this could be dangerous to me, but then, I intend to be dangerous to you, perhaps lethal, so a little parity is in order. Also, I don't want you hearing it from someone else.'

'Can one be a former count?'

'Oh, one can be anything.'

'And the Emniyet, do they know you're here?'

'They know, but they choose not to notice, for the moment, and I'm careful to do nothing within their borders.'

'What about, well, what we're doing here?'

'This is nothing.'

Polanyi, then. With a few questions, he'd led Serebin back through his life: his mother, fled from Paris to Mexico City in 1940, now waiting for a visa to the United States. His younger brother, fourteen years his junior, always a stranger to him and everybody else, a cosmetics executive in South Africa, married to a local woman, with two little girls. His father, returning to the army in 1914, taken prisoner, it was reported, during the Brusilov offensive in the Volhynia in 1916, but never heard from again. 'Too brave to live through a war,' his aunt said. Thus the history of the Family Serebin – life in their corner of the world spinning faster and faster until the family simply exploded, coming to earth here and there, oceans between them.

As for his mother's sister, Malya Mikhelson, a lifelong chekist. Her last letter postmarked Brussels, but that meant nothing.

'The INO, one would assume.' *Inostranny Otdel,* the foreign department of the secret services. 'Jews and intellectuals, Hungarians, foreigners. Not in the Comintern, is she?'

He didn't think so. But, who knew. He never asked and she never said.

They stared at each other, sniffing for danger, but, if it was there, they didn't see it.

'And money?'

God bless his grandfather, who had foreseen and foreseen. Maybe, in the end, it killed him, all that foresight. He had prospered under the Czar, selling German agricultural equipment up and down the Ukraine and all over the Crimea. 'Paradise, before they fucked it,' Serebin said. 'Weather like Provence, like Provence in all sorts of ways.' Old Mikhelson felt *something* coming, cast the Jewish tarot, put money in Switzerland. A Parisian office worker earned twelve hundred francs a month, Serebin got about three times that.

'Can you invade the trust?'

'No.'

'Ah, grampa.'

And the Germans? Was he not, a *Mischlingmann,* half-

Jewish?

No longer. His German friend had arranged for a baptismal certificate, mailed to the office of the Paris Gestapo from Odessa.

'You asked?'

'He offered.'

'Oh dear,' Polanyi said.

Serebin spent all day on the train, after a few hours of bad dreams at the Palas Hotel. There'd been a room reserved in his name. 'We will help you,' Polanyi said, 'when we think you need it. But Serebin you have always been, and Serebin you must remain.'

On 5 December, 1940, the Istanbul–Paris train pulled into the Gare de Lyon a little after four in the afternoon. There had been the customary delays – venal border guards at the Yugoslav frontier, a Croatian blizzard, a Bulgarian cow, but the engineer made up time on Mussolini's well-maintained track between Trieste and the Simplon tunnel and so, in the end, the train was only a few hours late getting into Paris.

I. A. Serebin, traveling on the French passport issued to the *étranger résident,* paused for a time outside the station. There was snow falling in Paris, not sticking to the street, just blowing around in the gray air, and Serebin spent a moment staring at the sky. The first driver in the line of waiting taxis was watching him. '*Régardez,* Marcel,' he said. 'This one's happy to be home.' Marcel, a lean Alsatian shepherd, made a brief sound in his throat, not quite a bark.

They were right. Serebin tossed his valise in the back of the cab and climbed in after it. 'In the rue Dragon,' he said. 'Number twenty-two.' As the driver started the engine, a woman came to the passenger side window. A Parisian housewife, she wore a wool scarf tied over her head and the ubiquitous black coat, and carried a string bag of battered pears and a *baguette*. She broke an end off the bread and offered it to the dog, who took it gently in his mouth, dropped it between his paws, and looked up at the driver before licking the crust. 'You are very kind, madame,' the driver said gravely, putting the car in gear.

He drove off slowly, down a street with a few people on bicycles but no other cars at all. The taxi was a *gazogène,* a tank of natural gas mounted upright in the lidless trunk, its top rising well above the roof. Gasoline was precious to the Germans, and the allocation for occupied countries was only two percent of their use before the war.

Across the Pont d'Austerlitz, then along the *quai* by the river, low in its walls in winter, the water dark and opaque on a sunless afternoon. For Serebin, every breath was gold. *This city.* The driver took the Boulevard St.-Germain at the Pont Sully. 'Come a long way?'

'From Istanbul.'

'Bon Dieu.'

'Yes, three days and nights.'

'Must have been a pleasure, before the war.'

'It was. All red plush and crystal.'

'The Orient Express.'

'Yes.'

The driver laughed. 'And beautiful Russian spies, like the movies.'

They drove very slowly along the boulevard, through the 5th Arrondissement and into the 6th. Serebin watched the side streets going by; rue Grégoire de Tours, rue de Buci – a shopping street, rue de l'Echaudé. Then the Place St.-Germain-des-Prés, with a Métro station and the smart cafés – the Flore and the Deux Magots. Then, his very own rue du Dragon. Cheap restaurant with neon signs, a club called Le Pony – it was clearly a nighttime street, with the usual Parisian tenements crowded together above the sidewalk.

'Here we are,' the driver said.

The Hotel Winchester. *Le Vanshestaire,* a hopeful grasp at English gentility by the owners of 1900, now run-down and drifting just below *quaint.* Serebin paid the driver and added a generous tip, took his valise and brief-case, and entered the musty old lobby. He greeted the *propriétaire* behind the desk and climbed five flights to his 'suite' – two rooms instead of one and a tiny bathroom.

In the bedroom, he went directly to the French doors that served as windows, opened them, and looked out into the street. His red geraniums, the famous *Roi du Balcon,* king of the balcony, had been dutifully watered during his absence but they were fast approaching the end of their days. In the room, a narrow, creaky bed with a maroon coverlet, an armoire, things he liked tacked to the wall – a Fantin-Latour postcard, an ink drawing of a nude dancer, an old photograph of the Pont Marie, an émigré's watercolor of the Normandy countryside, a publicity still from a movie theatre, Jean Gabin and Michelle Morgan in *Port of Shadows,* and a framed Brassaï of a pimp and his girl in a Montmartre café. He had a telephone, a clamshell used as an ashtray, a Russian calendar from 1937.

Serebin looked out at the wet cobblestone street, at the half-lit windows of the shops, at the gray sky and the falling snow.

Home.

8 December. The social club of the International Russian Union was on the rue Daru, a few doors down from the St. Alexander Nevsky Cathedral, the Russian Orthodox church in Paris. Inside, a few men played cards or read and reread the newspaper.

'I can't believe you came back.' Ulzhen looked gloomy, a Gauloise hung from his lips, there was gray ash on the lapels of his jacket.

Serebin shrugged.

'What's that supposed to mean?'

'I had to leave, but I didn't like it where I went, so I came back.'

Ulzhen shook his head – who could talk to a crazy man? Boris Ulzhen had been a successful impresario in St. Petersburg, staged ballets and plays and concerts. Now he worked for a florist on the rue de la Paix, made up arrangements, delivered bouquets, bought wreaths and urns from émigrés who stole them from the cemeteries. His wife had managed to smuggle jewelry out of Russia in 1922 and by miracles and penury they made the money last ten years, then tried to go to America but it was too late. Ulzhen was also the director of the IRU in Paris, nominally Serebin's boss but, more important, a trusted friend.

'Terrible about Goldbark,' he said.

'It is. And nobody really knows why it happened.'

'It happened because it happened. Next it will happen to me and, you know what? I wouldn't care.'

'Don't say that, Boris.'

'Send the crate of aubergines. I'll tip the deliveryman.'

Serebin laughed. 'You'll survive. Life will get better.'

'We hardly have heat. My daughter is seeing a German.' He frowned at the idea. 'Last year she had a Jewish boyfriend, but he disappeared.'

'Probably went to the Unoccupied Zone.'

'I hope so, I hope so. They're going to do to them here what they did in Germany.'

Serebin nodded, the rumors were everywhere.

'Better not to talk about it,' Ulzhen said. 'When's the magazine coming out?'

'As soon as I do the work. Maybe after Christmas.'

'Be nice for Christmas, no?'

'I suppose.'

'Got anything special?'

Serebin thought it over. 'About the same.'

'It's good for morale, what with winter coming. Not much festive, this year. So, at least a few poems. What about it?'

'I'll try.'

'I'd be grateful if you would,' Ulzhen said.

'Boris, I want to get in touch with Ivan Kostyka. I called at the office on Montaigne but they said he wasn't in Paris.'

For a long moment, Ulzhen didn't answer. 'What do you want with him?'

'It's business,' Serebin said. 'I met somebody in Istanbul who asked me if I could contact him. If Kostyka likes the idea there might be a little money in it for me.'

'You know what he is?'

'Everybody knows.'

'Well, it's your life.'

Serebin smiled.

'Let me see what I can do. Maybe stop by tomorrow, or, better, Thursday.'

'Thank you,' Serebin said.

'Don't thank me, it's not free. You have to try to get some money for us. We've got to do Christmas baskets, a hundred and eighty-eight at last count.'

'Jesus, Boris – so many?'

'Could yet be more. Now, I have a friend I can call, but, if Kostyka agrees to see you, you have to take that filthy sonofabitch by the heels and give him a good shake.'

'I will, I promise.' Serebin glanced at his watch. 'Look, it's almost one o'clock, let me buy you lunch.'

Ulzhen shook his head. 'Save your money.'

'Come on, Boris, I'm serious. Black market lunch.'

Ulzhen sighed. 'Three-thirty, I have to be at the store.'

9 December. Dinner at Chez Loulou, deep in the medieval lanes of the 5th Arrondissement. Before the

war, a mecca for the daring American tourist: checkered tablecloths, candles in wine bottles, expensive food, nasty waiters, bohemian adventure thick in the air. And not much had changed. Here was *Leutnant* Helmut Bach, of the city's most recent tourist invasion, arriving for dinner with a black turtleneck sweater beneath his satin-collared overcoat and a beret set at a rakish angle on his Teutonic head.

'Ilya! Am I late? I'm so sorry – the Métro . . .'

No, Serebin was early. And, not incidentally, two *pastis* to the good.

Beneath the Pigalle *apache* costume was a Saxon in his early thirties. Pale brown hair – cut close on the sides, wispy on top, blue eyes, brass rod for a spine, and an air of quivering anticipation, expectancy; something wonderful must happen, *soon*. A functionary in the diplomatic administration – it had to do with protocol, official visitors – Bach had come looking for Serebin not long after the combat Wehrmacht had been replaced by an occupation force. Serebin couldn't help liking him, and the biography of Rilke was real, an autographed copy on Serebin's bookshelf.

'Lately I'm working on Rimbaud. Ach, freedom. In the words, in, the *veins*. You don't read it, Ilya, you breathe it in.' His eyes were wounded, a rose flush across the tops of his cheeks. 'Why are we Germans not like that?'

So you can love that. But Serebin didn't say it. After all, this was only dinner talk, and not so bad. It went reasonably well with the *pâté* of hare, with the duck *aux olives* and cabbage fried in the dripping, with the pear tart. Helmut Bach *snowed* ration coupons, and ascended to fierce courtesy when Serebin tried to produce his own. Look, he was damned sorry that his unromantic countrymen had beaten the French army and taken Paris but really what the hell could either of them do about that?

Serebin liked the dinner, and he ate with pleasure, except for a few moments when the conversation scared him. Maybe *scared* wasn't the word, *alerted* might be better. In fact, he was only just beginning to understand what his affiliation with Polanyi was going to mean.

'You know, Ilya, I'm trying to teach myself Russian – the only way to understand why Russians love Pushkin, so they say. Would you be offended if I asked you to help me out? A word or a phrase, now and then? A rule of the grammar?'

That wouldn't have bothered the old Serebin, but now he wondered what, if anything, it might mean. Just as it wouldn't have bothered the old Serebin to ask Ulzhen a favor, because the old Serebin wouldn't have lied to a friend about what he was doing. But he had lied, and he didn't know exactly why. *To protect Boris Ulzhen.* Did it? Really?

And there was worse to come.

'So then, you must tell me about your journey to decadent Bucharest.' Were the papers correct, the accursed *Ausweis,* all that kind of thing? To think, that a man had to get permission – to travel!

He hadn't stayed long. Went on to Istanbul.

'Ah. And did you see your friend, your woman friend?'

Had he told Bach about Tamara? Well, maybe. He had all his life told all sorts of people all sorts of things. They crossed his mind like shooting stars, were said, forgotten. Could there be people who remembered, *everything?* God, he hoped not.

Bach's voice was delicate. 'Her condition, is improving?'

'Actually, it's not so good. One can only hope for the best.'

'Not so good, Ilya?'

'No.'

'You must not think me intrusive, but there is a famous doctor in Leipzig, an old friend of my family. He is known to be the most brilliant internist in Europe, with access to every kind of specialist, no matter where – Leipzig, Heidelberg, Berlin. As a favor to me, he will see her.'

'Very kind of you, Helmut.'

'What friends do! You could bring her to Leipzig, everything would be arranged.'

'Well . . .'

'Please, Ilya, think seriously about this. You might be asked to give a brief talk – with a translator, of course. Just coffee and cakes, a few of your admirers. Small price for a friend's health, no?'

Serebin nodded slowly, feigned uncertainty, a man not entirely sure of what he ought to do. The kitchen door thumped open and shut as a waiter came out with a tray. Bach threw his hands in the air, his face lit with excitement.

'Ilya! *Tarte aux poires!*'

14 December. The evening train to St. Moritz had only three cars and stopped at every mountain village, one prettier than the next. Strings of lights glistened on the snow, the harness bells of a horse-drawn sleigh jingled in the frozen air. Once, amidst the rhythm of the idling locomotive, Serebin could hear an accordion in a tavern by the station, where a Christmas wreath with a burning candle hung in a window. When the train left, crawling slowly around the long curves, there was moonlight on the forest. Serebin shared the compartment with two Luftwaffe officers, their skis and poles standing in the corner. In silence, they stared out the window.

From Paris to the eastern border, the towns were dark, streetlamps painted blue – landmarks denied to the British bomber squadrons flying toward Germany.

There'd been a long stop at Ferney-Voltaire, the last German passport *Kontrolle* in France, while Gestapo officers searched the train, looking for people who were not permitted to leave. Then another stop, even longer, at the border *contrôle* in Geneva, while Swiss officers searched the train, looking for people who were not permitted to enter.

Serebin dozed, tried to read a short story submitted to *The Harvest,* the IRU literary magazine, found himself, again and again, looking out at the night. He'd met the infamous Ivan Kostyka on four or five occasions, over the years. The first time in Odessa – a story assigned by *Pravda* on the visit of 'the renowned industrialist.' So, they'd wanted something from him, and sent Serebin along as a token of their high esteem. Then, in Paris, during a cultural conference in 1936, a lavish party at Kostyka's *grand maison* in the 8th Arrondissement. Next, a year later, in Moscow, where Serebin was one of twelve writers invited to an intimate dinner, essentially furniture, as Kostyka met with captains of Soviet industry. Finally in Paris, the spring of 1940, Kostyka embracing his Russian heritage at the IRU Easter party and making a donation that was just barely generous. But then, Kostyka was known to be a genius with numbers, especially when those numbers counted francs or roubles.

Or dollars, or pounds, or drachma, lei, or lev. By then, Kostyka knew who Serebin was, or, at least, the people around him did. Claimed he'd read Serebin's books and found them 'stimulating, very interesting.' It was possibly the truth. One of the versions of Kostyka's life had him born in Odessa, to a Jewish family, poor as dirt, called Koskin. However, cosmopolitan figures who moved in powerful circles were often believed to be Jews, and Kostyka had never revealed the secret of his birth. Another version had him born Kostykian, in Baku, of

Armenian descent, while a third favored Polish origins, Kostowski, somewhere near the city of Zhitomir.

But, anyhow, Russia, on that point at least the mythologists agreed. He was said to have run away from home and poverty at the age of fourteen, making his way to Constantinople, where he joined the *tulumbadschi,* the firemen, a gang that had to be bribed to extinguish fires, which, at times, when business was slow, they set themselves. From there, he graduated to brothel tout, then used his commissions to play the currency markets in the Greek *kasbahs*.

As a young man he'd gone to Athens, where he'd used every penny he'd saved to buy good clothing and an extended residency at the Hotel Grande Bretagne. He next contrived to court, then wed, a Spanish heiress. By this time he'd become Ivan Kostyka, accent on the first syllable, which either was, or was not, his real identity, depending on which of the stories you chose to believe. As for the truth, none of the newspaper reporters who tried to follow the trail in later years ever found a trace of him. Some people said that there had actually been someone with that name but, if he'd lived, he no longer did and any record of him had disappeared as well.

In Athens, Kostyka became intrigued by the potential of the Balkan wars and, speaking at least some of the languages, became a commission salesman for the Schneider-Creusot arms manufacturer of Lille. Selling cannon turned out to be his métier, and he discovered that the greatest profit was to be had by selling them to both sides. Kostyka prospered, having learned to use what was known as the *Système Zaharoff,* or *Système Z,* named for its originator, the greatest of all the arms merchants, the Russian Basil Zaharoff. The *Système Z* called for, first of all, the flattery of political leaders – 'If only the world knew you as you really are!' Then for a passionate appeal to patriotism, the same in all countries, and, finally, a reminder of the prestige that the possession of bigger and better armaments brought to statesmen of all nations.

But the key element in the success of the *Système Z* was the operation of a private intelligence service. This was crucial. Kostyka, and other powerful men, men of the world, had to know things. Who to flatter, who to bribe, who to blackmail. Mistresses had to be watched, journalists paid off, rivals destroyed. This was expensive, private detectives and bureaucrats and policemen cost money, but, if you could afford it, worth the expense.

Kostyka made millions. Had castles, paintings, lawyers, stories in the newspapers, had pretty much everything he wanted and, by 1937, Ivan Kostyka had become Baron Kostyka. But it was a Baltic barony, bought from an émigré Lithuanian, and bought in anger. He had, in the 1930s, lived in London, and faithfully served British interests, hoping for a *K,* hoping to become *Sir* Ivan Kostyka.

'But then,' Polanyi said in a Turkish whorehouse, 'he got into trouble.'

16 December. It was almost noon, Serebin shivered in his overcoat, the alpine sunlight sparkled on the ice of the St. Moritz municipal skating pond. The skaters were almost all women, slow and sedate as they circled the frozen pond. Serebin sat on a wooden bench, Ivan Kostyka at his side.

As Kostyka's mistress skated past, in fur hat and long fur coat, a silky little terrier in her arms, Kostyka gave her an indulgent smile and a discreet wave, a Swiss wave, and mouthed the words 'Hello, darling.'

When she'd gone by, he turned to Serebin. 'Who wants to know?'

'A small enterprise,' Serebin said. 'To stop this war.'

'From?'

'Britain.'

'Not France? Free France, as they call themselves?'

'No.'

'Perhaps you know the expression "false flag."'

'I've heard it. But, in this case, it doesn't apply.'

'You give me your word.'

'I do.'

'Can you prove it?'

'Perhaps I can, but not today.'

'I give you time, then. But, if you want my cooperation, I must have a signal.'

Serebin agreed.

'I will have nothing to do with the USSR – or
anyone else. Understood?'

'Perfectly.'

'My heart is with England, you see.'

He meant it. At seventy, he was bulky and short, had
gray hair, brushed back from his forehead in little waves,
and a face carved in pugnacious lines, chin and brow and
nose thrust out into a world he didn't like. 'These places,'
he said, his voice a mixture of sorrow and contempt.
'These Monte Carlos and Portofinos. Vevey, whatnot . . .'

Poor soul.

It was very quiet, the skates made a soft hiss on the
ice. Once again, the woman with the terrier came
around the circle, this time gliding to a stop in front of
the bench. 'Good morning,' she said to Serebin. Then, to
Kostyka, 'Take him, would you? He's getting restless.'

Kostyka accepted the dog, which sat on his lap, then
yipped and trembled as the woman skated away. 'Shhh,
Victor. Be nice.' He patted the dog with a big hand but
he wasn't very good at it. 'Oil,' he said. 'Not for me.'

'Risky, I expect.'

'Not even the word. And the men who run it, my God.
You know what Gulbenkian said about oilmen? He said
they were like cats, that it was hard to know from the

78

sound of them whether they were fighting or making love.'

Serebin laughed.

'Give me a steel mill,' he said. 'Or a railroad or some guns. I'll show you how to make money.'

'Well, the Germans need oil.'

'Oh yeah, oil and wheat, oil and wheat. Why didn't he just take Roumania and leave the rest of the world alone? Nobody would've cared, you know.'

'Hitler wants more.'

Kostyka snorted at the idea. 'He'll have shit.'

'So then, you'll help.'

No answer. Kostyka looked at Serebin for a moment, but whatever he saw there wasn't interesting, so he turned and watched the women as they skated and made a face like a man talking to himself and, Serebin felt as though he could almost hear it, almost see it, whatever machine was running in there was big and powerful and very fast. Eventually he said, 'You'll take lunch with us.'

Oh the mistress. At the grand Hotel Helvetia, lunch was set out on the balcony of Kostyka's suite by two waiters, who were tipped, then waved away. Kostyka, his mistress, and Serebin sat around the table and speared chunks of raw beef with their forks and cooked them in a chafing dish of bubbling oil. 'Fondue,' Kostyka said. It was like a eulogy for his life.

Kostyka's companion, introduced as Elsa Karp, was no powder puff. Not at all what Serebin would have expected. She was easily forty, and heavy, wide at the hips, with copious brown hair, a beak nose, a sullen, predatory mouth, and a sexual aura that filled the air and made Serebin almost dizzy. Or maybe that was the altitude, but he certainly felt it as he watched her eat, sitting across the table from him in front of an alp.

'Monsieur Serebin is from Odessa,' Kostyka said.

'We've been there,' Elsa said. 'It was . . .'

Kostyka dabbed his cooked beef in a dish of béarnaise sauce. 'Summer. A year ago? Two years?'

'Not last summer. The one before.'

Kostyka nodded. That was it.

'We stayed at the Czar's palace.'

Serebin was puzzled. 'Livadia palace?' That was in Yalta, at the southern end of the Crimea.

'We stayed a night there, darling,' Kostyka said. 'In Odessa we stayed with General Borzhov.'

'Oh yes, you're right. Mischa and Katya.' She looked at Serebin and said, 'Do you know them?'

'No, I don't think so.'

'She plays the violin.'

Odessa was elegant, she thought. Italian. White and southern. The famous steps. Eisenstein. The baby carriage. She was from Prague, near Prague. She found it much too gray there, too much *Mitteleuropa*. She loved their house in Paris, he must promise to come and see them. She was going to have it redone, but then, the war. Now they would have to wait. Of course, for a *city,* well, London, of course.

'For every man there are three cities,' Kostyka said, quotation marks in his voice. 'The city of his birth, the city he loves, and the city where he must live.'

Elsa Karp was animated. 'We loved the dinner parties, even with our poor English. Everyone so, brilliant. So clever, the way they, they make you talk.'

Band concerts. Bookstores. Eccentricity. The gardens! Kostyka's face froze, he was almost in tears. This was, to Serebin, extraordinary, a paradox of human nature – there were people in the world who lived brutal lives, yet, somehow, their feelings stayed close to the surface.

The beef was taking too long to cook. The three of them peered beneath the dish and Elsa Karp adjusted the wick, but the flame remained pale blue and unsteady. Kostyka was annoyed. 'Jean Marc!'

Jean Marc appeared from another room. A French aristocrat, a pure type that Serebin easily recognized – tall and slightly stoop-shouldered, with dark hair, his face vain and watchful.

'My *homme de confiance*,' Kostyka said. Confidential assistant, but much more – the title meant absolute discretion, absolute fidelity, the sacrifice of life itself when necessary. *He is armed,* Serebin thought.

Jean Marc turned the wick up as high as it would go, but it didn't help. 'It lacks oil,' he said. 'I shall call the waiter.'

Kostyka sighed, sat back in his chair, gave Serebin a certain look. *You see? How it is with us?*

By wireless telegraph:

17:25   16 DECEMBER, 1940
HOTEL HELVETIA/ST. MORITZ/SUISSE
SAPHIR/HELIKON TRADING/AKDENIZ 9/ISTANBUL/TURQUIE
PRINCIPAL REQUIRES LONDON CONFIRMATION HERE SOONEST
MARCHAIS

18 December. The Geneva/Paris night express was almost empty, only a few passengers leaving Switzerland for occupied France. Serebin took a stack of manuscripts from his briefcase and, with a small sigh, for himself, for the universe, began to work. *The Harvest* would not appear for Christmas, but maybe it could be done before the New Year. New Year also needed a boost for morale, didn't it? Of course it did, and their émigré printer was an angel sent from heaven, explicitly, Serebin thought, for the salvation of editorial souls.

Anyhow, he reminded himself, he liked working on trains. Here was Kacherin, 'To Mama.' Oh Jesus. The man never gave up – this poor sweet lady cooked potato pancakes, sat in a chair by her sleeping son, three or four times a year. *Love* rhymed with *above*, also with *stove*, well, it almost did. But then, what the hell, this wasn't *The Resounding Shell*, or any of the powerful Russian quarterlies. This was *The Harvest*, it had no Blok, no Nabokov. It had Kacherin and his sugar bun for mama. Who was Serebin to deny him his thirty-six lines? *Fix it!* Serebin went for the pencil, determined compassion burst like a bomb in his heart. Even in an imperfect world, *bedizened* didn't have to rhyme with *wizened*.

The pencil hovered, and died in his hand. He had no right to do this. Use it as it was, or leave it out. But then, Kacherin's dues paid for *The Harvest*, was it not just to include him? *Not really.* He put the poem aside – maybe in, maybe out, he would wait and see if they had room. And, if they didn't, and Kacherin didn't get published, he would at least get a banana.

Serebin carried a handsome check drawn on Kostyka's Paris bank, but the shaking-by-the-heels hadn't been easy. To Kostyka it was all the same, donating for Christmas baskets was no different than buying a lead mine, it was investment, and it demanded negotiation. How many baskets? What, exactly, was in these baskets? Serebin improvised. Cheese, a sausage, Ukrainian sweet bread, chocolate, every sort of festive delicacy. Kostyka looked grim. That was all well and good, but what about oranges? What about bananas?

Such things existed in Paris, Serebin admitted, but had to be obtained from German sources or on the black market – either way, very expensive. Kostyka didn't care, these were now *his* Christmas baskets, and *his* Christmas baskets would have an orange *and* a banana. Understood? Agreed? For a moment, Serebin was afraid he was going to have to sign something, but Kostyka stopped short of that. So, they'd find a way to buy the fruit. They had better, Serebin realized, because Kostyka would not forget their contract and would make it his business to find out if the IRU had met its obligations.

Serebin returned to work. He had a story from Boris Balki, called 'Tolstoy's Lizard.' This was good, and definitely in the winter issue. Balki was an émigré who worked as a barman at a Russian nightclub, the Balalaika, up in the tough Clichy district. He didn't much like Balki, who he found ingratiating and sly, and always up to something, but he wrote clean, steady prose. 'Tolstoy's Lizard' was a retelling of a true story about Maxim Gorky, who habitually followed people, secretly, in order to use them in his fiction. That was nothing new, Balzac had confessed that he did it all the time. Gorky, the story went, had once followed Tolstoy in the forest of Yasnaya Polyana. Tolstoy had stopped in a clearing to watch a lizard lying on a rock. 'Your heart is beating,' Tolstoy said to the lizard. 'The sun is shining. You're happy.' Then he became sorrowful, and said, 'I'm not.'

The train slowed suddenly, then jerked to a stop. Serebin looked up from the manuscript. Now what? They were only twenty minutes from the *Kontrolle* at Ferney-Voltaire, certainly not scheduled to stop at some village. Serebin peered out the window but there was only the dark station and the frost-whitened fields of the countryside. He put the manuscript aside and opened the door of his compartment in time to see three men in suits, speaking German in low, excited voices, hurrying toward the end of the car. Two of them carried small automatic pistols, barrels pointed safely at the floor. *Gestapo?* What else.

When they left the train, Serebin followed them to the door, stepped cautiously outside, saw that a few other passengers had done the same thing. Up beyond the locomotive, at the far end of the station, he could see flickering orange light. Serebin took a step along the

83

platform, then another. Somebody said, 'What's the problem?' Nobody knew. Slowly, they all walked toward the fire – nobody had said they couldn't.

Just beyond the end of the platform, an old Citroën had been pushed across the track and set on fire. Why? The three Germans returned, pistols now put away. One of them waved the crowd of passengers back toward the train. 'Don't worry,' he said in French. 'Go back to your seats, please.'

'What happened?'

'As you see.' He laughed. 'Some idiot threw a match in the gas tank. They'll have to wait for it to burn out before they can move it.'

'Sabotage?'

The German, still amused, shook his head. '*Folie,*' he said, and shrugged. *French madness.* Who could say what these idiots might do next?

By post:

Drake's
8 Grosvenor Square
London s.w. 1
18 December, 1940

The Right Honourable the Baron Kostyka
Hotel Helvetia
St. Moritz
Switzerland

Sir:
I write at the direction of Sir Charles Vaughn to offer our most sincere regrets that your name was erroneously omitted from the club's published list of members for the year 1940. You may be sure that this oversight will be corrected in the 1941 list.

Sir Charles hopes you will accept his personal apologies, and that you will agree to be his guest for dinner as soon as you are able to return to London.

Yours most respectfully,

J.T.W. Aubrey
Secretary

Come home, all is forgiven.

27 December.

The Parisian French had a grand passion for institutes, where people were known to be clever, and well-dressed, and subtly important, their offices located in fine, antique buildings in the fancy neighborhoods. The Institut National de la Recherche Pétrolière was a champion of the breed, the windows looked out over the bare trees of the Jardin du Ranelagh, just across from the Bois de Boulogne, on the majestic border of the 16th Arrondissement. 'We interest ourselves in numbers here,' Mademoiselle Dubon told Serebin. 'Economics. We don't actually touch the filthy stuff.' Her smile was tart and sunny, as was Mademoiselle Dubon.

From the moment they met, in her office on the top floor, Serebin thought of Mademoiselle Dubon as a nun. Of a certain age, she was conventionally dressed for business, a somber suit, a green scarf hiding her neck, but she wore nun's eyeglasses – delicate, gold spectacles, her fair hair short and severe, her rosy face innocent of makeup. There was, as well, a certain biting innocence in her manner – all sins known to her, and all forgiven. At least in the business of oil, but, Serebin suspected, perhaps well beyond that. 'So, monsieur,' she said, 'you are an old friend of the baron's.'

'We've met, here and there, over the years. Moscow, Paris. A conference, a dinner party.' Oh, *you* know.

She knew. 'I've had a note from his Paris office, hand-delivered, that suggests someone like you would call, and that I am to be, informative.' A dark cloud passed in front of the sun. 'So I shall be. But, monsieur, if you are not discreet, we shall both be shot, or whatever it is that the Boche do these days. Beheading, is it?'

'So they say.'

'Well, I'd prefer that mine stay where it is, if it's all the same to you.'

Serebin's smile was meant to reassure. 'I wonder if you could tell me,' he said, 'what happened to him, in London?'

'Nobody knows, not really. He was forcing his way up the ladder, as always, but it's thought he pushed a bit too hard, perhaps bested somebody who was better left unbested. They have rules there – they don't tell you what they are, but they have them. And, if you break them, doors close, people are out when you call, invitations don't come. A summer frost, it's all quite magical.'

'Nothing like Paris, of course.'

The irony was clear, but she said, 'We're perhaps more tolerant here, but you may be right. In any event, the British find themselves in difficulty, and perhaps not so particular about their friends. That's also in the rules, no doubt.'

'A footnote. But they will prevail, in the end.'

'God and Roosevelt willing, they shall. And sooner would be better. Now, that said, how can I be of service to you?'

'Friends of mine have an interest in the disruption of Roumania's oil exportation to Germany.'

'Oh do they? Well, I suppose it can be tried. Again.'

'If it will end the war it has to be tried, no?'

She thought for a moment before she answered. 'Oil is critical for Germany, especially in time of war. So, it excites them, inspires them to heroic effort. For example, during the evacuation of Dunkirk, the British bombed the oil storage facilities near Hamburg. The hits were not direct, but the tanks were punctured, and three thousand tons of oil leaked out. Almost all of it, however, was recovered, pumped back into the tanks. That, monsieur, that level of determination, is what your friends ought to be thinking about.'

'We know this, in Russia. The last, oh, three hundred years or so, when the moment was right, we would invite them to come over and help us out.'

She knew the history. 'National character,' she said. 'They *fix* things. For example, the last time the British went after Roumanian oil, they were quite successful. Have you ever heard the name Empire Jack?'

'No.'

'Colonel John Norton-Griffiths, member of Parliament, no less, and one of those delicious madmen produced by a rather sane race of people. Griffiths showed up in Bucharest in 1916, just ahead of the German cavalry. He came from Russia, in a two-seater Rolls which carried him, his valet, and several crates of champagne. He got the Roumanians to agree that the Ploesti oil fields had to be destroyed and, under his direction, they wrecked. I mean, they *wrecked*. Blew up the derricks, plugged the wells, broke into the pipelines, flooded the fields with oil and set it on fire. Griffiths worked alongside them, lit off the gas in an engine house and was blown out the door with his hair on fire. Didn't stop him for a minute. He got hold of a sledge-hammer and went for the derricks and the pipes like a demon. In the end, they smashed seventy refineries, burned up eight hundred tons of crude oil and petroleum products. The flames didn't die down for weeks.'

Serebin acknowledged the magnitude of the adventure but could sense the ending, the homily.

'But, by 1918, the Germans had production back up to eighty percent of the 1914 level.'

'Still, two years.'

'Oh yes, it hurt them. When the war ended, Ludendorff was headed for Baku after Caspian oil, with Turkey, Germany's ally, trying to break in from the south. At that moment, the army had only a two-month supply, the defense industries were out of lubricants, and the navy was barely able to function.'

'It worked.'

'With Roumanian help, I emphasize that, it did. The Allies held a conference, about ten days after the armistice, where a man named Bérenger, a French senator, made a speech that we don't, in this building, tend to forget. Oil, he said, "the blood of the earth," had become, in war," the blood of victory."'

'A dramatic image.'

'The Germans certainly thought it was. "Of course he's right," they told each other. "So now we'll find a way to make our own oil."'

'Synthetics.'

'The hydrogenation of German coal. The process developed by Bergius in the 1920s, acquired by IG Farben in 1926. Bergius got the Nobel Prize in chemistry, Farben sold a share of the process to Standard Oil of New Jersey, and Germany had oil. Some of it, anyhow. At the present moment – and here I remind you of that man in the top hat, raising his axe – the Bergius process provides ninety-five percent of the Luftwaffe's aviation gasoline. Still, they must have Roumanian oil. At the moment, they import a high volume from Russia but, if that should stop, they'll need Roumania. Even with fourteen synthetic fuel plants at work, the Ploesti field would account for fifty-eight percent of the German oil supply. Thus the Blitzkrieg: rapid invasion, no long-term demand for fuel. But, even if the Russian imports end, and even if the tanks stop, down on the roads, Germany can fight the air war, can bomb Britain every night.'

Mademoiselle Dubon studied the look on Serebin's face – it was not, apparently, unamusing. Her tone was gentle: 'You may say *merde,* monsieur, if you wish.'

'*Merde.*'

'And I agree. For war in these times, only partial solutions, and not very satisfying. Nonetheless . . .'

Serebin rose, walked to the window, looked out at the cold, empty park. Before the war, he would have seen British nursemaids and two-year-old French aristocrats, but they'd gone away. When he lit a Sobranie, Mademoiselle Dubon produced an ashtray.

'Have you met the tempestuous Elsa?' she said.

'I have. But no tempests, at least not while I was around.'

'They occur, I've heard, but Kostyka is smitten, she can do no wrong. And, adding spice to the gossip, there are those who say she is a Russian spy.'

Serebin returned to his chair. What would *that* mean? 'Is she, do you think?'

'Who knows. A man like Ivan Kostyka serves a life sentence of suspicion, he must assume that everyone he meets is trying to get to him. Sex, love, friendship, gratitude, respect, you name it – those are the tools of the trade. So, if she is a Soviet agent, he suspects it, he goes to bed with it, and worries about it in the morning.'

She paused to let that sink in, then said, 'And, speaking of Russia, you should keep in mind the events of last May and June. When Roumania chose Germany over Russia as her patron state – she had to pick one or the other – Stalin became very irritated and took Roumania's provinces of Bessarabia and the northern Bucovina. That made Hitler nervous, it put the USSR just on the doorstep of 'his' oil. So, don't be surprised if Hitler goes east, maybe sooner than you think.'

'Let's hope he does, because that will be the end of him.'

'Likely it will, but you can't count on it. Now, you

must be aware of what the British have already tried.'

'Some, certainly not everything.'

'In the fall of 1939, Britain and France offered the Roumanians money, as much as sixty million dollars, to destroy the oil fields, but they could never settle on a price. Then, that same winter, the British secret service sent a force of men from the British navy, posing as art students, up the Danube, to sink a line of barges and block the river. Since almost all Roumanian oil is barged to Germany, a logical solution.'

'That was in the newspapers. A loud snicker from Dr. Goebbels.'

'A justified snicker. The Germans fooled them – got them to go ashore, then stole their fuel. A *débâcle*. And there were other attempts; a plan to bribe fifty river pilots, to disappear, and murder the other ten. A guerrilla raid on the Tintea field, which is the high-pressure field, thwarted by diplomatic concerns. Some other plot, betrayed by an oil executive in London. There may have been more, that I don't know about and never will, but the lesson is clear, this is harder than it looks.'

'*Encore merde?*'

'With pleasure, a Wagnerian chorus of it.'

'And, when they're done, I have a rather simple-minded question.'

'Ask.'

'Why don't the Germans simply double their synthetic output?'

'Certainly there is such a plan in the economic ministry, and if they could wave a magic wand, they would. However, these plants take time and resources to build, and the Bergius process demands an extraordinary tonnage of coal – you don't want to starve the Krupp forges. No guns if you do that. They will certainly build more refineries, but they will also lose capacity to British bombing. So, today, they must have the Roumanian oil.

And, tomorrow. And, I believe, for a long time to come.'

'Mademoiselle Dubon. Tell me, what would you do?'

She thought it over for a time, then said, 'Well, I leave the miserable details to you and your friends, but there are only two possibilities, as far as I can see. If this is to be a secret operation, sabotage, then there must be, at some level, Roumanian complicity. The only other choice is waves of British bombers, willing to accept an obscene casualty rate from the antiaircraft protection. It took Empire Jack and his Roumanians ten days to do their work, so the small-unit commando raid isn't an option. And then, you are surely aware that the Roumanians and their German friends know you're coming. They are waiting for you, my dear.'

There was a silence when she stopped talking. He could hear typewriters in other offices, a telephone rang. Finally she said 'So,' raised an eyebrow, and left it at that.

'You've been very helpful,' Serebin said. She didn't, he could see from her expression, especially believe it.

A man appeared in the doorway, a dossier under one arm. 'Ah, excuse me,' he said, 'I'll . . .'

Serebin stood up. Mademoiselle Dubon said, 'You can come in, Jacques. This is Monsieur Blanc from the finance ministry, he was just leaving.' Over the man's shoulder, as he shook hands with Serebin, she mouthed the words *bon courage.*

29 December. When Serebin returned to his hotel, in late afternoon, there was a letter waiting for him at the desk. When he saw the Turkish stamps and the hand-written address, each letter carefully drawn in blunt pencil, he knew what it meant. He took the letter up to his room and sat on the bed and, after a time, he opened it.

'*Gospodin,* I am grieved to tell you that Tamara Pet-rovna was taken to the hospital. Doctor says it will only be a few days.' Serebin looked at the postmark, the letter had taken three weeks to get to Paris. 'She wanted me to write that she says farewell to you, that you must take care, that you are right in what you do.' The words Tamara had spoken were underlined. The letter went on. Could they stay at the house, for now? They must look for work. This was life. God watched over them all.

That same afternoon, in Istanbul, on the second floor of a waterfront lokanta called Karim Bey, Janos Polanyi ate a bland stew of chicken and tomatoes. Seated across from him was an English businessman, long a resident of the city, who owned entrepôts in the port of Uskudar, on the Asian shore. The Englishman was known as Mr. Brown. He was fattish and soft-spoken, a slow, comfortable man who smoked a pipe and wore, against the chill of the harbor, a pullover beneath his jacket. When he spoke, his French was steady and deliberate, a fluency that, Polanyi thought, one wouldn't have predicted on first impression. 'Something's needed right away,' he said.

'It's always like that,' Polanyi said.

'Well, yes, I suppose it is. Still, it's what they want.'

'We're doing our best.'

'Naturally you are. But you will have to do it quickly.'

'You know what happens, when one does that.'

'Yes.'

'We're not sure of Kostyka's people – it's been two years since he used them.'

'Who are they?'

'All sorts. Iron Guard and communist. Army officers, intellectuals. Jews. Café society. It wasn't built for politics, it was built for business, for information and influence.'

'Will Kostyka involve himself?'

'No.'

'A list, then.'

'Yes.'

'Did you ask him?'

'Indirectly. Serebin talked to him in Switzerland, then Marrano met with the *homme de confiance,* who gave him the list.'

'Annotated?'

'Here and there. But very briefly.'

'You may as well give me our copy.'

Polanyi handed it over. Brown looked at it briefly, then put it in the inside pocket of his jacket. 'How did you get it here?'

'By hand. With Marrano – he flew from Zurich.'

'We've offered you a w/t set. A suitcase.' He meant wireless/telegraph.

'We're better off without it. The German goniometry, their radio location, is too good, over there. And the Turks wouldn't care for it here.'

'Put it out in the country.'

'Maybe on a boat, but not yet. We're not so concerned about interception, with the Emniyet, they like to know what's going on, and we try not to offend them. *Modus vivendi.*'

'We protect you here, you know, and the rest doesn't matter, so you needn't be dainty about it.'

'I *will* lose people.'

'One does.'

'Yes, but I try not to.'

'Try what you like, but you can't let it interfere.'

Polanyi looked at him a certain way: *I've been doing this all my life.*

'We are losing the war, Count Polanyi, do you know that?'

'I know.'

'Hope you do.' Mr. Brown's chair squeaked as he moved it back.

He rose in order to leave, dismissed the food with a

93

glance, then began to relight his pipe. He met Polanyi's eyes for an instant and, through teeth clenched on the stem, said 'Mmm' and strolled toward the door.

30 December. Ulzhen and Serebin went up to the edge of the 9th Arrondissement to collect the winter issue of *The Harvest* from the saintly printer. They were not alone – always lots of volunteers, at the IRU. Russians liked to go someplace new and do something different, it didn't especially matter what it was, so there were three men and two women – 'We can push as well as you can' – in the cinder yard behind the printer's shop, along with a porter and handcart that Ulzhen had hired. In a slow, winter rain, they bundled *The Harvest* into stacks and tied them with cord, then set the bundles in the cart and covered it with a tarpaulin. They all shook hands with the printer, who had worked through the night, wished him *novym godom* and *novym schastyem* – best wishes and happy new year – and headed slowly down a narrow street toward the rue Daru, more than a mile away.

The Parisian porter wouldn't let them help, so they ambled along behind the barrow on the wet, shiny street. 'One place I never thought I'd be,' Ulzhen mused.

'The rue Trudaine?'

'The nineteenth century.'

One of the Russians had an extra *Harvest,* some of the pages bound upside down. He'd rescued the journal from a stack of spoiled copies, telling the printer that someone would be glad to have it. He thumbed through the pages, then began to recite. '"In Smolensk."' He paused to let them think about the title. '"In Smolensk, the gas lamps warmed the snow / Petya held a pitcher of milk / We could see the white breath of a cab horse / And the beggar by the church who played the violin / Played the wolf's song from Prokofiev / Played all that February evening / When we had nothing to give him/But some of the milk."'

'Not so bad.'

'It's good.'

'Who is it?'

'Vasilov.'

'Vasilov the taxi driver?'

'No,' Serebin said. 'He works at Renault.'

'"The penal colony!"' The émigré name for the huge Billancourt plant.

'May he burn in hell,' one of the women said, meaning Louis Renault. 'My poor brother-in-law died out there, worked to death.'

'How old?'

'Thirty-eight. After six years of it, *travail à la chaîne*.' Work on the assembly line. 'Like prison, he said.'

'He was right, rest in peace.' The man who'd read the poem made the sign of the cross. 'I tried it. You're photographed and fingerprinted, the timekeepers watch every move you make and, when they can't see you, they have spies in the cloakrooms, spies in the lavatory.' He spat into the gutter.

They were silent for a time, in memory. At the rue Blanche they had to wait, a German military policeman had halted traffic while a convoy of trucks rumbled past. After a minute or so he held up a white-gloved hand, the trucks stopped, and he waved the porter and his helpers across. *'Allons, mes enfants.'* Go ahead, my children. The porter jerked the handles of the cart and the Russians followed him across the street into the rue Ballu.

The man with *The Harvest* looked through the issue, now and again reversing the journal when the pages were upside down. '"Italian Influence on Three Paintings by Watteau."'

'Don't bother.'

'You're getting it wet, you know.'

'Oh, it doesn't care. How about . . . rhymed quatrains from Romashev?'

'No!'

'Very well, the parliament votes no. All right, then . . . Babel!'

'What? He gave you a story?'

'He's dead.'

Ulzhen stared at Serebin. 'Babel?'

'It's never been published,' Serebin said. 'An Odessa story. Somebody was handed a manuscript copy, he smuggled it out when he emigrated and gave it to me for safekeeping. I thought, well, nobody's read it, so, let it be in *The Harvest* for the New Year. Babel is in heaven. Believe me, if he's looking down he won't mind.'

'"Froim Grach."' They clustered around the man and slowed down. The porter looked over his shoulder, shrugged, and kept pace with them.

In 1919 Benya Krik's men ambushed the rear guard of the White Army, killed all the officers, and captured some of the supplies. As a reward for this, they demanded three days of 'Peaceful Insurrection,' but permission was not forthcoming, so they looted the goods in all the shops on Alexandrovski Avenue. After that they turned their attention to the Mutual Credit Society. Letting the customers enter ahead of them, they went into the bank and requested that the clerks put bales of money and valuables into a car waiting on the street. A whole month went by before the new authorities started shooting them. Then people began to say that Aron Peskin, who ran a sort of workshop, had something to do with the arrests. Nobody quite knew what went on in this workshop. In Peskin's apartment there was a large machine with a bent bar made of lead and the floor was strewn with shavings and cardboard for binding books.

The procession crossed into the elegant 8th Arrondissement, although for a time it was like the 9th, everything grimy and poor, with Gypsy fortune-tellers and private detectives and shops that sold cheap clothing and pots and pans. The porter stopped for a rest by the Gare St.-Lazare Métro and they gave him a cigarette and a drink of *marc* from a tin flask. Gathered around the cart, it was easier to listen to the story.

Peskin is murdered, then chekists come down from Moscow and shoot the killers, except for one who flees to the house of the bandit called Froim Grach.

Froim Grach was alone in his yard. He was sitting there without moving, staring into space with his one eye. Mules captured from the White Army munched hay in the stable and overfed mares with their foals were grazing in the paddock. Coachmen played cards in the shade of a chestnut tree, sipping wine out of broken cups. Hot gusts of wind swept the limestone walls, and the sunlight, blue and relentless, poured down over the yard.

Then, Froim Grach goes to the Cheka and asks them to stop shooting his men. The Moscow chekist is very excited, and rounds up all the interrogators and commissars to tell them who has come to see them, who is inside the building at that very moment.

Borovoi told them it was the one-eyed Froim not Benya Krik who was the real boss of Odessa's 40,000 thieves. He kept very much in the background but it was the old man who had masterminded everything – the looting of the factories and the municipal treasury in Odessa, the attacks on the White and Allied troops. Borovoi waited for the old man to come out so they could have a talk with him, but there was no sign of him. He went through the whole building and finally out into the yard at the back. Froim Grach was lying there sprawled under a tarpaulin by an ivy-covered wall. Two Red Army men had rolled themselves cigarettes and were standing smoking over his body.

The story ended soon after that, with a hint of regret, the twenty-two-year-old chekist from Moscow forced to admit that the old man was 'worthless to the society of the future.' The porter finished the cigarette and took up the handles of his cart and they moved off again, walking slowly in the rain toward the office near the cathedral on the rue Daru.

Serebin was wet and tired when he returned to the Winchester late that afternoon. There had been an impromptu party to celebrate the publication of *The Harvest*. Several bottles of cheap wine were bought, the journal was toasted many times, and people stopped by to get a copy and stayed to talk and laugh and drink wine.

On the top floor, Serebin found the door of his room unlocked, the light was on, a small valise stood by the window, and Marie-Galante was lying on the bed reading a fashion magazine. She looked up from the magazine and, after a moment, said, 'Hello, *ours.*' It was tender, the way she said it, he could tell that she knew about Tamara. 'You don't mind, do you? The manager let me in.'

No, he didn't mind. Heartsore as he was, it was good to have her there, propped on an elbow on his pillow, a little worried, and caring for him. For whatever reason, dark or sweet, caring for him.

He took off his wet overcoat and hung it in the armoire to dry. Then leaned over and kissed her on the cheek. The magazine was open to a photo of three models in tall, outlandish hats, the *Paris chic* answer to occupation.

'I was in Stockholm,' she said. 'So I've been on the trains for – *days*. Felt like it, anyhow.'

'A *wagon-lit?*'

'Coach, *ours*. Second class. And crowded, people everywhere – it's a busy war.'

'Well, consider yourself at home.'

She relaxed. 'You're gracious,' she said. 'You don't have a bathtub, do you.'

'There's a *salle de bains* for the rooms on the floor below, but it's, it's better to use it on Mondays, after the maid cleans. Otherwise, there's a basin under the sink, you're welcome to that.'

'Maybe later, I need to do something.'

'You have an apartment here, no?'

'Yes,' she said. 'Out in Neuilly.'

'I thought you did.'

She paused, then said, 'Can't go there right now.'

'Oh.' Of course. He understood. Say no more.

'No, no.' She laughed at him. 'It's not *that*, such things do not keep Marie-Galante from her tub. It's little men with mustaches, you know? Waiting on the corner? All day? Mostly one ignores them, but not right now. Right now it's better not to be in two places at once, so, I'm not in Paris. I'm in – Polanyi-land.'

Oh.

'Where you are in high regard. The gentleman was pleased, as much as he ever is, with your approach to the terrible Kostyka, so I come bearing, among other things, his gratitude.' She swung her legs off the bed, stood up, and stretched. 'All right,' she said. 'Whore's bath.'

She went into the bathroom, undressed, started to wash. Serebin took off his tie and jacket and lay down on the bed.

'Know what?' she called out.

'What?'

'We're going to Bucharest.'

'We are?'

'Tomorrow morning. Gare de Lyon.'

Serebin waited.

'Isn't that exciting?'

'Very.'

'I knew you'd think so.' She ran the water for a moment. 'It's almost warm, *ours*.'

'Can I ask why?'

'Absolutely you can. You're going to buy folk art. For your little shop on the rue de Seine, in arty Faubourg St.-Germain. And you're bringing your wife along. Difficult, the wife. Doesn't like the idea of your being footloose and fancy-free in sexy Bucharest.'

'Folk art?'

He could hear her sloshing water around, wringing the cloth out. 'Little wooden animals. Corn-silk dolls. Embroidered Gypsy shirts. Maybe, if you're lucky, a saint painted on a board.'

'Is there really such a shop?'

'Of course! Who do you think we are?'

'Am I me?'

'Heavens no.' She emptied the basin into the sink. '*Ours?*'

'Yes?'

'I'm going to put on clean underwear and sleep in your bed. You don't mind do you?'

'No, not at all.' Then, after a moment, 'It doesn't matter, but I wondered . . .'

'What?'

'On the boat? The first time?'

She laughed at him. 'Oh no! Was I told to do that? No, only to talk to you, the rest was my idea. I'm not – I've had lovers, *ours*, but not so many. I just, *liked* you, and, if we're being horribly honest, I liked also the boat, the night at sea, maybe the weather. You understand?'

'Yes.'

'Now that we've settled that, could you, maybe, go out and find us something to eat?'

'There's a restaurant nearby, not so bad.'

'Better not. One thing about Polanyi-land, one does spend time indoors.'

'Bread and cheese, then. Wine?'

She came out of the bathroom wrapped in a towel, her clothes in hand. 'Whatever you can get. And I think I saw a *pâtisserie* out on the boulevard and, unless it was a mirage, there were, in the window, éclairs.'

Just outside the railyards of Trieste, the night frozen and black and starless, it turned 1941. The engineer sounded the train whistle, more lost and melancholy than usual, the way Serebin heard it, and Marie-Galante looked at her watch and kissed him. Then they held on to each other for a long time – for hope, for warmth in a cold world, because at least they weren't alone, and it would have been bad luck not to.

They shared a first-class compartment, on that part of the journey, with a sallow young man reading an Italian book, dense and difficult by the look of it, who waited until they parted, then said, 'Please allow me to wish you both a happy and prosperous New Year.' They returned the Italian salutation in French, everybody smiled, life was bound to get better.

And maybe it would but, for the moment, they traveled incognito.

A month earlier, in the hours before he left the city of Izmir, Serebin, following the written instructions he'd found in his room, had two dozen passport photos made, then left at the portrait studio to be picked up later. Now he understood why. Marie-Galante had brought him a new identity, the passport of Edouard Marchais, well-used, with several stamps from here and there, an *Ausweis* permit for travel to Roumania, and various other documents Marchais would be expected to have. Marie-Galante, newly Madame Marchais, was dressed for the part in a black, belted overcoat, cut in the latest Parisian style, and a brown beret. On the subject of new identities she was exceptionally casual – paper was paper, it could be made to appear when you needed it. So, now that all he wanted was to be invisible, he could be whoever he liked.

They had to change trains in Belgrade, and waited for hours in the station, where they found, left on a bench, a *Paris Soir,* with the headline CIVIL WAR IN ROUMANIA? This did not sound like life getting better, unless you believed in question marks.

No evidence of that in Bucharest, at least not right away. It was dawn when they arrived at the Gara de Nord and took a taxi through the empty streets to the Athenée Palace on the strada Episcopiei. The city's grandest hotel, infamous for having cards on its dining room tables that forbade political discussion, and much loved by cartoonists, whose spies peered out from the potted palms, at slinky seductresses and confidence men and cigar-smoking tycoons.

But, too early for them to be out at that hour. There were only maids, plodding down the endless corridors, and one yawning room service waiter, with a tray of glasses and whiskey bottles, for some guest determined not to let the night end just yet. Serebin and Marie-Galante unpacked and fell into bed and made love, made love like lovers, the slow, affectionate, and tired version of the thing, then slept like the dead until the winter sun lit the room and woke them up. 'So now,' she said, 'we will order coffee. Then we must go to our hideout. A breath of fresh air for us, and some leisure for the Siguranza to search the luggage.'

They walked a few blocks, to the strada Lipscani, then down a lane to a small building in the Byzantine style – lime green stucco, with a steep roof covered in fish-scale slates. *Some Ottoman bey lived here,* Serebin thought. Inside, it smelled of spice and honey and mildew, and there was a cage elevator – a gold-painted coat of arms mounted atop the grille – that moaned like a cat as it crept slowly to the fourth floor.

The apartment was almost empty. On yards of polished teak floor stood three narrow beds, and a marquetry chest filled with Swiss francs, gold coins, Roumanian lei, a map of Roumania, a map of Bucharest, two Walther automatics and two boxes of ammunition, valerian drops, rolls of gauze bandage, and a horrible knife. There was also a large Emerson radio, with an antenna cable run through a hole in a window frame and out into the thick ivy that covered the wall above a tiny garden.

'This is the safe place to talk,' she said. 'Don't say too much in the hotel room – keep it down to a whisper – and for God's sake don't say *anything* in the lobby of the Athenée Palace. It has one of those acoustic peculiarities; what you say in one corner can be clearly heard in the opposite corner.' She sat on the edge of a bed, produced five sheets of paper from her purse, and handed them to Serebin. It was a typewritten list of names, numbered 1 to 158, with a few words of description by each name:

Senior official, Defense ministry
Private investigator
Sofrescu's mistress
Assistant manager, Bucharest branch of Lloyd's Bank,
   Hungarian

Former ambassador to Portugal, silk stockings
Siguranza, financial specialist
Colonel, General Staff, ordnance acquisition
Publisher, friend of the playwright Ionesco
Journalist, gossip and blackmail

A hundred and fifty-eight times.

Some of the entries had numbers beside them, a price quoted in Swiss francs.

'The British,' Marie-Galante said, 'call this an Operative List of Personalities.'

'A kind of poem,' Serebin said. 'The way it runs down the page.' He couldn't stop reading.

The idea amused her. 'Called?'

'Oh, how about, 'Bucharest'?'

Now she was amused. 'Don't kid yourself,' she said.

They needed to know, she told him, who would work for them, which meant who would work against German interests in Roumania. Before the war, the operation had been run as the Roumanian branch of a Swiss company – DeHaas AG – with a local representative, who paid people and accepted information, but it was known that DeHaas AG was Ivan Kostyka. 'The network has been dormant since '39,' she said. 'It's our job to see if any of it can still be used.'

Visit a hundred and fifty-eight souls?

'Not in this life,' she said. 'We know who we want to contact. And for God's sake don't say what we're doing.'

They talked for a time but didn't stay long, it was not a comfortable place to be. Out in the street he noticed a man walking toward them, who met Marie-Galante's eyes for a moment, then looked away. In his late twenties, with the straight back of a military officer and, Serebin thought, perhaps a Slav, maybe Czech, or Polish.

'Someone you know?'

They turned off the strada Lipscani and headed for the hotel. 'We're not alone here,' she said. 'That's not the way it's done.' They walked in silence for a few minutes, then she said, 'And if by chance you should see Marrano, pretend you don't know him.'

'Anyone else?'

'Not right now, that you need to know about. Maybe later, we'll see.'

10:30 P.M., the Tic Tac Club, in a cellar on the strada Rosetti. By the doorman – in a uniform that made him at least a general in that army – a signboard with glossy photographs of Momo Tsipler and his Wienerwald Companions, and the local songstress, Valentina – 'the toast of Bucharest!' Also playing: the comedian Mottel Motkevich, of whom the *Zagreb Telegraf* said 'Kept us in stitches!' And, 'Special every night – those naughty Zebra girls!'

The maître d' bowed at the money Serebin put in his hand, and Marie-Galante, in clouds of Shalimar, with hair in a French roll, and evening makeup, took every eye in the room as they were shown to the large table in the corner with a card that said *Rezervata*. Somebody said '*Ravissant!*' as they walked by, while Serebin, at the rear of the procession, produced a rather compressed public smile.

Onstage, the Momo Tsipler nightclub orchestra, five of them, including the oldest cellist in captivity, as well as a tiny violinist, wings of white hair fluffed out above his ears, Rex the drummer, Hoffy on the clarinet, and Momo himself, a Viennese Hungarian in a metallic green dinner jacket. Momo turned halfway round on his piano stool, acknowledged the grand entry with a smile, then nodded to the singer.

The sultry Valentina, who rested her cigarette in an ashtray on the piano, where the smoke coiled up through the red spotlight, took the microphone in both hands, and sang, voice low and husky, '*Noch einmal al Abscheid dein Händchen mir gib.*' Just once again, give me your hand to hold – the first line of Vienna's signature torch song, 'There Are Things We Must All Forget.'

Valentina was well into her third number, Cole Porter's 'Let's Do It, Let's Fall in Love,' when Colonel Maniu – *senior official, national gendarmerie,* and his wife joined the party at the corner table. She dark and taut and bejeweled, he handsome and imposing in evening clothes. Craggy and leonine, he would play the king, not the prince. They came to the table as 'Argentines, without means,' did it – their arrival accompanied by a small commotion in whispers.

'We're so pleased . . .'

'Madame Marchais, Madame Maniu.'

'*Enchanté.*'

'Colonel, come sit over here.'

'Madame Maniu, allow me.'

'Why thank you.'

'My pleasure.'

'We've just come from the opera!'

'What was it?'

'*Rigoletto.*'

'Good?'

'*Long.*'

Serebin and Marie-Galante were drinking Amalfis – the choice of *tout Bucharest* – vermouth and Tsuica, the national plum brandy. The colonel ordered expensive scotch, and Madame a glass of wine, left alone after one sip.

For a time they smoked and drank and listened to Valentina; another throaty Viennese love song, then, as finale, Piaf's 'L'Accordéoniste.' This drew immediate and thunderous applause in the crowded cellar. It was clearly sung as a political anthem, for love of that cruelly occupied city nearest the Roumanian heart. Serebin looked over at Marie-Galante, who stared fiercely at the stage, eyes shining, close to tears. On the final note, Valentina put a hand to her heart, the drummer beat a military flourish, and the audience cheered.

Serebin the romantic was moved, Maniu the policeman was not. 'Nightclub patriots,' he said.

'And tomorrow?'

Maniu shrugged.

Madame Maniu gave him a look.

'Well, colonel,' Marie-Galante said, 'you know the people here, but I think she meant it.'

'She certainly did,' Madame Maniu said.

'May I invite her over?' the colonel said. 'You would enjoy meeting her, and she knows all sorts of interesting people.' He took a card from a leather case, wrote on the back, summoned a waiter, and told him what to do. Then he said, 'So, how is our mutual friend?'

'As always. He doesn't change,' Serebin said.

'And he gave you my name? Personally?'

'He did.'

'Why would he do that, if you don't mind my asking.'

'He's a good friend of ours — we share an interest in how life will go here.'

'It will go very badly, as it happens. The legionnaires — the members of the League of the Archangel Michael, called the Iron Guard — will fight Antonescu, *and* his German allies. To the death.'

'They are madmen,' Madame Maniu said.

'For them,' the colonel said, 'Antonescu and Hitler are insufficiently fascist. The Legion is drunk with some kind of national mystique, and their position reminds one of the Brown Shirts in Germany, in 1934, who were so crazy, who were such, well, *idealists,* that Hitler had to destroy them. When Codreanu, who originally organized the Legion — and he was known as 'God's executioner' — was killed in '38, with thirteen of his acolytes, the legionnaires took to wearing little bags of dirt around their necks, supposedly the sacred earth on which their leader fell. And some of the peasants believed, truly believed, that Codreanu was the reincarnation of Jesus Christ.'

The Companions of the Wienerwald began to play a kind of drunken elephant theme, which signaled the appearance of Mottel Motkevich, who, to a series of rim shots from the drummer and an expectant ripple of laughter, staggered to the middle of the stage. The spotlight turned green, and for a time he stood there, swaying, his flabby face sweating in the overheated room. Then he closed his eyes and shook his head, clearly overwhelmed by it all – *I just woke up in the maid's bed with the world's worst hangover and somebody pushed me out on the stage of a nightclub.*

He peered out at the audience for a time, then said, 'Where am I, Prague?'

'Bucharest!'

'Hunh.' He sighed, then said, 'All right, Bucharest. Say, know where I was last week?'

A different volunteer: 'Where?'

'Moscow.' He rolled his eyes at the memory. *'Oi vay.'*

Laughter.

'Yeah, you *better* laugh. Did you know, by the way – and this is actually true – they have a perfume factory there, and they make a scent called Breath of Stalin.'

Laughter.

'Can you imagine?' He gave them a moment to think about it. 'So, of course, when you're in Moscow, there's always a parade. That's fun, no? Hours of it. When they come to the end, they run around the back streets and march again. Anyhow, I'm standing there with my old friend Rabinovich. Rabinovich is no fool, he knows where his bread is buttered, if he *had* bread, if he *had* butter, and he's holding up a big sign. 'Thank you, Comrade Stalin, for my happy childhood.' So, time goes by, and a couple of policemen come over and one of them says, 'Comrade, it's a swell sign you got there but tell me, how old are you?' 'Me?' Rabinovich says. 'I'm seventy-five.' 'Well then,' the policeman says, 'I have to point out to you that when you had the happy childhood, Comrade Stalin wasn't even born.' 'Sure,' Rabinovich says, 'I know that. That's what I'm thanking him for."

It went on. Russian jokes, Polish jokes, Hungarian jokes. Maniu had another scotch. A police car went by in the street, its high-low siren wailing, and Mottel Motkevich paused for a moment. Then, as the routine neared its end, he looked: offstage, gaped in mock horror, and held his hands to the sides of his face – *if you could see what I see!*

'Now the fun begins,' the colonel said.

'Thank you, Prague!' Mottel called out, and waddled off to the elephant theme as Momo Tsipler clapped and said, 'Let's hear it for Mottel Mot-ke-vich!'

As the applause died away, Colonel Maniu said, 'Well, what's going on here is not so funny.'

Serebin ordered another Amalfi.

'My advice to you,' the colonel said, 'is, stay out of the way.'

'Oh,' Serebin said, 'we just want to talk to people, people who've helped in the past.'

'Surely not the same thing, not now. That was just, business. Commercial information, a little money in the right hands. I don't think anybody really cared – it's a way of life here.'

'What's so different?'

'Everything.'

The old cellist lit a cigarette, holding it with thumb and forefinger, and smoked blissfully, leaning back in his chair, off in some other world. Serebin thought about what to say next. *Do the best you can,* Marie-

Galante had told him on the train. *You'll just have to get your sea legs.*

'We are realists,' Serebin said. 'And we know it's not the same, we know that some of the sources are no good now. And you're right, colonel, this isn't commerce, it's politics, and that's always been dangerous. But we do have money, and we will take good care of the people who help us. As you know, in times like these, money can mean, everything. So, if it used to be, say, five thousand Swiss francs, now it's fifteen, or twenty.'

Momo Tsipler hit a dramatic chord on the piano and the Companions swung into the Offenbach theme, the *Mitteleuropa* version, clarinet leading the way, but emphatically the cancan. *'Animierdamen!'* Momo sang out – nightclub girls. *'Die Zebras!'*

A dozen women came prancing and neighing onto the stage, then out into the audience. They were naked, except for papier-mâché zebra heads and little black and white shoes made to look like hooves. They went jiggling among the tables, playing with the patrons – a pat with a hoof, a nudge with a muzzle – whinnying from time to time, then galloping away.

The colonel's voice rose above the hilarity. 'Yes,' he said, 'for some, perhaps, that would be sufficient.'

Madame Maniu leaned toward the colonel and spoke briefly in Roumanian.

Maniu nodded, then said, 'I trust you understand our position in this. We will, of course, do whatever needs to be done.' His tone had stiffened, as though he were defending his honor.

'Well, yes, of course,' Serebin said.

One of the zebras came bounding to their table and, as she bent over the colonel and began to unknot his tie, Serebin found himself staring at an excessively powdered behind, which waggled violently and threatened to upset his Amalfi. Maniu smiled patiently, being a good sport his only option, while Serebin whipped the glass away and held it safely in the air. He was unaware of the expression on his face, but Marie-Galante watched him for a moment, then burst into helpless laughter. The zebra finally got the tie off and went cantering away with it, held high like a prize.

Marie-Galante wiped her eyes and said, 'Oh dear God.'

The colonel persisted. 'What I was going to say, was that we are very much indebted to Ivan Kostyka, but it has nothing whatever to do with money.'

In the center of the room, a great commotion. A zebra had snatched a pair of eyeglasses from a very fat man with a shaved head, who turned pink and tried desperately to look like he was having fun. And while he was perhaps too embarrassed to try to retrieve the glasses, his wife clearly wasn't. She ran shrieking after the girl, who danced away from her, then climbed up on a table, put the glasses on the zebra head, and did a vivid dance on the general theme of myopia. Meanwhile, the Companions played away at full volume, the clarinet soaring to its highest register as the crowd cheered.

Maniu started to speak, but his wife put a hand on his arm, and they all sat back and watched the show. In time, the zebras went prancing off and, a few minutes later, a waiter appeared at the table, bearing Colonel Maniu's tie on a silver tray.

'Our local amusements,' Madame Maniu said.

'Not so different in Paris,' Marie-Galante said. 'It takes people's minds off their troubles. Do you suppose that poor little man got his glasses back?'

'I expect he did,' Madame Maniu said.

'I promise you he did,' the colonel said. 'That poor little man is something or other in the German legation.'

'Always politics,' Serebin said.

'Well, here anyhow,' Madame Maniu said.

'No, it's everywhere.' Serebin finished his drink and looked around for a waiter. 'Maybe time for the desert island.'

'I'll go with you,' the colonel said. 'But we better learn to speak Japanese.'

'You were telling us a story, colonel,' Marie-Galante said.

'Yes,' Maniu said, a sigh in his voice. 'I suppose you should hear it. What happened to us was this: in the spring of '38, Codreanu and his followers were arrested. Codreanu himself had murdered the prime minister, at the railway station in Sinaia, and he and his thugs were plotting to overthrow the king and take the country for themselves. So, certain trusted officers, and I was one of them, one of the leaders, managed this arrest, done in such a way that there was no violence. But the Iron Guard wouldn't go away. Cheered on by their support-ers − philosophy professors at the university, civil servants, just every sort of person, they assassinated Cali-nescu, the prime minister who'd ordered the arrest. Six months later, as the uprising continued, somebody lost patience with the whole business and Codreanu and his followers were executed. 'Shot while trying to escape.' Now that's the oldest story in the world, and for all I know they may actually have been trying to escape, but true or not doesn't matter. Codreanu was a threat to the state, so it was either that, or have him as dictator.

'The Iron Guard vowed revenge, it was like some-body had knocked down a hornets' nest. One of their responses was to let it be known that I was involved in the original arrest. They didn't come after me − maybe more couldn't than didn't, I was very careful − but our two daughters, in school in Bucharest, were harassed. By schoolmates and, far worse, even by some of the teach-ers. I mean, they *spit* on them, on *children*. When Kostyka found out about this, he arranged for them to go to boarding school, in England, where they are now. I suppose we could have gone as well, but I wasn't going to be thrown out of my own country, you understand, not by these people. So, you see, our friend helped us when we were in trouble, and paid for it. Now, if we're needed to do this work again, we'll do it. But please, for God's sake, be careful.'

'For now,' Serebin said, 'we need only to know who we can trust.'

'For now?' The question mark was barely there – Maniu's irony well tempered by courtesy.

'We'll have to see,' Serebin said. 'There may . . .' He stopped short as he saw the singer Valentina, working her way toward them through the crowd.

A waiter brought two chairs, and they all squeezed in together. The second chair was for the singer's gentleman friend, gray and diffident, older – maybe fifty to her thirty, with stooped shoulders and a hesitant smile. 'Gulian,' he said, introducing himself with a nod that passed for a bow, and said little after that. Across the table, Valentina was not much like the typical *chanteuse*. A studious girl, beneath the rouge and mascara, soft and pretty, probably Jewish, Serebin thought, and conservatory-trained, working as a nightclub singer because she needed the money.

Serebin ordered champagne, and Marie-Galante proposed a toast to Valentina. 'To thank you for your song,' she said. 'I am *Parisienne*.'

'Piaf is inspiring,' Valentina said. Like most educated Roumanians, she spoke reasonably good French. 'I heard her in Paris. Twice. Before the war.'

'We're at the Athenée Palace,' Serebin said. 'Buying folk art for our shop on the rue de Seine.'

'Yes? That must be interesting.'

They managed to make small talk, just enough, Marie-Galante coming to the rescue each time it faltered, then Valentina excused herself – she must have a few minutes before the next show started.

When they'd gone, Serebin said, 'Who is he?'

'A businessman,' Maniu said. 'Very rich, one is told. And very private.'

Conversation continued, but Serebin's mind wandered, here and there. The evening was winding down, he could feel it. Madame Maniu glanced at her watch and Colonel Maniu mentioned that he had a car and driver and offered them a ride back to the hotel, but Marie-Galante caught Serebin's eye and he declined. Not long after that they said good night, and Serebin asked for the check.

As they headed for the door, Serebin looked back at the table. The waiter had collected what remained of the bottle of champagne, and the half-empty glasses, and was carrying them, very carefully, back to the kitchen.

It was long after midnight when they left. Snow was falling, soft and heavy in the night air, and the street lay in the still silence that comes with snow. A *trasuri,* a horse-drawn cab, stood alone in front of the Tic Tac Club.

Serebin helped Marie-Galante up the step. 'The Athenée Palace,' he told the cabman. They sat close together on the old cowhide seat, and Marie-Galante rested her head on his shoulder. The cabman, in heavy mustache and crushed hat, flicked the reins and they moved off down the street.

It was so quiet they did not speak. The cold night smelled good after the smoky cellar. Serebin closed his eyes and, for a time, there was only the squeak of the turning wheels and the steady trot of the horse on the snow-covered pavement. When the horse slowed, abruptly, Serebin looked up to see where they were. They had come to an intersection, where the strada Rosetti met the Boulevard Magheru. Not far from the hotel, he thought. The horse went a little further, then stopped, its ears pricked for a moment, then flattened back against its head. *Now what?* The cabman made a clicking sound but the horse didn't move, so he spoke to it, very gently, a question. Suddenly, Marie-Galante's hand went rigid on his arm, so tight he could feel her fingernails, and he smelled burning. In the distance, a muffled snap, then another, and a third.

The cabman turned and looked at them. Calmly, Serebin waved him on, saying 'Just go ahead' in French. The cabman called the horse's name and it took a few steps, then stopped again. Now the cabman spoke to them. They didn't understand the words but they could see he was frightened – of what lay ahead but, also, of disobeying well-dressed people who came out of night-clubs. 'It's all right,' Marie-Galante said. 'It's all right.'

He tried once more, this time cracking a green leather whip above the horse's withers. The horse lowered its head and moved off at a fast trot. A minute went by, maybe whatever was going on, a few blocks away, was over. But it wasn't. Somewhere in the next street, a sharp crack and a rolling echo, cut by the rhythmic thump of a machine gun, followed by shouted orders. The air above the cab sang for an instant and the horse twisted in its harness and reared up as the cabman fought the reins. The cabman's eyes were wide when he turned around. '*Va rog, domnul,*' he pleaded. Serebin knew at least this much Roumanian, it meant 'please, sir.' Up ahead, Serebin saw two shadows, running low from one doorway to the next. '*Va rog, domnul,*' the driver said, pointing to his horse. He repeated it, again and again, and Serebin could see he was crying.

'We have to get out,' Serebin said.

He climbed down, and helped Marie-Galante, who tried a few steps in the snow, then took her shoes off and walked quickly beside him. Behind them, the cabman turned the *trasuri* in a wide circle, then disappeared back down the street.

'I hate Bucharest this time of year,' Marie-Galante said, breath coming hard.

'Are you all right?' he said.

'For the moment.'

'Over there,' he said, heading toward the arched entryway of an apartment building. The arch covered a porte cochere, which ran some thirty feet back to a massive door with a griffon's head on the iron ring that served as a handle. Serebin tried the handle, then pounded on the door.

He gave up, after a while, and they settled against the wall that supported the arch, deep in shadow. 'I better put these back on,' Marie-Galante said, hanging on to Serebin and forcing one wet foot at a time into the suede heels. There was a brief silence, then the machine gun started up again, a series of three-round bursts that went on and on, and were joined first by scattered rifle shots, then a second machine gun, sharper and faster than the first.

The smell of fire intensified until Serebin's eyes began to water, and a drift of black smoke floated over the snow. Across the street, a window on the top floor was cranked open, the creak of rusty metal absurdly loud against the background of gunfire. A silhouette with rumpled hair thrust itself out the open window, shook its fist, and shouted angrily. A second voice, a woman's voice, shouted even louder, the silhouette disappeared, and the window was cranked shut.

Serebin laughed. Marie-Galante said, 'And don't ever, *ever,* let me catch you doing that again!' Then, a moment later, 'You don't suppose it's going to be a *long* coup d'état, do you?'

'What we want now is daylight, that usually makes a

difference.' He looked at his watch. 'Almost two, so . . .'

'Three hours. Want to beat on the door again?'

'No.'

'Sing 'Frère Jacques'?'

A beam of yellow light appeared on the street. It swept from one side to the other, returned, and went out. From the same direction, back toward the nightclub, came the irregular beat of an old car engine. '*Merde,*' Marie-Galante said. 'We're on the wrong side of this thing.'

The car crawled toward them, they pressed themselves against the icy stone wall beneath the arch, as far as possible into the shadow. 'Don't cross over,' Serebin said.

The car came into view, then stopped almost directly in front of the entryway. Painted on the door was a fiery crucifix crossing a dagger. 'The Iron Guard cavalry,' Serebin said.

'Shh.'

The searchlight was mounted on the roof. As the car idled, it snapped on, probed the entryway, crept up the side of the building, then went off.

'They know,' Serebin whispered. *The door. A telephone call.*

The car door opened, the dome light went on, somebody swore, and the door slammed. They heard footsteps crunching in the snow.

He was sixteen, Serebin thought. With a strange, elongated face – something wrong with him. Hair cut high above the ears, armband with symbol. He carried a rifle and, when he saw them, he lazily pointed it at Serebin's heart and spoke a few words, his voice edgy and tight. They raised their hands. He beckoned, they stepped toward him, and he backed up until all three were just under the edge of the arch.

He stared at them for a moment, swung the rifle back and forth, from one to the other, then worked the bolt.

''Bye, *ours.*'

The boy spoke again, irritated. And again.

'What's he want?' Marie-Galante said.

Serebin had no idea.

The boy pointed to his eyes, then away.

'He means,' Serebin said, 'don't look at me while I do this.'

'Fuck him.'

A voice from the car, a question.

An answer, fast, thick with tension.

Again, the voice from the car.

The boy with the rifle answered, querulous this time.

The car door opened, then slammed shut. Somebody spoke, and the searchlight hit Serebin full in the face. He had to close his eyes.

But he'd seen that the second one was older, and had a pistol of some sort in his hand. That meant command. 'Lei,' the man said. 'Francs, pounds.'

Serebin thought of saying 'Reichsmarks,' which would save their lives, but he didn't have any. Instead, he reached slowly into his pocket and threw money, mostly lei, on the snow. Marie-Galante took off her watch and her necklace and dropped them on the money. The man pointed to her hand, she added her wedding band.

'Passportul.'

Serebin produced his passport and tossed it on the ground. Marie-Galante searched her small evening bag, swore, mumbled something about the hotel room, then found hers. The older man picked them up, along with the money and the jewelry. He paged through the passports, saw the *Ausweis* and other German documents, then said *'Franculor,'* French, and tossed them away.

He spoke to the boy with the rifle. It sounded like a man talking to someone he knows is crazy – soothing, but firm. The boy lowered the rifle. The commander turned to Serebin and Marie-Galante, said, 'Hotel,' and jerked his head in the direction they'd been going in the cab. When he saw that Serebin understood, he said, *'La revedere, domnul,'* good evening, and the two returned to the car. The searchlight went off, the car turned around and drove away.

Serebin saw the boy again, a few days later. Or maybe not, there was no way to be sure. He'd been hanged from an iron bar that held the sign for an umbrella shop, and the face was quite different, but Serebin rather thought it was him.

THE
GREEN
SALON

5 January, 1941.

They watched it go on, for the next few days, sometimes from the tall windows in their room, the red and gold drapes tied back with braid, sometimes through the doors in the lobby, which looked out on an empty square and a statue of a brass king on a brass horse.

No windows in the lobby itself, only yellow marble pillars, settees in raspberry plush, Bordeaux carpets, mirrored walls, and, through a pair of arches, a green salon, with foreign newspapers laid out on low marble tables, and a gold-framed photograph of King Carol on an easel. In the green salon, one ordered Turkish coffee and listened to the fighting; around the royal palace, just next door, or the nearby police station. It was old Europe in the green salon, it smelled of araby – the scent, like violets, worn by Roumanian men, smelled of leather, of Turkish tobacco.

Sometimes the fighting stopped, and in the silence some of the guests went out for a breath of air and wandered through the streets, though not *too* far, to see what they could see. At dusk, on the third day of fighting, in the strada Stirbei Voda, Serebin came upon a bloodstain on the snow and a burning candle. He walked another block and saw, chalked on a wall, *Homo homini lupus est.* Hobbes's phrase, 'It is man who is the wolf of mankind.' And what heartbroken citizen had dared, in the hours of street fighting, to do such a thing? Well, he was Serebin's friend for life, whoever he was.

When the attack began – the traditional occupation of the national radio station, followed by the traditional plea for public calm and the traditional proclamation of a new regime – the Bucharest police, armed with pistols and rifles, had fought back, but they were no match for the legionnaires. Then the army appeared. Much the subject of rumors in the hotel lobby – *the army has refused to leave its barracks, the army has gone over to the Guard.* But then, very late on the second night, Serebin woke to the sound of cannon fire and saw a spectral Marie-Galante, nude and pale, staring pensively out the window. 'At last, the army,' she said.

He joined her. Down on the strada Episcopiei, a group of artillerymen, in the sand-colored uniforms of the Roumanian army, were firing a field gun; a tongue of flame at the barrel, a shell tearing through the sky, then a distant explosion. And, on both sides of the street, as far as he could see, infantry, running from doorway to doorway, one or two at a time, going wherever the shells were going.

'It's over,' Serebin said.

And, a day later, it was. In Bucharest, anyhow. For the time being.

Elsewhere, it continued. There were maps in the newspapers every day, and in some apartments, all across the continent, there were maps pinned to the kitchen wall. So it could be followed, studied, day after day, the war that went here, then there. To Libya, where British troops fought Italian units at Tobruk, to Albania, where Greek troops pushed Italian divisions back across the Shkumbi River and headed for Tirana. To northern Italy, where British warships from Gibraltar entered the Gulf of Genoa, shelled the city's port, and bombarded the oil refinery at Leghorn.

That story was in the *Tribune de Genève,* which Serebin read in the green salon, while eating a large sugared bun studded with raisins. At the next table, a thin woman wearing bright red lipstick, a fur stole around her shoulders, spoke German to a friend. 'My dear, I cannot *abide* this Marshal Antonescu, 'the Red Dog' I think they call him. Is that because he is a communist?'

'No, my dear, it's his hair, not his politics.'

'Is it. Well then, I *do* so hope the Guard will, ah, put him down.'

They both laughed, gaily enough, but it was not to be, and, a day later, as the snow melted beneath a winter sun, the captured legionnaires were taken away in trucks, or dealt with in the street. Still, it wasn't over yet, not according to the hall porter on the fifth floor, who shook his head and was sorry about the way people were now.

That afternoon, Serebin and Marie-Galante went to the strada Lipscani house to make telephone calls. Rather vague and general – *an acquaintance in Paris suggested . . . Would so-and-so be at home?* Then Serebin took a tram out to a neighborhood of opulent homes, where a retired naval officer had coffee served in the conservatory and said he had never heard of DeHaas AG.

Serebin got away as quickly as possible, and found Marie-Galante waiting for him at the Lipscani house, just back from an hour with a prominent lawyer.

'What did he say?' Serebin asked.

'He said that some people preferred to make love only in the afternoon.'

'And then?'

'That some women required a firm hand to make them passionate.'

'And *then?*'

'I mentioned DeHaas. He gave up on the firm hand in the afternoon, and explained that the Roumanian legal system was dynamic, not static, that it followed the French, not the English model, particularly with respect to contracts concerning the disposition of agrarian lands.'

'Well, good, I was worried about that.'

'He went on. And on. Eventually, he showed me to the door, told me I was beautiful, and tried to kiss me.'

Dr. Latanescu, the economist, was dead.

And the Hungarian bank employee had returned to Budapest. But Troucelle, the French petrochemical engineer, seemed pleased with a French telephone call – made by Marie-Galante, the native speaker – and invited them to lunch at the Jockey Club. 'I'm free tomorrow. Can we say, one o'clock?'

He waved and smiled when they came through the door, clearly delighted at the prospect of lunch. Which was quite good; a puree of white beans, boiled chicken with sour cream and horseradish, and a bottle of white Cotnari, from Moldavian vineyards on the Black Sea.

'The Burgundy *négociants* needn't worry,' he said, tasting the wine, 'but they don't do so badly here.'

He was terribly bright, Serebin thought. Young and brisk and competent, a classic product of the Sorbonne's Polytechnique, wandering abroad, like so many Frenchmen, to make his fortune in foreign lands. Over lunch they followed, as best they could, the Gallic prohibition, *no discussion of work or politics at table,* and made it just past the chicken – a considerable achievement given the situation in the city. Then Troucelle said, 'I have to confess, I've thought and thought, but I don't believe I actually know this Monsieur Richard you mentioned.'

'No?' Marie-Galante said. 'He was here maybe two or three years ago, with a company called DeHaas.'

'Hmm. Could he have used another name?'

'Well, he could have. But why would he?'

Troucelle had no idea. 'Of course you never know, with people, especially abroad.'

'No, that's true.'

And there she let it stay.

A waiter pushing a pastry cart arrived at the table. 'Just coffee, I think?' the civilized Troucelle suggested. From Marie-Galante, the Genghis Khan of the dessert table, civilized agreement.

'After Poland,' Troucelle said, 'I remember thinking, 'I expect someone from DeHaas will turn up here.' Appears I was right, no?'

'Logical, really, when you think about it.'

'I enjoyed my connection with Kostyka,' Troucelle said. 'One only met his *people,* of course, he never appeared in person. Always the *fusées.*' It meant fuses, in French political slang, intervening layers of aides and assistants who would 'burn out' before an important person could be reached by the law. 'And in the end,' Troucelle continued, 'the whole thing didn't amount to much, a few research reports on the petroleum industry. And they were quite generous about it.'

'Even more so, now, I would think.'

'Yes, it's only logical, as you put it. What sort of information do you suppose they'd want?'

Marie-Galante wasn't sure. 'Perhaps what you gave them before, but it's not for us to say. The war was a shock to the commercial world, even though everybody could see it coming, but business can't just stop dead. So it's mostly a matter of flexibility – I suspect that's the way DeHaas would see it. Find a way to adapt, to adjust, then get on with life.'

The waiter brought tiny cups of coffee, a dish of curled lemon peels, and little spoons.

'Going up to Ploesti?' Troucelle said.

'Think it's a good idea?'

'I don't see why not. It's all *there,* you know, it was a real, honest-to-God oil town before the war, Texas riggers and all. They used to have contests on Saturday night, get drunk and see who could shoot out the most streetlights. A little bit of Tulsa, east of the Oder.'

'We have business in Bucharest,' Serebin said, 'and our time is limited. But, maybe, if we have the opportunity . . .'

'It would be my pleasure,' Troucelle said. 'I'd enjoy showing it to you.'

'Nazi bastard,' Marie-Galante said – but by then they were out in the street, walking back toward the hotel.

'How do you know?'

'I know.' And, a moment later, 'Don't you?'

He did. He couldn't say how he did, it was just, there. But then, he thought, that's why they'd hired him. *I. A. Serebin – Minor Russian writer, émigré.*

After midnight, in the room in the hotel, Serebin stared up at the ceiling and smoked a Sobranie. 'Are you awake?' he said.

'I am.'

'Just barely?'

'No, I'm up.'

'Want me to turn on the light?'

'No, leave it dark.'

'Something I want to ask you.'

'Yes?'

'Did DeHaas actually do something? Or did it just, exist?'

'I believe they were in the business of building steam mills. Flour mills.'

'Were they built?'

'That I don't know. Probably the office functioned, sent letters, telegrams, talked on the phone. Maybe they built a few mills, why not?'

'But these people, Maniu, the lawyer, they knew what they were doing.'

'Oh yes.'

'And Troucelle, of course he knew. And he knows what we're doing now, and that it has to do with Roumanian oil – all that business about Ploesti.'

'Yes, the instinct of the *agent provocateur*. And, they're going up to the oil fields, why not arrest them there?'

'So?'

'So it's a problem, and it has to be solved. He may just want to be bribed, and, if that's it, we'll bribe him. Or, he may go to the Siguranza, but that's not the end of the world. You see, Polanyi calculated that we'd talk to the wrong person, sooner or later. But he counted on two things to keep us safe, two forms of reluctance. If Troucelle turns us in, like a good little Vichy fascist, he turns himself in as well. Why do these people, who want to spy on Roumania, come to him? Because he used to spy on Roumania himself. Oh really, they'll say, you did? When? What did they pay you? Who else did it? You don't know? Sure you know, why won't you tell us? Clearly, he'd best think things through very carefully before he goes singing to the Roumanians.

'And then, the second kind of reluctance is in the Siguranza itself, up at the top. They'd better have a meeting, because they'd better talk about how it's going to go here. Today's enemy may be tomorrow's ally, then what? Seven months ago, Germany wouldn't dare attack the mighty French army behind its impregnable Maginot Line. Seventeen months ago, Germany wouldn't dare to attack Poland, because the Red Army would go to war against them and in six months the Mongolian hordes would be fucking the Valkyries in the Berlin opera house. The world has come undone, my love, and this thing isn't over, and, when it is, quite a considerable number of people are going to discover they jumped into the wrong bed.'

'All right. But what if he goes to the Germans?'

'Well, a lot depends on which Germans he goes to. If he's best pals with the chief of Gestapo counterintelligence in Roumania, that's the end of us. With the others, the SD or the Abwehr, it's not so bad. They'll watch and listen and wait – they'll want *more,* there's always *more.* And, the way Polanyi has it planned, we have a good chance to disappear while that's going on. As it is, we're only here for a few more days, then out. If you don't have time to do it right, Polanyi figured, do it wrong, do it fast and ugly, break all the rules, and run like hell. That's why you're called Marchais, my sweet, so you can return as Serebin.'

'Well, it *sounds* good,' Serebin said. 'Safe in bed, it sounds good.'

'Polanyi is a kind of genius, *mon ours,* dark as night, but what else would you want? He's done these things all his life – that's *all* he's done. He once told me that he'd been taken to some kind of lawn party, at the Italian legation in Budapest, where he made his way to a certain office and stole papers from a drawer. He was, at the time, eleven years old.'

'He went with his father?'

'He went with his *grandfather.*'

'Good God.'

'Hungarians, my sweet, Hungarians. Swimming for ten centuries in a sea of enemies – how the hell do you suppose they're still there?'

Readily enough, the Princess Baltazar agreed to receive the friend of Monsieur Richard in Paris. As though, he told Marie-Galante, such calls were commonplace. The house was not hard to find, a white, three-story frosted cake, with turrets and gables, overlooking the botanical gardens. Once upon a time he had played on a beach in Odessa, and a little girl had taught him to take liquid sand from the edge of the sea and drizzle it through his fingers to decorate the top of a castle. The house of the Princess Baltazar reminded him of that.

She was somewhere beyond forty, blond and curly, pink and creamy, with a bosomy décolletage on a purple dress just tight enough to suggest the elaborate and complicated flesh beneath it.

'Monsieur Richard,' she said. 'With the *pince-nez?*'

Who else?

'Such a brilliant man.' Would Monsieur care for coffee? Something to eat? There was a bit of Moldavian Swiss roll, she thought, or was it just too close to lunch?

'A coffee,' he said.

She left the room, haunches shifting high and low, and he could hear her making coffee in a distant part of the house. No maid? The tabletops in the parlor were covered with little things; china cats and porcelain dairy-maids, demitasse cups and saucers, bud vases, ashtrays. And photographs in standing frames: Princess Baltazar with King Carol, Princess Baltazar with various signifi-cant men – minor royalty, chinless aristocrats, and two or three nineteenth-century types with grandiose beards and decorations.

'So many friends,' he said, when she returned with the coffees and thick slices of the dangerous-looking Moldavian pastry.

'What other pleasures in this life?' she said, sitting next to him on the couch. 'Will you relent on the roll, monsieur?'

Serebin smiled as he declined. 'And who is this?' he said, pointing at one of the photographs.

'Ah, if you were Roumanian, you would not have to ask,' she said.

'A well-known gentleman, then.'

'Our dear Popadu, the economics minister, a few months ago, and a great friend of Elena's.' She meant Lupescu, the former king's mistress. 'I am told he is lately in Tangier.' Sad for him, to judge from her expression.

'And this?' The man he pointed to looked like a Ruritanian minister in a Marx Brothers film.

Why that was Baron Struba, the well-known diplomat. 'Poor man. He was on the train with Carol and Elena, and he was shot in the – well, he couldn't sit down for a month.' Serebin knew the story. When Carol had abdicated in September, he'd had a train filled with gold and paintings, even his collection of electric trains, then made a run for the Yugoslavian border. Along the way, units of the Iron Guard had fired on the train and, while Lupescu, a real lioness, had remained resolutely in her seat, Carol had gone into exile cowering in his cast-iron bathtub.

'You seem to know,' Serebin said, 'everybody.'

The princess was demure on that point, eyes lowered, saying volumes with a modest silence. When she looked up, she rested a hand on the couch by his side. 'And what brings you to Bucharest?' she said. Her smile was inviting, her eyes soft. He was, if he let on that he was rich or powerful, going to be seduced.

'I am here to buy art,' he said.

'Art!' She was delighted. 'I can certainly help you there. I know all the best dealers.' He could return to Paris, he realized, with a trunkful of fake Renoirs and Rembrandts.

'Then too, I wanted to do a favor for a friend of mine, who used to work for a Swiss company here. Called, what, DeHaas, I think, something like that.'

Her eyes changed, and there was a longish silence. 'What sort favor?' Her French was dying.

'To see old friends. Get back in touch.'

'Who are you, monsieur?' she said. She bit her lip.

'Just a Parisian,' he said.

Her eyes glistened, then a tear rolled down her cheek.

'I will be arrested,' she said. She began to cry, her face contorted, a thin, steady moan escaping her compressed lips.

'Don't, please,' Serebin said.

Her voice rose to a tiny, choked-back wail. 'The matrons.'

'No, no, princess, no matrons, please, don't.'

She began to fumble with the back of her dress, her face had turned a bright red. 'I will please you,' she said. 'I will astound you.'

Serebin stood. 'I am so sorry, princess.'

'No! Don't go away!'

'Please,' he said. 'It was a mistake to come here.'

She sobbed, her face in her hands.

Serebin left.

Outside, as he walked quickly away from the botanical gardens, he realized that his hands were shaking. He headed for a café on the Calea Victoriei, sat on the glass-enclosed terrace, thought about a vodka, ordered a coffee, then took a newspaper on a wooden dowel from a rack by the cash register – a copy of *Paris Soir*, the leading Parisian daily.

Reading the paper did not make him feel better. The German propaganda line was not overt, but it was everywhere: *we are crusaders, out to rid Europe of Bolsheviks and Jews, and, regrettably, have been forced to occupy your country. Please pardon the inconvenience.* Thus twenty minutes of *Paris Soir* gave Serebin a bad case of traveler's melancholy – what one learned not to see up close was unpleasantly clear from a distance. Life in Paris, said the paper, had always been amusing, and it still was. There were reviews of films and plays – romantic farce much the current taste. Recipes for stewed rabbit and turnips with vinegar – it may be all there is to eat, but why not make it delicious? Interviews with 'the man on the street' – what ever happened to plain old common courtesy? There was rather hazy news of the campaigns in North Africa and Greece, with expressions like 'mobile defense' and 'strategic readjustment in the battle lines.' And news of Roosevelt, urging Congress to loan money and ships to Britain. Gullible people, the Americans, how sad.

And so on. From local murders, robberies, and fires, to indoor bicycle racing, and, finally, the obituaries. Which included:

The artistic community of Paris has been saddened to learn of the death of the Polish sculptor Stanislaus Mut. Turkish papers reported yesterday that his body had been found floating in the Bosphorus, death having occurred from unknown causes. Istanbul police are investigating. Born in Lodz in 1889, Stanislaus Mut lived much of his life in Paris, emigrating to Turkey in 1940. Two of his works, *Woman Reclining*, and *Ballerina*, are on display at the Art Museum of the City of Rouen.

Serebin recalled meeting Stanislaus Mut, who'd been courting a Russian woman at the *cocktail Américain* on Della Corvo's yacht. What happened? An accident? Suicide? Murder? Did his presence at the party make him an associate of Polanyi's? Serebin returned the paper to its rack and paid for his coffee. *Fuck this day, nothing's going to go right.*

But maybe it was only him. Back at the Athenée Palace, Marie-Galante had good news. She had visited with a professor of botany at the university. 'He will do anything,' she said. 'We have only to ask.'

'What can he do?'

That she didn't know.

Well then, why was he there in the first place?

'He said he reported to DeHaas on developments in Roumanian science and technology.'

'Oh.'

'Don't look at me like that. What happened with

Princess Baltazar? Were you charmed? Were you – naughty?'

Serebin described the meeting.

'Maybe I should have gone with you,' she said, slightly deflated.

'You think it would have made a difference?'

She hesitated, then said, 'No, probably not.'

The next two days were a blur. Life got harder: a number of calls went unanswered, and a few of the people who did answer spoke only Roumanian, managing an apologetic word or two in English or German, then hanging up. The heat went off in the Lipscani house, Serebin and Marie-Galante worked in their coats, breath steaming. The eight German names on the list were not telephoned. A police detective threatened to arrest them if they came anywhere near his house, while three people didn't know a single soul in Paris or in France for that matter yes they were sure.

The wife of a civil servant thought they were selling bonds, which she made it very clear she didn't want to buy. At the hotel desk, no contact from Troucelle, which was either good or bad, they couldn't be sure. An accountant, from an office that worked on the books of the oil companies, said, 'I cannot meet with you, I hope you will understand.'

'If the question is,' Serebin said to Marie-Galante, 'can Kostyka's intelligence *apparat* be brought back to life, perhaps we have an answer.'

'Don't give up,' Marie-Galante said. 'Not yet.'

Through the concierge at the Athenée Palace they hired a car and driver to take them up to Brasov, in the foothills of the Carpathians north of the city. 'Dracula country,' Marie-Galante said. 'Vlad Tepes and all that, though these days it's mostly ski resorts.' And antique shops, where peasant arts and crafts were for sale. Serebin understood that Monsieur and Madame Marchais, having come to Roumania to buy folk art, had, eventually, to go and buy it. Still, he did not look forward to the excursion.

The driver told them his name was Octavian. A candidate, Serebin thought, for the oiliest man in Bucharest, which was no small distinction. His mustache was oiled to sharply pointed ends, oily curls sprang loose from his hair. Octavian welcomed them to his humble car – an old but highly polished Citroën with a plume of rich, blue smoke throbbing from its tailpipe, rubbed his hands like a concert pianist, grasped the wheel firmly and, after a moment of meditation, began to drive.

The road to Brasov took them through Ploesti, as it happened, where army officers manned checkpoints and demanded a special pass, required to enter the city, which they did not have. Octavian went off for a private chat with the commanding officer, then returned to the car and told Serebin what it cost. Could it be that much? Marie-Galante shrugged. Roumanian army officers were paid a daily wage of thirty lei, about six cents in American money, so bribery was a way of life. It had always been a poor country, too often conquered, too often plundered. The Russian General Kutuzov, preparing to invade Roumania in 1810, said of the Roumanians that he 'would leave them only their eyes to weep with.'

Driving through Ploesti they could, now and again, get a view of the oil fields in the distant haze: the tops of the towers, and the natural gas flares, seen as wobbling air against a pale sky. A mile further on they reached the final checkpoint, at the northern edge of the city, with the usual crowd of Roumanian soldiers supplemented by two German SS officers. The Germans were curious, took the passports and examined them at length, made notes in a ledger, asked what brought them this way, and why no pass. Better not to have it, Serebin realized. Better to be hapless art dealers, confused and uncertain when it came to official papers and difficult things like that. The taller of the SS men was affable enough, until he asked Serebin for his wife's maiden name. Serebin laughed nervously, then gave the name that Marie-Galante had insisted he memorize. 'So,' she said as they drove away, 'now you see.'

The road narrowed after Ploesti and wound through woods and farmland, the Carpathians looming high in the distance. Serebin's spirits rose, it always surprised him how much he needed fields and trees. A city dweller, he thought himself, craving places where they kept cafés and conversations and books and love affairs. But he did not take sufficient account of his Odessan heart, eternally warm for a city that had, with its dirt streets and wild gardens and leaning shacks overgrown with vines, its own heart in the countryside. Marie-Galante felt his mood change, and took his hand in both of hers. At which moment Octavian met Serebin's eyes in the rearview mirror and gave him an immensely oily and conspiratorial smile. *Women, always women, only women.*

Brasov was a small city, still, at its center, more or less in the thirteenth century. 'See there,' Octavian said. 'The Black Church. Very famous.' It was black, an ashy black, like charcoal. 'Toasted by the Austrians in 1689,' he explained, his French failing him for a moment.

In a narrow lane behind the church they found a row of antique shops, the owners, not expecting much business in January and civil war, called down to do business by Octavian shouting in the street. Serebin and Marie-Galante bought a large wooden trunk plastered with the labels of long-vanished steamships, then looked for folk art to pack inside, Octavian sometimes signaling to them with agonized glances when the price was too high.

Serebin bought toys. A wooden ball bound to a stick with a cord – though how a child would contrive to play with such a thing was completely beyond him, and a variety of spinning tops. Also wood carvings: a hut, a sheep, a few saints, and several hounds, some lying with crossed paws, others bounding after prey. Marie-Galante added embroidered vests, wooden and ceramic bowls, and a set of woodworker's tools that could have been centuries old, then bought a Persian lamb hat for herself. She tried it on, setting it at various angles, as Octavian and the shopkeeper and Serebin looked on, and asked them did it look better like this? Or this?

Serebin had called the number earlier, with no success, and drawn a line through the entry: *Gheorghe Musa – senior civil servant.* On the right-hand side of the page, no indication of payment. Now, the morning after they returned from Brasov, he tried one last time. Dialed, then stared out the window and waited as the double ring, a dry whispery vibrato, repeated itself again and again. It would, he knew, never be answered.

But it was.

'Yes? Who's calling, please.' It was the voice of an old man. Perhaps, Serebin thought, an old man whose phone had not rung for a long time.

'I hope I'm not intruding,' Serebin said.

'No, sir, you are not.'

'My name is Marchais, I happen to be in Bucharest, and I'm calling at the suggestion of a friend in Paris.'

'Marchais.'

'Yes, that's right.'

In the silence on the telephone Serebin could hear the silence of the old man's apartment. *He knows,* Serebin thought. Knows perfectly well what kind of telephone call this is, and he's thinking it over. At last, a voice. 'How may I help you?'

'Would it be convenient for us to speak in person?'

Another pause. 'All right. Would you want to come here?'

Serebin said he did, and Musa gave him a tram number, a stop, and an address.

The apartment occupied an entire floor, up six steep flights of stairs. Inside it was dark, and so quiet that Serebin was conscious of the sound of his footsteps. It immediately occurred to him, though he could not have said how he knew, that no woman had ever lived there. Gheorghe Musa was a small man, frail, with a few wisps of white hair and a pleasant smile. 'You are a rare visitor,' he said. For the visit, or perhaps it was his usual habit, he had dressed formally; a heavy, wool suit, of a style popular in the 1920s, a white shirt with a high collar, a gray tie.

Musa walked slowly to a room lined with bookcases that reached the ceiling. When he turned on a lamp, Serebin could see, by his chair, well-used editions of Balzac and Proust, a Latin dictionary, a set of German encyclopedias.

'And, so, what brings you to Bucharest?'

Serebin mentioned folk art, Brasov, then DeHaas.

'Oh yes,' Musa said. 'Some years ago, I used to see a gentleman who worked for that organization. Owned by – he calls himself Baron Kostyka now, I believe. We used to pass information to them, now and then. Depending on what we wanted them to do.' His smile broadened in recollection. 'Influence,' he said. 'A ministry word.'

'We?'

'Oh I worked for several ministries, over the years. I was at Interior for a long time, then, eventually, the Foreign Ministry, with various titles, until I retired. 1932, that was.'

'It's that old?'

'DeHaas? Oh yes, very old, and venerable. A local institution, really. And why not? Kostyka's financial arrangements were large enough to have an effect here, in this country. We tried to make sure his manipulations were favorable to Roumania. We didn't always succeed, but that's the game, as I'm sure you know. One must always try.'

'So, you're retired.' Serebin prepared to leave.

'Yes. For a time I stayed active — a special assignment, once in a while, but that's all gone now. I'm a Jew, you see, and that's entirely out of fashion here.'

'Like Germany.'

'Not quite that bad, not yet. But there are, restrictions. I had to give up my radio, last month, and one does miss it terribly. But you wouldn't want Jews having radios, would you. We are also forbidden servants, and, lately, there's talk about housing. I have no idea where I'll go if they take this place away from me.'

'What would they do with it?'

'Give it to their friends. It's a way they've found to improve their lives. You're surprised?'

'Unfortunately, no. It's everywhere, Germany's influence.'

'Yes, that, but we have our own enthusiasts. The Legion staged a grand event last November, the Day of the Martyrs they called it. The remains of Codreanu and his henchmen were supposedly dug up, two years after their execution, and reinterred, here in Bucharest. Fifty-five thousand Iron Guardsmen marched and a hundred thousand sympathizers cheered them on. The schools were closed, Codreanu and his thirteen followers were declared 'national saints' by the Orthodox church, the newspapers were printed in green ink. The ceremony was attended by official delegations from all over fascist Europe — Hitler Youth from Germany, Spanish Falangists, Italians, even a group of Japanese. As the coffins were lowered into a mausoleum, German war planes flew overhead and dropped funeral wreaths — one of them hit a legionnaire on the head and knocked him out cold. Then the Legion marched for hours, singing their anthems, while, in the streets, people wept with passion.'

He paused, and Serebin realized that he had actually seen it.

'Yes,' Musa said. 'I was there.'

Serebin could see him in the crowd, old, invisible.

'I had to do something.'

After a moment, Serebin said, 'Will Roumania be occupied? Like France?'

'We are occupied, sir. The Germans began to arrive in October, even before the king ran away. Just twenty or so, at first, in residence at the Athenée Palace, their boots lining the hall at night, set out to be cleaned and polished. Then more, and more. 'The German Military Mission to Roumania,' a euphemism taken from the language of diplomacy. A few thousand of them, now, housed in barracks, and they keep coming. But it will never be an official occupation, we've signed up as allies. The only question that remains is, who will govern here? The Legion? Or Marshal Antonescu? It's Hitler's choice, we await his pleasure.'

'Will there be, resistance?'

Musa smiled, a sad smile, and shook his head very slowly. 'No,' he said softly. 'Not here.'

Serebin didn't want to go, but sensed it was time to leave. Gheorghe Musa would do for them whatever he could, but what that might turn out to be was for others to decide.

'Perhaps you will tell me something,' Musa said.

Serebin waited.

'What precisely interests *you*, at this moment?'

Serebin hesitated. *Hard to know, right now. Of course, as events unfold* . . . That was the established line and Serebin knew it was correct – the question had to be deflected. But then, for a reason he couldn't name, he said, 'Natural resources.'

'Oil and wheat.'

'Yes.'

Musa stood and walked to the bookshelves on the other side of the room, peering at a long row of red cardboard binders with handwritten labels on their spines. 'If I have to leave here,' he said, 'I suppose I will lose the library. It's not the kind of thing you can take to, to – wherever it might be.'

He turned to a floor lamp, tugged on the chain again and again until the light went on, then went back to the binders. 'One thing about governments,' he said, 'think of them what you will, but they do write reports.' He ran his finger along the row. 'For example, wheat and rye production in the province of Wallachia in 1908. Read that one? Bet you haven't. There's a drought in the final chapter, it will keep you up all night. Certainly kept *us* up. Or, let's see, *Ethnic Census of Transylvania* – the date gives that one away, 1918, after they chased the Hungarians out. Or maybe you'd like . . . *Petroleum Production and Transport: Report of the General Staff.* The date being, uh, 1922.' He slid the binder out, brought it over to Serebin, and handed it to him.

Serebin turned the pages. The text in Roumanian he couldn't read, but he found a map, with boundaries in dotted lines, and underlined names. Astra Romano. Unirea Speranitza. Dacia Romana. Redeventa Xenia. Standard Petrol Block. Romana Americana. Steaua Romana. Concordia Vega.

'The oil fields,' Musa explained. 'With the names of the concessions.'

'What is it?'

'A study of our vulnerabilities, undertaken by the General Staff of the army. After the British raid of 1916, we had to look at what happened, what had been done to us, and what might happen in the future. For the British, of course, the destruction was a great success, a triumph. But for us it was a national humiliation, the more so because we did it to ourselves, we were forced to do it, and we had to ask, will this happen every time we go to war? Can we stop it? It's our oil, after all. It's owned by foreigners, but they must pay us for it, and it belongs to us.'

Serebin read further; long columns of numbers, percentages, paragraphs of explanation, a map of the Danube, from Giurgiu in Roumania all the way up to Germany.

'That's the transport route,' Musa said.

Serebin leafed through the pages until he came to the end, then offered the report to Musa.

'Oh, you might as well take that along,' Musa said. 'It's no use to me anymore.'

It snowed again, that night.

Serebin had the concierge book them a ten o'clock table at Capsa, the city's most popular restaurant, famous for its Gypsy orchestra. The hotel doorman helped them into a taxi and told the driver where they were going. Halfway there, two blocks from the Lipscani house, they said they had to stop for a few minutes and asked the driver to wait. Then they walked, hunched over, fighting the bitter wind that blew down from the mountains. Serebin carried the report in a briefcase that Marie-Galante had sent him out to buy earlier that afternoon.

'Cold,' Marie-Galante said.

Serebin agreed.

'Talk to me,' she said. 'We're lovers, going out for the evening.'

'What will you have?'

'Udder in wine.' A Roumanian specialty.

'Will you? Really?'

'God no.'

'There's nobody around,' Serebin said. The city seemed deserted, white snow on empty streets.

'Talk anyhow,' she said.

He talked.

In the lane that led to the Lipscani house, the young officer was shivering in a doorway.

'Our guardian – how does he know to be here?'

'I make a telephone call. To a number that is never answered.'

They entered the Lipscani house and rode up in the moaning elevator. Marie-Galante took the briefcase from him, checked one last time to make sure the report was in there, then placed it by the desk.

They left, heading back toward the waiting taxi. From the darkness, a man in an overcoat came toward them on the other side of the street; head down, hands in pockets, bent against the wind-driven snow. As he hurried past, Serebin saw that it was Marrano.

Back in bed, thank heaven. The long, heavy meal eaten, and no work till morning. It had been a loud Gypsy orchestra, with copious Gypsies – Serebin couldn't count them because they never stopped moving; leaping about the stage in their baggy pants and high boots, a whirl of fiendish grinning and shouting, singing and dancing, and savage, implacable strumming. *Can you play 'Shut Up and Sit Still,' traditional ballad of the Serebin clan?* Nothing worse than nightclub Gypsies when you weren't in the mood, and Serebin wasn't, he was dog tired, period.

Marie-Galante yawned and settled herself on her pillow. 'Thank God that's over,' she said.

'What happens now?'

'Marrano is off to Istanbul. On Lares, the Roumanian airline – may the gods protect him. Polanyi will be pleased, or maybe not, one never knows. Maybe he's had a copy for years, or the information is too old, or it was all wrong to begin with. Still, it can't stay here, and we can't afford to get caught with it. But the important thing is that Musa trusted you.'

'I guess.'

'Oh, he did. It's in your nature.'

'What is?'

'Honor, good faith. You are who you are, *ours*, man without a country, soldier of the world.'

'All that?'

'Well, he saw something.'

'He didn't care, love, he would've given that thing to a gorilla.'

'Maybe. But it happened, didn't it, and it could be important.'

'Or not.'

'Or not.'

She yawned again, rolled over on her stomach, closed her eyes.

From the ballroom, far below them, Serebin could hear the orchestra playing a waltz.

14 January. It was just after eleven when they walked through the lobby, on their way back to work. From the corner of his eye Serebin saw an assistant manager, forefinger held stiff in the air, coming toward him, trying to get his attention. He was a tiny man, unsmiling and formal, who wore a gray cravat with a pearl pin and a boutonniere in his lapel, a pink tea rose that morning. 'Monsieur Marchais? A moment, please, monsieur, if I may?'

The request had a certain pitch to it, an undertone of discretion, which meant, in the mysterious alchemy of hotel protocol, that what he had to say was for Serebin's ears alone. Madame Marchais, the dutiful French wife, continued on her way to the door, while the assistant manager leaned close to Serebin, his voice infinitely confidential.

'Monsieur, your, ah, friend – she did not leave her name,' he paused for a delicate clearing of the throat, 'telephoned last night. Rather late. She did sound terribly, *distressed,* if you'll forgive me, and asked that you call her as soon as you can. She left a telephone number for you.'

The man pressed a slip of paper in Serebin's hand. 'It seemed quite urgent, monsieur.' *Your slut is pregnant, now show some gratitude.*

Which Serebin, magnanimously, did.

Well, would that there had been a slut, he thought later, and the problem *the little problem.*

They hurried to the Lipscani house and Serebin called the number. A woman answered – a cultured voice, but very frightened. 'I am a friend of the colonel,' she said. 'Of the family, you understand?'

He said, 'Yes.' Then mouthed the name *Maniu* to Marie-Galante.

'They've left the country.'

'Why?'

'They had to. He was betrayed. Something about people he used to work with.'

'Did he say what happened?'

'A little. He approached the wrong person.'

'And?'

'They were almost arrested. But they got away, with the clothes on their backs.'

'Do you know where they went?'

'Over the border. I am to tell you that he regrets what happened, that he is sorry. Also, that he wants an old friend to know. You understand this?'

'Yes.'

'He said, "A visa for England."'

'We will do what we can, but we'll have to know where he is.'

She thought about it. 'This is all I can do,' she said.

'Of course. I understand.'

Her voice wavered. 'I would do more, I would do anything, everything, but I cannot. I must not. Other people could suffer.'

'You have to do what's right.'

'I can explain . . .'

'No, don't. Better that you don't.'

'All right, it's finished.'

'It never happened.'

'Then, good-bye.'

'Good-bye.'

'I wish you success. I don't know anything, but I wish you success.'

'Thank you,' Serebin said.

He hung up, then repeated the conversation for Marie-Galante.

'*Merde,*' she said. 'At least they got away.'

'How would he get a visa?'

'We tell Polanyi, he tells the people he's working with in London. The British legations are informed, and they – Lisbon, Madrid – wait for him to show up. That is, if the British are willing to take him.'

'Is it possible they won't?'

'Yes, sad to say.'

'How could that be?'

'Can be, often is. Nature of the world,' she said. 'That world.'

They returned to the Athenée Palace at four. Troucelle called from the lobby. He happened to be passing by. He wondered how they were doing. Serebin said they'd be down in a few minutes.

Marie-Galante sat in a chair, put her face in her hands.

'Are you all right?'

'Tired,' she said. She looked up at him. 'Well, there it goes. What is it, fourteen days? Maybe that's good, I don't know. These things always come apart. If they're built slowly, carefully, they can last a long time. If not, the roof falls in.'

'Escape through the kitchen?'

She shook her head. 'Laurel and Hardy. No, we'll find out what he wants. Let it just be money.'

'Will we be arrested?'

'Always a possibility, but not like this, this is a probe. I think we'll have coffee. Very civilized. Don't make it easy for him, but let him know we're prepared to listen to a proposition.'

'We don't have that much, do we?'

That didn't worry her. 'Cable to Istanbul.'

'What do we offer?'

'A year's money, maybe. Not a lifetime – that makes us too important. In American dollars, say, five thousand. Twenty-five thousand Swiss francs.'

Downstairs, a table in the green salon. Turkish coffee in little cups without handles, cream cakes, toast with butter, Moldavian roll. Outside, beyond the mirrored walls, twilight on a winter afternoon.

Troucelle sprang to his feet when he saw them coming. Under pressure, he was a caricature of himself – too bright, too clever, his smile radiant. 'Allow me to present Domnul Petrescu,' he said. The name Petrescu was the Roumanian version of Smith or Jones, the man who stood beside him somebody he would never have known. Pencil mustache, bad teeth, olive green loden jacket.

'So pleased to meet the friends of Jean Paul,' he

said. Serebin thought he saw at least one more of them, sitting in a wing chair in the far corner, reading a newspaper.

'Domnul Petrescu is a devotee of the peasant crafts,' Troucelle said. He already regretted what he'd done, Serebin thought. There was a bead of sweat at his hairline, he wiped it away with his thumb.

'It's your interest?' Petrescu said.

'Our business,' Marie-Galante said.

Petrescu looked at her a certain way. With anticipation. If things went right . . . Reluctantly, he turned his attention to Serebin. 'You are born in France?' Then, an afterthought, 'Monsieur?'

'In Russia.'

Marie-Galante put a spoonful of sugar in her coffee, stirred it around, then took a sip.

'Where was that?'

'St. Petersburg. I left as a child.'

'So, you're a Russian.'

'In Paris a long time,' Serebin said.

'Marchais is a Russian name?'

'Markov, domnul. My father changed it.'

'Your father.'

'A grand old gentleman,' Marie-Galante said. 'A poet,' she added, admiration in her voice.

'Of course, once he came to France he had to work in a factory,' Serebin said. 'At a lathe.'

'And you, domnul?' Marie-Galante said.

'Me?' He was startled at her impudence.

'Yes. Your father, what did he do?'

Petrescu stared at her, his mouth worked as though something was stuck between his teeth. 'We are from the countryside.'

'Ahh,' Marie-Galante said, sentimental for the land.

Troucelle laughed – how pleasant to have a good conversation!

Petrescu needed time to think. He reached for a buttered toast. Serebin could hear him eating it.

'Delicious, don't you think?' Marie-Galante said.

'Tell me, domnul,' Serebin said, 'is there a particular aspect of the peasant crafts that interests you?'

Petrescu put the remainder of the toast triangle back on his plate and patted his lips with a napkin. 'Wood carving,' he said.

'I seem to recall,' Troucelle said, 'that you were contemplating a visit to Ploesti.'

Serebin and Marie-Galante looked at each other. Us? We were? 'I believe it was you who mentioned it,' Serebin said. 'No?'

'You need permission to go there, don't you?' Marie-Galante said.

'You do?' Troucelle said.

'Didn't someone tell us that?' she asked Serebin.

'It's no problem,' Petrescu said. 'Really, you should go. The craftsmen there are known to do excellent work, and I can help you get a pass, if you like.'

'Something to think about,' Marie-Galante said to Serebin.

'It's an interesting city,' Troucelle said.

'Maybe on our next trip,' Serebin said.

'But it's very kind of you to offer to help us,' Marie-Galante said. She looked at her watch, then said to Serebin, 'My dear?'

'Yes, you're right,' Serebin said. He stood, so did Troucelle and Petrescu. 'I regret our visit had to be brief, but we really must leave.'

'I hope I shall have the pleasure of meeting you again,' Petrescu said.

'Well, he did it,' Marie-Galante said, back in the room.

'Why?'

'To improve his position here? I don't know. *Il faut se*

défendre – it's an article of faith, for some. "First above all, watch out for yourself." '

'What was all that Russian business?'

'Your accent. Troucelle told them about it.'

'They think we're Russian spies?' Serebin sat on the edge of the bed and began to take off his shoes.

'They might.'

Serebin unbuttoned his shirt.

'They're scared of the Russians,' she said. 'They'll be cautious, if they think they're dealing with Moscow.'

'Didn't seem cautious.'

She opened the armoire, took out a daytime dress on a hanger, then put it back. 'When you get dressed,' she said, 'put on whatever you want to keep.'

By wireless telegraph:

18:10   14 JANUARY, 1941
BURO DI POSTA E TELEGRAMMA/STRADA TRAIAN/
    BUCURESTI/ROMANIA
SAPHIR/HELIKON TRADING/AKDENIZ 9/ISTANBUL/
    TURKIYE
CONFIRM RECEIPT YOUR ORDER #188
CARLSEN

The Hotel Luna.

On a sign above the door, a naked wench sat cross-legged in the curve of a quarter moon, smiling down on a street of bars and women in doorways. *The hotel of the moon.* Serebin paused in the doorway and stared up at the wench. Like a mermaid with legs, he thought; rosy, prominent tummy, cascade of golden hair that covered her breasts, and a certain smile – demanding and forgiving, yes, both, and mysterious. The model was probably the artist's girlfriend, but Serebin knew a muse when he saw one.

Marie-Galante, waiting at the door, said, 'Somebody you know?'

The desk was in the vestibule. To the clerk, they were only one more couple, coming in out of the night. Marie-Galante in her Persian lamb hat, Serebin dark and studious in his steel-rimmed glasses, maybe from different worlds but Eros couldn't care less about that and, for a few hundred lei, neither did the clerk at the hotel of the moon. No bag for the porter to carry, key for Room 38, staircase over there, carpet as far as the first floor.

It had been a leisurely flight from the Athenée Palace. In the room, Marie-Galante made two calls to the number that never answered, counting on her fingers as it rang. One last look around, then a ride in the elevator, and a casual walk through the lobby. They stopped at the desk, picked up a letter, and strolled out the door. Next they took trams and taxis, here and there, into quiet neighborhoods with empty streets. Once they were sure they weren't being followed, they went to a café where, in the WC, Serebin picked up an envelope from the young officer. Inside, a new identity: *Carlsen,* a Danish passport with travel permissions from the Gestapo office in Copenhagen. Finally, a visit to a post office in the strada Traian for the wire to Polanyi – Marie-Galante explaining that *188* meant it was time for them to get out. From there, they walked to the Hotel Luna.

Small room, sagging bed, rust-stained sink, and a line of pegs on the back of the door where they hung their clothes. Beneath the window, an ancient radiator hissed and banged, warming the room to a point where they could walk around in their underwear.

'Your best?' Serebin said. Her bra and panties were ivory silk, snug and expensive-looking, that favored the warm color of her skin.

'From Paris, I think. Can you see?'

He turned the hem down in back and squinted at the label. '"Suzi," it says.'

'Rue St.-Honoré.'

He stretched out on the bed and clasped his hands beneath his head. 'How long do we stay here?'

'We'll know when the wire comes.'

'What if it doesn't?'

She settled herself beside him. 'We languish.'

'Oh.'

'Forever, *ours.* A new life, just you and me.'

Serebin was taken by a sudden fit of elation. He stared up at the yellowed ceiling; lightbulb on a cord, cracks in the plaster, spiderweb in the corner. Nobody in the world knew where they were.

'You're having thoughts,' she said.

True.

With the light out and the window shade up, Room 38 was lit blue by the neon sign of a bar across the street. There was a jazz band playing in the bar, guitar and violin, maybe the local Django and Stéphane, who never made it to Paris.

'Do you know this song?' she said.

He waited a moment for the refrain. 'Yes. "I don't stand, a ghost of a chance, with you." He almost sang, the English words rough in his Russian accent.

'Ghost? A specter?'

'An idiom. Almost no chance.' The band spent a long time with the song, the guitar improvised, then the violin.

'What's it like for you,' Serebin said, 'in Neuilly?'

She thought for a while. 'The apartment is just so. Very proper, everything exactly as it should be. It seems cold, to me, *haute bourgeois,* stuffy, but that's by necessity. Labonniere has to entertain there, diplomatic dinners, things like that.'

'Boring?'

She nodded. 'One says nothing, but it must be said cleverly.'

'And the Germans?'

'Of course they're included, but it's not so bad. They've worked out a kind of unspoken courtesy for the occupation, a sort of wistful regret. Now and then, of course, you get a real Nazi, and that makes for a long evening, especially when they drink.'

The song ended, there was applause and a drunken shout or two from across the street. 'Not so bad, the Luna,' she said. 'Comes with free nightclub.'

He moved so that his lips were on her shoulder. She put her hand on the back of his neck and, very gently, began to comb his hair up with her fingers.

By wireless telegraph:

09:40   15 JANUARY, 1941
HELIKON TRADING/AKDENIZ 9/ISTANBUL/TURKIYE
CARLSEN/POSTE RESTANTE/BURO DI POSTA E
    TELEGRAMMA/
STRADA TRAIAN/BUCURESTI/ROMANIA
SHIPMENT ARRIVES 18 JANUARY/PIER 5 PORT OF CON-
    STANTA
SAPHIR

The owner of the Hotel Luna had a brother-in-law who, it turned out, drove a taxi and he, for a thick wad of lei, took them ten miles east of the city to the town of Branisti, where they could catch the 8:22, the last train to Constanta. 'One place we cannot go is the Gara de Nord in Bucharest,' Marie-Galante explained. 'You may be sure that, since last night, when we didn't return to the hotel, Petrescu and all the little Petrescus are looking for us, and that is the one place they are sure to look.'

In Branisti, they sat in the taxi, across the street from the station, until 9:50, when the 8:22 finally showed up, then ran for the train. A bribe to the conductor in the first-class car produced tickets and a reserved compartment which they shared with a well-dressed woman and an elderly cat in a wicker basket. The woman was exceptionally polite, and spoke to them, and to the cat, in a language that neither Serebin nor Marie-Galante could identify. This, however, did not deter her for a moment, and she continued the conversation for quite some time. Eventually, she wrote the number three, and a word that could have been January, with her finger, in the film of grime that covered the window. She had, apparently, been traveling for two weeks, and Serebin and Marie-Galante were relieved when she got off the train at the next stop, leaving them alone in the compartment for the five-hour trip to Constanta.

The train moved slowly across the plains of Dobrudja, the waning moon hidden by cloud, the fields dusted with snow, a long way from everywhere. When they asked for something to eat, the conductor summoned a dining car steward, who brought them coffee and wine and warm brisket sandwiches on thickly buttered rolls. The man seemed apologetic, perhaps wanted to serve them a grand Roumanian supper, but Serebin and Marie-Galante ate like wolves and had to fight hard not to fall asleep once the dishes were taken away.

They talked idly, for a time, then Serebin said, 'By the way, I don't think you ever told me what was in the letter.'

'What letter?'

'That came to the hotel.'

Marie-Galante swore, horrified at the lapse.

'There was a lot going on,' Serebin said.

'No excuse,' she said, hunting through her purse. She took it out, a thick envelope that implied invitations to formal dinners or weddings, tore it open, then turned on the lamp by the window in order to read it. 'From Valentina,' she said. 'She's performing tomorrow night at the Tic Tac Club and has reserved a table for us.'

'That's it?'

She turned the letter over to reveal blank paper. 'That's it.'

'What could she want?'

'I can't imagine. Maybe she liked you. Anyhow, we'll never know.' Deliberately, she ripped the letter and the envelope into smaller and smaller pieces, saying, 'Better not to have this with us.'

Serebin took the handful of torn paper off down the corridor, walked silently past the snoring conductor, opened the door at the end of the car and stood over the coupling. The steady hammering of the locomotive was loud in the open space between the cars, and the icy air, scented with coal smoke, felt good on his face and woke him up. They passed a village, a cluster of shadows by a dirt road, gone in a moment. Then he extended his arm and opened his hand, the bits of paper were taken by the wind, and fluttered away into the darkness.

18 January.

At dawn, in the port of Constanta, gulls circled the winter sky, their cries sharp and insistent in the morning silence. There was a heavy sea running, out beyond the jetty, and the yacht *Néréide* rocked gently on the harbor swell. In the forward cabin, the writer I. A. Serebin opened his eyes, took a moment to figure out where he was, then sat up in bed and lit a Sobranie cigarette.

His life, he realized, had come round again, circling back to the Constanta waterfront, where he'd boarded a Bulgarian freighter some two months earlier, and he once more found himself in a ship's cabin with the woman who slept beside him. Carefully, he slid out of bed, retrieved his glasses from the night table, put on his shirt and pants and shoes, and climbed a stairway to the upper deck.

To Serebin, the day was familiar. Rolling cloud in gray light, stiff wind, sea breaking white against the jetty rocks. He knew this weather, it meant he was home. Or as close as he was ever going to get. Rust-dappled freighters, broad-beamed fishing boats – nets slung over their bows, seagoing tug, Arab dhow, oil tanker; a Black Sea harbor, an Odessa harbor. Not quite the same, of course; two patrol boats, gunmetal gray, flew the swastika. And, also different, the lone figure leaning on the *Néréide*'s railing. It struck him as odd, somehow, a Hungarian count wrapped in a sailor's duffel coat, his hair blowing in the breeze. Polanyi turned toward him and nodded, Serebin joined him, they shook hands in silence.

The gulls were fishing. One of them landed on the rocks with a herring and had company right away.

'How was it?' Polanyi said.

'*Bordel*.' Whorehouse.

'It's the war.'

'Is it.'

Polanyi spread his hands. 'Not so good for your view of human nature, this work.'

'There were exceptions.'

'Well, one, anyhow.'

'More.'

Polanyi reached into a flap pocket on his coat and handed Serebin a telegram, wired care of André Bastien, with an Istanbul address. It had been sent to Marie-Galante a week earlier, and it was from Labonniere. Dry and to the point: he had been appointed second secretary at the French legation in Trieste, he needed her by his side.

Serebin handed the telegram back to Polanyi.

'Officially, you haven't seen that,' Polanyi said. 'But I thought you should see it.'

'When will you give it to her?'

'Right away.'

Serebin watched a fishing boat in the channel, its engine pounding as it fought the incoming tide.

'Working together like that,' Polanyi said. He looked over at Serebin, wondering if he needed to say more and saw that he didn't. 'She'll have to come back to Istanbul with us.'

'When?'

'Late tonight, I think. We plan for you to leave Constanta tomorrow, by train.'

'Yes?'

'Back to Bucharest.'

Serebin nodded.

'You can say no, of course.'

He didn't bother to answer.

'You should buy clothing, whatever you need, in Constanta. We'll have someone take you to the store. But, before you do that, we'll talk about everything that went on. You'll find it tiresome, everybody does, but that can't be helped. Would eleven suit you?'

'Eleven,' Serebin said.

Polanyi put both hands on the railing, hesitated, then walked away, heading toward the staircase that went to the cabins below.

Serebin spent a half hour on deck, then returned to the cabin. Marie-Galante was seated at the dressing table, putting on lipstick. She wore a slip and stockings, a towel wrapped around her hair. He saw that she'd made the bed, emptied the ashtrays, neatened up as best she could.

'Hello, *ours*.' She meant *good-bye,* her voice deeper than usual, tired, resigned.

He sat in a chair in the corner.

'I have to go away.' She pressed her lips together, turned them in for a moment, studied her image in the mirror. Not so good, but she didn't care. 'I have a wire from Labonniere. He's been promoted, sent to the legation in Trieste. Ever been there?'

'Once or twice.'

'What's it like?'

'Italian, Slovene, Croatian – everything, really. Very sunny and bright, at least when I was there.'

'Sunny and bright.'

'Yes.'

'That's always good. Cheerful.'

She met his eyes in the mirror.

'I have to go,' she said. She undid the towel and began to rub her wet hair.

'I know.'

He walked over to her, she rose and put her arms around him, her damp hair against his cheek. They stayed like that for a time, then she let him go.

They sat around a table in the salon: Polanyi, Marrano, Serebin, Marie-Galante, and a young man in a silvery gray suit worn over a black sweater, with a sharp face and water-combed hair, introduced as Ibrahim. As Marrano began his report on Bucharest, both he and Polanyi took notes.

Serebin watched Marrano as he spoke. *The Renaissance assassin*. Dark eyes, pitted face, a thin line of beard that traced his jaw. His story did not sound so very different from theirs. A woman who slept with important men – lately, Marrano said, a German general. The manager of a telegraph office. A gossip columnist. A Siguranza officer. The last, after agreeing to meet with Marrano, had disappeared. Marrano telephoned late at night and talked to the man's sister, who, very agitated, said nobody knew where he was.

'I did manage to see an assistant to Kobas, who was the oil minister until Antonescu took over. He was terrified, but brave. We met after midnight, in an abandoned building. He guessed right away what we were up to. "Don't try anything," he said. "The fields are closely guarded. They're just waiting for somebody to show up."'

Polanyi nodded, he knew.

Marrano went on. Editor of a newspaper, who said that only the Legion could save Roumania from the Jews. A retired diamond merchant, in a wheelchair. A mystery woman, contacted through a Gypsy vendor at a street market. 'Ilona, that's all I know. I had to book an entire compartment on the train for Ruse, in Bulgaria. She appeared after the first stop, we talked for, maybe, five minutes, then she left. Very curious. Long, black hair, worn loose, dressed all in black, a scar by one eye, a gold wedding band on her right ring finger. She wore a purse on a shoulder strap, the way it hung I thought, *something* in there, am I to be shot? I think, maybe, if I'd said the wrong thing, it might've happened. She was very determined.'

Polanyi raised an eyebrow.

'She was paid a great deal of money,' Marrano said, 'according to the list. And no last name, not even there. I believe DeHaas may not have known who she was.'

'Political?'

Slowly, Marrano shook his head. "If the job is worthy of me,' she said, 'I will do it."

Polanyi looked at Serebin.

'She did not say very much. Mostly she made me talk, and stared into my soul. Then she left at Daia station, suddenly, just as the train was about to leave. And I got off at the last stop in Roumania, Giurgiu.'

'The pipeline from Ploesti ends in Giurgiu,' Polanyi said.

'I knew that, so I decided to take a little walk, just to see what I could see. What I saw was the inside of a police station. For a very long hour, then a man in a suit showed up. A man who spoke French. Who was I? What was I doing there? Who did I know?'

'What did you tell them?'

'A woman.'

'They believe you?'

'Well, I'm here.'

Polanyi turned to Serebin and Marie-Galante. '*Mes enfants,*' he said. Marie-Galante began, Serebin joined in. Colonel Maniu. The lawyer. Troucelle, Princess Baltazar. Gheorghe Musa. The oil field study.

'We managed to have most of it translated,' Polanyi said. 'Depressing, really. The vulnerabilities the General Staff saw in 1922 were exploited by the French in 1938, and by the British a year later. Without success. The French tried to lease the oil-barge fleet, the British mined the fields – but they never used the detonators. What they tried instead was to outbid the Germans for the oil, and that worked very well indeed. Too well, in fact. The price of Roumanian oil went through the roof, and the Germans couldn't afford it. So they threatened to occupy the country. The Roumanians caved in, and gave them an exclusive sales agreement.'

'Where does that leave us?' Marrano said.

Polanyi sighed. 'On the river, I suppose.'

'Broad and flat.'

'Yes. We're on the wrong fucking end,' Polanyi said. 'Maybe up toward the Iron Gates.'

'I would think,' Marrano said, 'that the British have been over that ground.'

'They have. But, my friend, you must understand, it's our turn.'

'Whatever it is, it won't be permanent.'

Polanyi wasn't ready to admit that. 'The right catastrophe . . . But, you're not wrong. More likely I will offer them time, weeks, and at least the potential for repetition. Of course we all dream of the great coup – we have to do that, no?'

Just after midnight, Serebin stood on the pier as the *Néréide* departed. Watched it motor out the channel into the Black Sea, where, a few minutes later, the light at the stern grew dim in the mist, then disappeared. Marie-Galante had said a final good-bye on deck; reserved, steadfast, a farewell in time of war, tears forborne to preclude the memory of tears.

At the Hotel Tomis, on the Constanta waterfront, he drank, to no effect, and busied himself with housekeeping: committing names to memory, turning phone numbers into letter code concealed in journalist's notes. Thus his new identity: a French journalist, with the notional assignment of a story on a French traveling circus playing in Bucharest. *Crowds of children, clapping their hands in glee as they follow Caca the Elephant in the circus parade.*

He burned his notes when he was done, washed the ashes down the sink, turned off the light, stared up at the world. He had met privately with Polanyi for an hour or so, and toward the end of the discussion Polanyi had said, 'Labonniere is one of us, Ilya. Please understand. And while it is always preferable for a diplomat to be accompanied by his wife, it is crucial for a diplomat who is engaged in secret work. Crucial for this diplomat, anyhow, and, especially, this wife.'

The Hotel Tomis. By the Portul Tomis, the ancient Latin name for Constanta, infamous as the city of exile for the Latin poet Ovid. Who wrote a love poem that an emperor didn't like. Thinking about that didn't make Serebin feel any better, and it didn't put him to sleep. But with time, and persistence, the vodka did.

In Bucharest, they'd found him a room in an apartment – a long way from the Athenée Palace and the center of the city – which belonged to an elegant, distant woman in her sixties who owned a jewelry shop. The strada Lipscani house was out of bounds, he'd been told, and the Hungarian operative, no Slav it turned out, sent back across the border. Serebin had two or three days' work to do, then *la revedere, Bucuresti*. He sat on the bed in his room, unfolding two new shirts, squashing them this way and that to get rid of the creases, which resulted in rumpled shirts with creases.

To see the British foreign correspondent James Carr was not difficult. Serebin called the Reuters bureau, said he was an émigré with a story to tell, left a transparently common Russian name, and was in the office an hour later. He could have done the trick at the Associated Press or Havas – Carr was a freelance journalist and filed for any paper that needed a Bucharest dateline.

When Serebin arrived, Carr was half-sitting on the wooden railing in the reception area and telling a secretary some story that made her smile. He seemed, on first impression, a standard of the breed: tall and stooped, handsome face with a touch of Anglo-Saxon decadence, lank hair, dirty blond and too long unbarbered, a clever smile and a good blazer. The trench coat, hung carelessly on the clothes tree in the corner, was certainly his. 'Jamie Carr,' he said, extending a hand with fingers yellowed by nicotine.

He ushered Serebin to a room in back. 'All for us,' he said ruefully. It was too quiet – no sound of typewriters or telephones. 'Looks like I'm going to be the last one out.'

'You're leaving?'

This was in French. Carr answered in English, but slowly, so that Serebin could understand. 'I damn well better,' he said. 'I'm only here by virtue of an Irish

163

passport. Neutral, you see. Officially. But that's not true and the Legion knows it.' He settled himself in a swivel chair, Serebin sat on the other side of the desk. 'Would you believe, somebody shot my bed? From the apartment below mine. Came home in the morning and there was a hole in the bloody thing.'

He offered Serebin a stubby Roumanian cigarette, lit one for himself, then produced a pad and pencil. 'So then, what do you have for me?'

Serebin said he'd come to Bucharest to talk to people who'd done business with a company called DeHaas.

'No! That vulgar little shit. What'd he do, put my name on a list?'

Serebin nodded.

Carr opened a drawer, peered inside, found a tin ashtray. 'Must be an interesting sort of a list, care to sell it?'

No point answering that.

Carr made a face, mock horror at the perfidy of it all. '*Quid pro quo,* was what that was. A private inquiry agent, so-called, and he told me a good deal more than I ever told him. But, lie down with dogs, get up with fleas. He was probably blackmailing half the sinners in Bucharest. Which is half the city.' He grinned. 'Jesus Christ you only had to look at him.'

'Was it Zarrea?' The name was on the list.

Carr tapped his notepad with the pencil eraser. 'Say, you know a lot.'

'Not much, just Kostyka's *apparat*. Some of it, anyhow.'

'All right, so what do you want with me?'

'We might need your help, later on.'

'Oh? And who would I be helping, then?'

'Your English friends.'

Carr burst out laughing. 'Jesus I hope not!' Then he stared at Serebin for a time. Puzzled. Something he couldn't figure out. 'You mean the real thing, don't you.

Out of some little office in London.'

'Yes.'

He drew a face on his pad. 'Well, maybe I believe it but no matter, it's a moot point. I won't be here long enough to help anybody.'

Serebin started to rise, discussion over, but Carr waved him back down.

'Not oil, is it? It can't be that.'

'Why not?'

'Been tried. And it don't work. They sent a couple of their knights-errant out here in '39 and they got shipped home in their underwear.' He started to say more, thought better of it, then went ahead anyhow. 'You know,' he said, 'they can blow it up any time they want.'

'They can?'

'Oh yes. But they haven't, have they, and that means they don't want to. Because, fact is, there are plenty of RAF bombers at British airfields in Greece, as we sit here, and they can go up to Ploesti and bomb the oil fields tonight. What is it, maybe five, six hundred miles? They have the range, there and back, no problem. But, somehow, it isn't done. Now what does that mean, do you suppose? To me it means that somebody important says no. *Stop* the oil, sure, don't let it reach Germany, but don't bomb the wells. So they've got you sniffing around whorehouse Roumania instead, and all you're going to get for your trouble is the clap.'

'Britain and Roumania are not at war,' Serebin said. 'Not yet.'

'Balls,' Carr said. 'A matter of weeks, a technicality. No, what's going on here isn't diplomacy, it's money and influence, it's business, and it happens every day. Back in 1916, for instance, the Allies were in cannon range of the steel mills at Thionville, in the Lorraine. The mills were behind the German line, at that point, the Germans were using them to make artillery shells, and we knew it.

But, nothing happened. And that was thanks to the intervention of Baron de Wendel and his friends on the Comité des Forges – which meant Zaharoff and the rest of the arms merchants. These were *their* mills, so they wanted them back, in good condition, when the war ended.

'After the armistice, of course, there was hell to pay. Questions in Parliament, newspapers saying rude things. So up jumps Lloyd George, and he claims that the government didn't want the war to end with a destroyed industrial base in France and mass unemployment. That leads to comm-u-nism. Which was major bloody nonsense, you know? Because what it really was, was money, getting what it wanted, which it always does. No shock to anybody over the age of five, I suppose, but British soldiers died from those shells, just like they'll die from Panzer tanks running on Roumanian oil.'

A brief silence, in honor of the way things were, then Serebin said, 'I'm sure you're right.' *Though it doesn't matter if you are.*

Which Carr perfectly understood. 'Doesn't change anything, does it.'

'No.'

It meant *of course not,* the way he said it, and Carr perfectly understood that as well, because in a very particular way they were the same.

'Who are you?' Carr said. 'I mean, as much as you can say.'

'Russian émigré. A writer, sometimes.'

'Well,' Carr said, 'I wish I could help you . . .'

'But?'

'But . . .' He hesitated, wanted to say something he knew he shouldn't say. Finally he wheeled the swivel chair forward as far as it would go and leaned on the desk. 'It's no secret,' he said quietly, 'you could ask around, the right people, and they'd tell you, because there *are* no secrets in this place, that I'm already doing what you want me to do.'

Serebin was amused. 'The same people?'

'Maybe different offices in the same building,' Carr said. 'Hell, I don't know.'

'It's the war.'

Serebin put his cigarette out and rose to leave.

'Want some advice?' Carr stood up and walked Serebin toward the door. 'Watch out for yourself. All right?'

'Always,' Serebin said. 'Story of my life.'

'No, I mean now, tonight. This whole thing, Antonescu, the Legion, it's about to explode.'

'You're sure?'

Carr shrugged. 'Just be careful where you go. Who you're with.' They shook hands in the reception area. The secretary was on the phone, speaking rapidly in Roumanian. She looked up at them, then went back to her conversation.

'Well, good luck.'

'Thank you,' Serebin said. 'To both of us, I think.'

It was restless, the city, Serebin felt it, yet not a sight or a sound explained anything. *Race of ants. Telepathic – we know, we just know.* It was cold, he raised the collar of his coat, people hurried past, eyes on the ground. A policeman on the corner took a moment to admire himself in a pocket mirror. Not unusual in Bucharest, Serebin had seen it often.

Polanyi had told him to stay off the street, to work at night, if he could. He came to a movie theatre, paid, and went in. It was practically empty, a romantic comedy on the screen. He dozed, then woke suddenly at the sound of a newsreel – somber music, a voice taut with melodrama. A destroyer stood bow up in the sea, black smoke pouring from its deck. Then an auto race, a man at the finish line waving a checkered flag. *Valentina.* When did she arrive at the club? Eight? Nine? She would be early, he thought. *Maybe she likes you,* Marie-Galante had said, teasing him. But women never joked about things like that, not really.

Idly, he considered it. She was dark and serious, an *artiste,* likely capable of fierce excitements once she broke free of herself. But not at his hands. Because she would never go after a man that way. Never. No, this was something else. What? She knew virtually nothing about him, except that he'd come from Paris and, presumably, was going back there. Was that it?

He looked at his watch. On the screen, two women spoke confidentially in a parlor, one of them dabbed at her eyes with a handkerchief, a man, about to enter, his hand on the doorknob, overheard them, and stood there, eavesdropping. What did he hear? Serebin couldn't understand a word of it. Once again, he looked at his watch. He would try in an hour – he could always occupy himself for an empty hour. Then what? Go to the nightclub? Alone? Have his hair ruffled by a Zebra? No. Foolish, dangerous. Stage door, then. There was always a stage door, even at the Tic Tac Club.

He came out of the theatre into swirling snow and white streets. Two women held on to each other, taking timid steps on the slippery pavement. Usually, the sidewalks were shoveled right away. But not tonight. On the other side of the avenue, Floristi Stefan, a light in the window shining on the flowers. He waited while an army truck rolled past, then crossed the street and entered the shop.

Inside it was warm and fragrant, and two young girls in blue smocks said, *'Buna seara, domnul.'* There was a radio playing softly at the end of the counter, a string quartet, Mozart, or maybe Haydn, he could never tell them apart. One of the clerks came over to help him and he pointed to a tall bucket of long-stemmed red roses. He held up ten fingers, then two, she nodded with approval and said something like 'Ah, she's lucky, your lady friend.'

She drew a length of gold paper from a long roll, spread it on the counter, and began to make a bouquet, now and then adding a branch of small green leaves. Suddenly, the music stopped. The other clerk went over to the radio and began to work the tuning knob but, wherever she paused, there was only a low, steady hum. She kept trying, then decided the problem was in the radio and gave it a hard slap on the side of the case. That didn't work either, and the girl making the bouquet said a few sharp words, so she gave up and returned to the counter. When the roses were securely wrapped, the paper folded cleverly into itself, Serebin paid, and left the shop.

Where was he? The next cross street was the strada Roma, he thought the club might be somewhere to his left, maybe not too far. He wandered for a time, then spotted a corner of the Athenée Palace. He immediately changed direction, but at least he knew where he was and, a minute later, headed off toward the nightclub.

The street he took was unlit, and unnaturally silent, any sound of life lost in the hiss of the snow. There were only a few shops and they were closed for the night, wooden shutters rolled down and locked. On some of them, the owners had nailed hand-printed placards. He stopped to have a look, and discovered that the words were close to French. *Roumanian Shop,* the first one said. Then, next door, *Christian Property.*

Fifteen minutes later, the Tic Tac Club. No cabs, no customers in sight, only the generalissimo doorman, hands clasped behind him, rocking back and forth as he waited for his night to begin. Serebin walked past the club, then turned right into the side street until he found the alley he was looking for. Halfway down the alley, a triangle of yellow light illuminated falling snow and an iron door. The door was set inside a small alcove, and Serebin stood in its shelter and tried to brush the snow off his roses.

A few minutes later, a man hurried down the alley, one hand holding on to his hat in the stiff wind. He turned into the alcove, breathed a soft 'Ach' in disgust at the weather, saw the flowers, and gave Serebin a conspiratorial wink. He pulled the door open, letting out a powerful gust of roasting meat and garlic, and disappeared inside.

Next to arrive, Momo Tsipler and one of the Wienerwald Companions, a violin case under his arm. Catching sight of Serebin and his bouquet, Tsipler said, in German, 'Tonight she will be his,' and the violinist laughed. He threw his cigarette into the alley and Tsipler opened the door, holding it ajar so that Serebin could go in. 'You'll freeze it off, out here,' he said.

Serebin shook his head and smiled.

As the door closed behind them, Valentina turned the corner at the end of the alley. Serebin left the alcove and met her halfway. She was wearing an old fur coat, and a wool muffler as a head scarf.

'Valentina,' he said.

She peered at him, then seemed startled when she figured out who he was. 'Oh, it's you.'

He offered her the bouquet.

'What's this?'

'Can we get out of the snow?'

The building across the alley from the club had a matching alcove and there was just enough room for them to stand facing each other.

'I had to have a reason to wait here,' Serebin said.

Relieved, Valentina said, 'Oh,' and took the flowers from him. 'You surprised me,' she said. 'Anyhow, thank you. They're beautiful.' Then, 'What are you doing here?

The hotel operator said you'd left.'

'We did. But we got your note.'

'It's Gulian,' she said. 'He wanted to see you.'

'Why?'

'Well, to offer his services.'

'To do what?'

'Maniu talked to him, before he had to leave. He thinks you're here to work against the fascists. He's wrong?'

'No. Where is he?'

'Home. He'll be along later, but you shouldn't wait.'

'I can.'

'No, don't. Something's going on. There was a murder, earlier today. A German major was sitting in a café and a man walked up to him and shot him dead. The man was arrested, a former boxing champion, called Axiotti.'

'Why did he do it?'

'Maybe provocation. It's the Legion – don't try to understand, just get off the street.'

'What about you?'

'I have to be here.' She looked at him for a moment, then said, 'Well, that's how it is.'

'Can I contact Gulian?'

'Do you have something to write with?'

Serebin found a pencil and gave it to her. She tore a corner off the gold paper on the bouquet and began writing. 'I give you his home and his office. But please, be careful.'

'Why is he doing this?'

'He hates them. Since '33, when Hitler took over. Hates what they've done to the Jews, what they've done to Europe. It's just the way he is.'

She handed him the scrap of paper. She'd written two addresses and two telephone numbers. No name.

'Can you read it?'

'Yes. I think so.'

'All right, good. Go with God.' She kissed him on the cheek and walked quickly across the alley to the door of the nightclub.

Serebin needed the Number Six tram to reach his apartment. He walked north until he found a boulevard, then east to a tram stop – a bench on an island in the middle of a broad avenue. A small crowd of men waited impatiently, stamping their feet to keep warm, peering down the track into the snow. Serebin stood next to a tall, spindly man with professorial briefcase and umbrella. A narrow face, ascetic and prim. *The professor,* he thought. A conjecture supported, perhaps, by the fact that the man spoke reasonably good French.

'Waiting a long time?' Serebin said.

'Almost an hour,' the man said. 'It's later than usual, tonight.' He took an apple from his briefcase and began to eat it. Somewhere in the distance a bell rang. Once. A church bell, Serebin thought, its voice deep and heavy as the echo faded away.

'Did you hear that?' Serebin said.

The professor chewed his apple for a moment, then swallowed. 'Excuse me,' he said. 'It's called the Great Black Bell.'

'A church bell?'

'Yes. The church is occupied by the Legion, and one ring means that one legionnaire has died in battle.' He ate another bite of his apple. 'A huge bell,' he said, 'it takes twenty-nine men to make it ring.'

A man standing nearby said, 'They must be fighting.'

'Somebody said they were. This afternoon, in Vacaresti.'

'Oh.'

'Where is that?' Serebin said.

'The south end of the city,' the professor said.

Looking down the track, Serebin thought he saw the dim glow of a light. Somebody said, 'Here it comes.'

The light grew brighter, and Serebin could hear the motor.

'It's about time.'

On the other side of the boulevard, a figure appeared from the shadow of the buildings, walking quickly, almost running, toward the tram stop. He paused to let a car go by, its wheels sliding in the snow as it passed, then crossed the street. An older man, with a full beard, and the broad-brimmed hat and tight leggings worn by Orthodox Jews. He was breathing hard, and his face was white. He stood at one end of the island, pressed a hand to his side, then examined it, squinting as though he had lost his glasses.

The tram approached going full speed, swaying around a curve, its bell ringing wildly. Serebin stepped back from the track as it rushed past, half empty, to angry shouts and curses from the crowd.

Serebin watched it disappear. 'Maybe there's another one.'

Some of the men began to leave.

'Doubtful,' the professor said.

'Are you far from home?'

'Far enough.'

Serebin looked around for the bearded man, but he was gone. 'I guess we'll have to walk,' he said.

They set out together, following the tram track in the middle of the boulevard. 'Where do you live?' the professor said.

'Out this way. About a mile or so.'

'My wife will be frantic,' the professor said.

'Can you telephone? From a café, perhaps.'

'I tried earlier, but the phones aren't working.'

They trudged along in silence. The snow was well over the tops of Serebin's shoes and his socks were wet and cold against his skin. All along the boulevard, people were walking home – apparently the city's buses and trams had stopped running. Sometimes a car passed, very slowly, its hood and roof capped with snow. The amber light of a café appeared in the darkness, but the owner was closing up for the night. 'Sorry, gentlemen,' he said.

A block further on, Serebin stopped. 'Is that, singing?' They were men's voices, a lot of them, strong and confident.

The professor muttered something that Serebin didn't hear, sped up for a moment, then began to run. Serebin ran after him, saw that he was headed for the cover of the buildings. *Christ, he's fast.* The professor ran with stiff back and long strides, snow flying in his wake. He pumped his arms, briefcase in one hand, furled umbrella in the other, his hat bobbing precariously on his head, finally tumbling off. They were both breathing hard when they reached the brick wall of an apartment house.

'My hat.'

'Leave it.'

He was infuriated, could see the hat lying forlorn in the street, was barely able to keep himself from retrieving it.

Across the boulevard, some fifty or sixty men, marching in formation with rifles held across their bodies. They sang well, Serebin thought, liked doing it and were good at it.

The song stopped. Replaced by the throb of a heavy engine and clanking treads. The reaction was immediate; frantic, chaotic. And, Serebin thought, comic – *the Men's Chorus of the Iron Guard run for their lives.* The riflemen broke ranks and fled into a narrow street off the boulevard. But not quick enough – the tank jolted to a halt and the turret traversed as the cannon tracked the running shadows. The professor said, 'My God.' Serebin threw himself on the snow. A long flame lit the street, and the flat *crump* deepened as it rolled back to them off the sides of the buildings.

Serebin shouted, 'Get down.'

The professor wasn't so sure. He wore a good tweed overcoat, there would be hell to pay if he ruined it. Compromise: he dropped to one knee and rested the briefcase by his side.

In silhouette, the hatch on the top of the turret was flung open and a man with a submachine gun began to work the street, the flare at the barrel flickering on and off with each burst. The cannon shell had meant nothing, zooming away into an unlucky wall, but now the legionnaires were in trouble, and pinpricks of light sparkled from the doorways. Serebin heard it, the air ripped like cloth above his head and he burrowed into the snow as a sliver of brick stung him on the neck and flew away.

Suddenly, the machine gun went silent. Serebin looked up and saw only darkness above the open hatch. The cannon fired again, and again, right and left, broken glass showered down from the windows and a shop began to glow with orange light.

The rifle fire from the legionnaires thinned, then stopped. Serebin managed to get himself turned around so that he could see the professor. He lay on his back, one leg folded beneath itself. Serebin slid closer, but there was nothing he could do. The man had a red hole beneath one eye, the other stared up at the falling snow.

Why wouldn't you lie down?

Serebin heard the tank move off down the boulevard and, very slowly, got to his feet. The man's arm had jerked savagely when he'd been hit and his briefcase had come open and stood on end. Inside, there was only a newspaper.

★

All night long the Black Bell rang as Serebin worked his way across the city, the smell of burning stronger and stronger as the hours passed. At one point, the air-raid sirens went off, whining up and down for an hour. He walked, mostly, sometimes ran, and crawled when he had to. Once down a street where the twelve-story telephone exchange faced an eight-story apartment building, the former occupied by the Legion, the latter by the army and police. In between, the bodies of three legionnaires who'd tried to rush the army position. He waited as they fought, exchanging fire window to window, the ricochets singing off into the night, then circled through a park where two soldiers were carrying a third to a taxi with a red cross painted on its side. He was not alone, he saw others, caught out in the storm, bent low, running from cover to cover, trying to go home.

There was no sunrise. The street simply turned gray, the low sky heavy with winter cloud. He was then at a large square, the piata Obor, and not far from the apartment. He started to cross, then thought better of it and slid beneath a car. The square was held by men wearing the green armbands of the Legion. They had a Model A Ford pickup with a machine gun mounted on a tripod, and had built a barricade of overturned cars and buses, dressers, desks, and beds, across one end of the square. Two of the men sat on a red couch.

Which way to go? *Back out, try another street.* He was almost finished, he thought, exhausted and soaked and cold, and he had to wait for a minute and gather his strength.

Before he could leave, the barricade was smashed open by a huge tank with a swastika on its side. The tank was followed by an armored car, the commander standing behind the driver, a pair of binoculars hanging down the front of his leather coat. He raised his arm and waved it forward, and a motorized Wehrmacht unit advanced into the square and sealed off all but one street.

The legionnaires thought the Germans had come to help them, and shouted, *'Sieg Heil'* and *'Heil Hitler'* and *'Duce! Duce!'* but the Germans did not respond. When the square was fully controlled, the commander shouted an order and, after a few moments of shocked silence, the Legion began to leave, walking slowly away down the open street.

When Serebin finally turned his key in the door, the woman who owned the apartment was sitting in her bathrobe, listening to the radio. She leapt up, a hand pressed to her heart, threw her arms around him and wept. When he'd put on dry clothes, she told him the news. The Legion had held the city all night, had murdered hundreds of Jews, at the Straulesti abattoir and in the Jilava forest, and looted and burned the Jewish quarter. Then, at dawn, Antonescu's forces, supported by German units, had beaten them back; had retaken the radio station, the palace, the railyards – all of Bucharest.

'It's over,' she said. 'The Legion is finished. I cannot believe my own words, but, for this night at least, thank heaven for Adolf Hitler.'

At nightfall on 22 January, Serebin took a train to Giurgiu and crossed the river into Bulgaria.

POLANYI'S
ORCHESTRA

In Bulgaria, they called Russia Uncle Ivan and he was their favorite uncle, because he'd rescued their Slavic souls from the Ottoman devil in 1878 and they never forgot it. So the French journalist who boarded the Danube ferry in Roumania became, when he reached the Bulgarian port of Ruse, the Russian émigré I. A. Serebin, who, glancing back toward the far shore with evident distaste, earned from the customs officer a fraternal slap on the back.

They were pleased to see him, at the border post, where they'd had a steady stream of Roumanian refugees all night long and didn't really know what to do with them. 'A writer?' the officer said, looking at his papers. 'You ought to go up to Svistov.' Where, it was explained, they had a museum dedicated to the memory of the assassinated poet Konstantinov, his pierced heart exhibited in a glass box. 'It will inspire you,' they said.

There was not a room to be had anywhere in Ruse but, for one of Uncle Ivan's wandering lads, a nearby hotel had a bowl of soup, an army blanket, and a couch in the lobby where he was guarded the long night through by the hotel dog. In the morning, he wired Helikon Trading and received his answer *poste restante* by the end of the day. *Arriving Central Station Edirne 17:25 on 24 January.*

Serebin spent a long day with the Bulgarian railroad, crossed into Turkey, walked around Edirne for an hour, and entered the railway station waiting room just after five, where Polanyi's assistant Ibrahim found him and took him off to a caravansary hotel by the Old Mosque.

Polanyi had taken care to make things nice for his

returning warrior. There was a crackling blaze in the fireplace, a plate of things on toasted flatbread, a bottle of Polish vodka. Serebin was surprised at the depth of gratitude he felt. 'Welcome home,' Polanyi said. 'How bad was it?'

Bad enough. Serebin described his time in Bucharest, Polanyi listened carefully and, now and then, took notes. 'It's no surprise,' he said, rising to put a fresh log on the fire. 'We thought they would support Antonescu. It's basic German policy, they've certainly said it often enough. "Peace and quiet in the raw material zone." Stability is what they want, and they couldn't care less about Roumanian politics, to them it's comedy, farce. They want the oil and the wheat, forget the ideology. And no Balkan adventures.'

'They are there in force,' Serebin said. 'Tanks, armored cars, everything.'

'And more to come, as they get ready to attack Russia.'

'Will they?'

'They will. And soon, likely after the spring floods.'

The prediction wasn't new. A drift in war conversation since Poland in '39, and Serebin saw always, when it came up, the same images. A thousand Ukrainian villages, shtetls, peasants, who had no shoes, who, some days, had nothing to eat, nothing. And *then* the soldiers came, as had Serebin, *then* the huts and barns burned and the animals died. To Polanyi he could only say, 'Poor Russia.'

'Yes,' Polanyi said. 'I know. But the divisions are moving east, in Poland, and, soon, in Roumania. Bulgaria will sign up with Hitler – Czar Boris will, at any rate – and he already has Hungary, as much as anyone can ever have it, including the Hungarians. Britain has offered to send troops to Greece, but they've refused. For the moment. Right now, they think they can chase the Italian army all the way back to Rome, but Hitler won't allow it. By spring, you'll see the swastika flying over the Acropolis, and southern Europe will be essentially secured.'

'Except for Yugoslavia.'

'A thorn in his side. And the Serbs never go quietly.'

'Will he invade?'

'Well, he won't sneak in. Coup d'état, more likely.'

Polanyi settled back in his chair and took some time to light a cigar. 'So, Ilya,' he said, 'tell me how you propose to halt oil shipments to Germany and bring an end to this wretched war.' The edge of amusement in his voice wasn't subtle – caught in a hopeless cause that couldn't be abandoned, one had better be amused.

'Blow up the river,' Serebin said. 'Or block it.'

'How?'

'Not like the British in '39.'

'Meaning?'

'No commandos.'

'What then?'

'Plausible accident.'

'Ten days. Maybe two weeks.'

'Then another.'

Polanyi sighed. 'Yes, if you can't attack the fields, you have only the transport system. We're all agreed about that.'

'Marrano?'

'Everybody. My last two people should be out by the end of the week.'

'How many were there?'

'Ilya, please.'

Serebin laughed. 'Sorry.' Then he said, 'It doesn't have to be forever, does it?'

'No. We don't have to win, we have to play. Slow him down – an inevitable problem with supply. Make him think about timing, with his Russian invasion, wait for the Americans, or maybe he'll choke on a cauliflower.'

For a moment, they watched the fire.

'Who could ever have imagined,' Polanyi said, 'that the man who came to burn down the world would be a vegetarian.'

'We'll need people in Roumania,' Serebin said.

'We have them. Just barely, but we do.'

Serebin didn't believe it.

'We didn't fail in Bucharest,' Polanyi said. 'Not quite.'

Lunch was ordered in the room. Polanyi and Serebin went round and round, what and how and when and back to what. No final conclusion – the gods on Olympus would have to be consulted – but plenty of false trails pursued to the end. *What Can't Be Done,* that dreary epic, written this day in the form of notes by Count Janos Polanyi. Eventually, for Serebin, an assignment in Paris, *thank God,* and, finally, parting gifts. Balkan Sobranies, sugared plums from Balabukhi – just as he'd given Tamara Petrovna – and, for the long ride west, a copy of Lermontov, *A Hero of Our Time.*

Was this a shrewd choice, Serebin wondered, or the only Russian book in the store? *Maybe shrewd,* he thought, as the train clattered toward Sofia. Lermontov had been banished from the Guards Hussars, after writing a poem that attacked the Russian oligarchy for the death of Pushkin, and exiled to the Caucasus as a regular army officer. Was there cited for bravery, in 1837, but the Czar refused him the medal. Eventually, he was killed in a duel, as witless as any in literary history, at the age of twenty-six. A disordered life, in detail not anything like Serebin's, but chaotic enough.

'Have you spent long in Cechnia?'

'I had about ten years there with my company in a fort near Kamenny Brod. Do you know it?'

'I've heard of it.'

'Ah, those cutthroats gave us a time of it! They're quieter now, thank heavens, but once you went a hundred yards from the stockade there'd be some shaggy devil on the lookout, and you'd only to blink an eyelid and before you knew where you were you had a lasso round your neck or a bullet in your head. Grand chaps!'

He looked up to see a girl with a basket waiting for the train to go past. Well, whatever else might be true, Polanyi had chosen a book that every Russian had read, but that every Russian liked reading again. And, by the time he reached Subotica, in Yugoslavia, the Balabukhi plums were more than welcome, to Serebin and his fellow travelers, since there'd been practically nothing to eat at the station buffets where the train stopped.

28 January. In Istanbul, Janos Polanyi sat at a table on the second floor of a waterfront lokanta called Karim Bey. He drank a glass of raki as he waited, staring out at a long line of Turkish porters, struggling up the gangplank of a freighter beneath immense burlap sacks.

He was not at all pleased to be there, and he did not look forward to lunch – with the fattish and soft-spoken Mr. Brown and his relentless pipe. His infuriating pipe, a device used to stretch silent pauses out to uncomfortable intervals where disapproval hung in the air amid the fruity smoke. Polanyi unfolded his napkin and refolded it, he was tense and apprehensive and he didn't like it. What he had to offer Mr. Brown was the best that could be offered but he feared, expected, the usual reaction: a cold, tolerant silence seasoned with contempt. For who he was, for what he did, and for the quality of his proposals. As a social attitude it was, of course, beneath him: an aristocrat from a thousand-year family need not concern himself with the Mr. Browns of the world. But, applied to secret work, this contempt could kill.

Polanyi had always suspected that Mr. Brown was an *amateur* of chess. That he saw a world of pawns and bishops and helpless kings. But the people who did what Polanyi asked of them were not pawns. They lived, Serebin and Marrano and Marie-Galante and the rest, and he meant for them to keep living. But it would better suit Mr. Brown, he believed, if he could be made to suppress this instinct and sacrifice the occasional pawn for a stronger position on the board.

Polanyi was on the verge of making himself really angry when Mr. Brown approached the table. Fortunately for everyone, perhaps, he was not alone. 'This is Mr. Stephens,' he said.

Polanyi stood up and, as they shook hands, the man said, 'Julian Stephens.'

A first name! A minor adjustment in the introduction, but it implied a change of style, a change of attitude, and Polanyi's spirits rose. Stephens took the floor immediately. He was pleased to meet him, had heard such good things about him, was anxious to work with him, Istanbul was an extraordinary city, was it not, and so forth, and so on. Social talk. But, as he spoke, Polanyi began to understand who he was.

A man of some depth, and some cruelty. No, not quite, more the capacity for cruelty. He was maybe thirty-five, a boyish thirty-five, pale, with thin lips and straight hair, straw-colored, cut short above the ears and combed back from a part on the side. And there was something in his manner that brought to mind a story Polanyi had heard long ago, to do with savage contests of intellect that took place at high table at Oxford. No quarter asked and none given, a reputation made or ruined, in a world where reputation meant everything. Had he, in fact, come from the university? Not really any way to know that. Law, or banking, or commerce, the possibilities were endless but, whatever it was, he had been to the wars, and, Polanyi sensed, won them.

'I believe,' Mr. Brown said, 'that the two of you will get on well together.'

'I would think so,' Polanyi said.

'What we've done,' Mr. Brown said, 'is to create a new and different kind of office. At the direction of the prime minister himself, I should add. That will specialize in operations meant to damage the enemy's industry – particularly war-related industry, his transport, and communications.'

'An office for sabotage,' Polanyi said.

'Yes,' Stephens said. 'With the kind of technical support that will make it work.'

Polanyi nodded. This was a good idea, if they meant it. 'In the Balkans?'

'Everywhere,' Stephens said. 'In the occupied countries.'

'So Switzerland will be left alone.'

'For the moment,' Stephens said, with a thin smile.

'My office will continue as it always has,' Mr. Brown said. 'But we will deal strictly with intelligence. In that regard, you and I may work together again, but, for the present, Mr. Stephens is your man.'

Mr. Brown rose and offered Polanyi his hand. 'I will leave you to it,' he said. His demeanor was amiable enough, but Polanyi wasn't persuaded. Whatever else this was, Mr. Brown took it as defeat. Somewhere, in some distant office in the green and pleasant land, there'd been a battle of meetings and memoranda, and Mr. Brown's side had come off second best.

Stephens watched as his colleague left. Then he said, 'So then, here we are. I'd better tell you right away that I'm new to this, ah, this sort of thing. I expect you know that. But, I tend to learn quickly, and the people in

London will let me do pretty much whatever I want. For the time being, anyhow, so we'd best take advantage of the honeymoon, right?' He opened the menu and peered at it. 'I suppose we should order lunch.'

'Probably we should.'

He read down the page and closed the menu. 'Haven't the faintest idea what any of it is, would you order for me? Nothing too ambitious, if you don't mind.'

'Perhaps a drink, to start.'

'I daresay. What are you having?'

'Raki.'

'Is it very strong?'

'It is.'

'Splendid.'

Polanyi signaled to the waiter, standing idle in the corner. 'And then, lamb?'

'Yes, lamb, good.' He folded the menu and placed it beside him, then took a pen and a small pad from his pocket, unscrewed the top of the pen, and opened the pad to a clean page. 'Now,' he said, 'on the way down here I had an idea.'

A quiet afternoon in January. The Parisian weather, lately come to its senses, cloudy and gray and soft. One of the city's favored weathers, this gloom, good for making love, good for idle speculation and small pleasures. This was at heart a southern city, a Latin city, its residents forced to live in the north, between Englishmen and Germans, energetic souls who liked bright sunshine and brisk mornings. Well, they were welcome to them. The true Parisians, and Serebin was one of them, woke happily to damp twilight and, even in an occupied city, believed that anything was possible.

In a narrow street by the Place Bastille, the elegant Brasserie Heininger was closed on Mondays, its red and gold affluence lost in darkness, its gallant waiters home with their wives, its glorious platters of *langouste* and sausage only aromatic memories in the still air. At the infamous Table Fourteen, where a bullet hole in the mirror served as memorial to a Bulgarian headwaiter assassinated in the Ladies WC, the chairs leaned forward, propped against the table. All was silent, waiting for Tuesday.

But not quite. The kitchen was alive. By some vaguely defined *droit de chef,* the talented but fulminous Zubotnik served Monday lunch, a banquet of leftovers, to his émigré friends. Zubotnik had never actually *thrown* his cleaver at anybody but he shook it, often enough, and screamed in six languages. He had ruled the kitchen at the Aquarium restaurant in St. Petersburg, made his way to Paris in 1917, worked as a sous-chef for a month, then, when the incumbent chef fled to Lyons, crying out as he went through the door, 'No human man can turn that color,' had, at a horrendous rise in salary, agreed to replace him. Papa Heininger had regretted that decision for twenty-three years but Zubotnik was a genius and what could you do.

Serebin attended the Monday feast whenever he could. He had, since childhood, a passion for second-day delicacies. They got better overnight, and tasted better yet when eaten in the kitchen instead of the dining room.

'Here, you,' Zubotnik said from his white beard. 'Take some of this.'

Serebin carefully sawed a slice off half a beef Wellington, the crust still flaky after a night in the refrigerator. He put a teaspoon of Zubotnik's brutal mustard beside it, and considered a second until Zubotnik growled, 'Don't murder it, Serebin. And give Anya some mousse.'

'Thank you but no, Ivan Ivanovich,' Anya said.

'Just do what I tell you,' Zubotnik said to Serebin.

'Only a little,' Serebin said, commiserating. The salmon mousse had been chilled in a fish-shaped mold and Serebin gave her one of the tail fins.

'While you're up,' Ulzhen said, extending his plate.

They sat at the long wooden table in the kitchen. Serebin, Boris Ulzhen, the poet Anya Zak, the taxi driver Klimov and Claudette, his Franco-Russian girl-friend, and Solovy the robber.

Serebin poured himself a glass of red wine from the large flask. There were various *appellations* and vintages in the flask, blended by chance from bottles unfinished by Sunday night's patrons. Zubotnik and his friends could eat whatever they wanted at the Monday lunch but Papa Heininger would clutch his heart in an alarming way when Zubotnik visited the cellars so the chef, realizing that life would go better if the *propriétaire* remained aboveground, had forsworn the bins.

'To the Zubotnik '41,' Klimov said, raising his glass.

'Na zdorov'ye!'

'Na zdorov'ye!'

'Ilya Aleksandrovich,' Anya Zak said, 'please to continue your story.' She waited attentively, her bright, nearsighted eyes peering at him through old-fashioned spectacles. Solovy began to roll a cigarette, taking long strands of tobacco from a cloth pouch.

'So,' Serebin said, 'we came to Bryansk at dawn. We'd heard that Makhno's people had occupied the city, but we didn't hear anything. They were always loud, those people, fighting or not, women's screams and pistol shots and great shouts of laughter. But it was very quiet in the city. A little smoke from the burnt-out houses, not much else. "Take a squad," the captain said, "and go see what's what." So off we went, using whatever cover we could find, just waiting for the snipers, but nothing happened. You could see the looters had been there, stuff they didn't want dropped in the street. Clothes and toys and pans, half a painting. Then I saw the goat, it came walking toward us, casually enough, staring at me with those strange eyes, just going about its business until somebody came and put a rope around its neck. Something funny about this goat, I thought. I looked closer, and saw a long shred of yellow paper hanging out of its mouth, with the printed words *Genius and Dissipation*. My sergeant saw it at the same time I did and we both started to laugh, almost couldn't stop. We'd been fighting for a day and a half and we were a little crazy, the way you get. He had to sit down in the street, there were tears running down his cheeks. All this made the goat self-conscious and it began to finish the paper, *Genius and Dissipation* rolling up into its mouth as it chewed.

'One of the men called out from a doorway, "The hell's gotten into you?" but we couldn't answer. I mean, go try and explain something like that. And we really couldn't figure it out, just then, not for about thirty minutes. Then we got into the center of the city and saw the posters. Stuck up on the wall of a theatre with flour glue, which goats like. The posters announced the appearance of the actor Orlenev, coming to Bryansk to play the role of the English tragedian Edmund Kean in the play called *Kean, or Genius and Dissipation*.'

Solovy snorted with laughter, but he was the only one.

'Bryansk was the worst,' Ulzhen said.

'Berdichev,' Zubotnik said. He cut a piece of *baguette*, put smoked salmon on it, then a drizzle of oil, and handed it to Claudette.

'Still,' she said to Serebin, 'you miss it, your terrible Russia.'

'Sometimes.'

'They all came through Berdichev,' Klimov said. 'Taken and retaken twenty-seven times. Makhno's band,

Petlyura's band, Tutnik's partisans. "And," they used to say, "Nobody's Ninth Regiment."'

'You remember everything,' Solovy said.

'I remember,' Klimov said. 'Jewish prayer shawls used as saddlecloths.'

Claudette ate her salmon with a knife and fork. Serebin poured wine for Ulzhen and Anya Zak. 'Oh, thank you,' she said.

'The winter *Harvest* was a great success,' Ulzhen said to Serebin. 'I've been wanting to tell you that but you haven't been around.'

'Yes, very good,' Solovy said.

'The Babel, of course,' Ulzhen said. 'Everybody talked about it. That, and Kacherin's poem to his mother.'

'No,' Serebin said. 'You're joking.'

'Not at all.'

'It had feeling,' Zubotnik said. '*Real* feeling, sincerity, what's wrong with that? Didn't you have a mother?'

'So now,' Ulzhen said, 'you have only to worry about spring.'

'Anya Zak will be in that one,' Serebin said. He knew better. Zak published only in the best quarterlies, she would never, *never*, submit to a magazine like *The Harvest*.

'Will she?' Zubotnik said. He gave money to the IRU.

Her glance at Serebin was covert, and not amused, *how could you?* 'I wish I had something,' she lamented. 'I've been working on a long piece, for weeks, the whole winter, but, we shall see, maybe, if I can finish . . .'

'We would, of course, be honored,' Ulzhen said, lingering on the *would*.

'You should try the salmon, Tolya,' Claudette said to Klimov.

'Mm,' Zubotnik said. He cut some bread and salmon and passed it across the table.

Ulzhen set his napkin down. 'Excuse me for a

moment,' he said. As he stood up, he met Serebin's eyes, *come with me.*

Serebin followed him from the kitchen out to the bar that bordered the darkened restaurant, then into the men's room. Ulzhen looked for a light switch on the wall but he couldn't find it.

'I'll hold the door for you,' Serebin said.

'Doesn't matter.'

Serebin held the door ajar while Ulzhen used the urinal. 'Ilya Aleksandrovich,' he said, his voice echoing faintly off the tiled wall, 'we need your help.' He finished, began to button his fly.

'All right,' Serebin said.

'A committee,' Ulzhen said. He went to the sink and turned the water on. 'Only four of us.' He mentioned two people that Serebin barely knew – the widow of a German industrialist, very rich, who had come to live in Paris years earlier, and a thin, serious, older man who hardly said a word to anybody. To Serebin, this made no sense at all.

'Committee?'

'She has the money,' Ulzhen said. 'And he was an officer in the military intelligence.'

'To do what?'

'For our Jews, Ilya.' He washed his hands, then began to dry them with a towel from the stack on the attendant's table. 'Eighty-nine of our members, as far as we can determine. And their families, that number we don't know. But we've decided to get them out, if they want to go. First into the Unoccupied Zone, the Vichy zone, in the south, then to Nice. There are still boats that will take passengers, we'll provide documents and whatever money we can manage. We know we can get them to Spain, at least that far, then, maybe, South America. So, it's a very quiet committee.'

'Secret.'

'Yes.'

Serebin felt ill. He had to go to Marseilles in two days, then God only knew where after that. He heard laughter from the kitchen.

'Why me?' That loathsome phrase, out of his mouth before he could stop it.

'Why you?' Ulzhen had heard it loud and clear. 'Because you don't flinch, Ilya. Because the fact that you can take care of yourself means that you can take care of people who can't, and, most of all, because I want you there with me.'

'Boris,' he said.

To tell? Not to tell? Excuses poured through his mind like water, this lie or that, one worse than the next.

'Yes? What?' Ulzhen dropped the towel in a basket by the table.

'I can't.'

'Of course you can.'

Now he couldn't say anything.

'What is it, some business you're doing with Ivan Kostyka? Is that it? You want money, all of a sudden?'

Serebin didn't answer.

'Look, this has everything to do with Poland, I don't need to tell you the stories, and it's coming here. Nothing wrong with chess tournaments and magazines, Ilya, but we're responsible for these people. They're coming to me, they're asking for help. What am I to tell them? You're busy?'

'Boris, I have to do something else. I *am* doing something else. For God's sake don't make me tell you more than that.'

'You are?' He was going back and forth – truth or cowardice?

'Yes.'

'Swear it to me.'

'I swear. On anything you like. Please understand, as

long as I'm in Paris, I'll do whatever you want. But I cannot promise to be in such and such a place at such and such a time, and, in what you're talking about, that's everything.'

Ulzhen took a deep breath and let it out. It meant concession – to disappointment, betrayal. That betrayal came for some noble reason, ghostly, beyond explanation, did not matter.

'How did this happen?' Ulzhen said, defeat in his voice.

'I got involved,' Serebin said.

Ulzhen wanted to argue, then thought better of it. 'Well, you have to do what you think is right,' he said.

'I know.' Serebin looked for words, to somehow bridge the space that had opened between them, but all he could say was, 'I'm sorry, Boris.'

Ulzhen shrugged. So life went.

It was almost five when they left. Klimov and Claudette, Anya Zak and Serebin walking together for a time, then parting at the rue de Turenne, where Anya Zak headed off into the Eleventh and Serebin went with her. To a street that reminded Serebin of the tenement districts of Russian cities, old and poor and silent, where Anya Zak had a room above a tailor shop. 'It isn't much,' she said, 'but you can come up if you want.' He did. He was very lonely, and he couldn't face going back to the Winchester just to be by himself.

A small room, cluttered and warmed with things she liked. A fish bowl filled with mussel shells on an upturned crate, Bal Musette posters and Victorian silhouettes tacked to the wall. Books everywhere, a glass of dried weeds, a copper lion.

They talked idly for a while, then she read him a poem. 'No title yet,' she said. 'For me, that is always difficult.'

She settled herself into the corner of an easy chair, drew her feet up beneath her bulky skirt, and read from a paper in one hand while the other held a Sobranie, its blue smoke curling straight up in the airless room. The poem was intricate, about a lover, more or less, the lines simple, declarative, and opaque. She'd been, sometime, somewhere, easy prey. Was still? Didn't care? 'But the heart was blind that summer,' she recited, inhaled the cigarette, spoke the next line in puffs of smoke. Loss in a crowded room, in a storm, a dream, a shop. She had long dark hair, with a few silver strands, that hung down around her face, and, as she read, she would tuck one side of it behind her ear but it didn't stay. She looked up at him when she finished and said, 'Awful, isn't it.'

'No, not at all.'

'A little awful, admit it. One's intimate self is, you know.'

She was narrow-shouldered and lean on top, broad below the waist, heavy-legged. On the windowsill by the bed, half a burned candle, its wax congealed in a saucer. 'You are looking at me,' she said.

'True.' He smiled at her.

'Tell me, are you working?'

'I wish I could, but life takes sharp corners, lately, so all I do is watch the road. A line sometimes, now and then, but who knows where it belongs.'

She understood. 'They are killing us,' she said. 'One way and another.'

'What will become of you, Anya?'

'Such a question!'

'Forgive me, I didn't mean . . .'

'No, it's all right,' she said. 'I know what you mean. In fact, I think I've been offered a way out, if things go wrong here. About a year ago I met this couple. Nice enough, *haute bourgeois* types, but sweet. They were rich and social, before the occupation. Likely still are, now that I think about it. Anyhow, they somewhat adopted me, the saintly poetess, poor as a mouse, you know how it is. Sunday afternoons, they would have me up to their apartment, in Passy, all kinds of sexy nonsense in the air though nothing *said,* of course. Then, about a month ago, they told me that they had a little house in a village, in Normandy somewhere, at the end of a road, and if life went bad in Paris, I was invited to go up there and hide out for as long as I needed to.'

'I hope it doesn't come to that,' Serebin said. 'Still . . .'

'What about you?' she said.

'I don't think I'll have to run,' he said. 'Of course, you can never be certain.'

'No you can't. Not about anything, ever. You and I know all about that.' She took her spectacles off, blinked at a fuzzy world, folded them up, and put them on the table beside her.

More would come off, he imagined. Everything. By the light of the candle on the windowsill. And, as time went by, she would wear the very same smile she wore at the moment, opening, as her eyes closed, to a shape he dearly loved to see. Stripped, languid, appetitious, a true partner in crime, no saintly poetess at all and very pointed about it. Oh, his heart might be a little somewhere else, but that he couldn't help and there was no way on earth she could know about it.

'Well,' she said.

As he stood up, she leaned her head back against the top of the chair. 'Getting late,' she said. 'Would you like to come and kiss me good night?'

As he walked toward the hotel, a long way away, it occurred to him that maybe she did know. Sensed it, understood him better than he thought possible. But, whether she did or she didn't, it had been a long kiss goodnight, warm and elaborate, and a lot happened while it was going on. Was it possible they'd had a love affair? A thirty-second love affair? Well, why not. He stopped at the far end of the Pont Marie. *I'll do anything you like.* She hadn't said it out loud but even so she'd told him that. He wasn't wrong. He could turn around, go back, she'd be waiting for him. No, he thought, that's crazy. Don't think about it, go home to bed.

A direct order, half of which he obeyed.

Polanyi's Orchestra.

Performing the Roumanian Symphony, Opus 137.

Was it 137? One hundred and thirty-seven opera- tions? He'd tried, now and then, to count them all, but it never worked. What to include? What to leave out? It wasn't always clear, so, in the end, he declared it to be, over thirty years, some number not far from that, then burned the notes – jotted initials and dates, typically on the backs of envelopes – and got rid of the ashes.

This one had, at least, a name. Medallion. Or, Opera- tion MEDALLION, as it would appear in the records. Not that any of the people involved would ever be allowed to know it, that was for him and Stephens, and the warlords in London. Medallion. He hoped it sounded noble and enduring, in English. It certainly sounded damned strange in Hungarian, but then what didn't.

It was by his own initiative that Jamie Carr played in the orchestra. In fact, he belonged to a different operation, with another name, yet, even so, he played. When inspi- ration struck he was with Girlfriend Three, a tall Polish nightclub dancer with penciled eyebrows. They were alone in an office, the street outside deserted on a Sunday morning.

Time to leave, they'd told him. The British legation in Bucharest would close down on the 10th of February, be gone by then. So, he'd packed. Taking along much more than he'd planned – what a lot of *stuff* he'd acquired! Clothes and books and papers and whatnot from the apartment. The iron lamp in the parlor, for example. Lots of memories in that lamp, couldn't just leave it behind. And, of course, he'd take a few things from his desk at the office, good friends, with him for two long years of writing and conniving.

Once in the office – Girlfriend Three had spent the night and come along to keep him company – he thought, *well, pity to leave all these files.* Press clippings, cabinets packed with them. He wanted, at first, a few for his own purposes. He liked them. Taken together, they constituted a sort of surreal history of his life in Roumania. Here was Zizi Lambrino, King Carol's paramour and the subject of great *scandale* before Lupescu snatched the king for her own. And here was Conradi, chief of the Gestapo in Roumania. Crippled below the waist, with the head of a Roman emperor and a huge chest, he lay in bed all day long and received a steady stream of informants.

The stack grew higher and higher. 'What good this?' Girlfriend Three said, looking through the columns of newsprint glued to yellowing paper. He wasn't entirely sure, but how else to remember Sofrescu and Manescu and Emil Gulian? For a moment, he had visions of taking it all – let the porters come and put the cabinets on the train. These offices were going to close, forever, these offices were going to be in the middle of a fiery war. But then, he thought better of that and took only the best, the strangest, stacking them carefully as a sullen Girlfriend Three sat in a swivel chair and shot paper clips out the window with a rubber band.

Marrano, after a difficult night at sea, was in Beirut.

In the bar of a small hotel near the harbor. A lizard slept on the wall, strips of flypaper hung from the ceiling, a French naval officer in the corner was drinking *absinthe,* and Professor Doktor Finkelheim, late of Vienna, sat across the table, a cup of tea cooling in front of him. Finkelheim, wearing a brown shirt and a green tie with a stain on it, looked like a hamster.

At the moment, a gloomy hamster. Sad to say, he told Marrano, his research materials had been abandoned in Vienna, he'd escaped with his life and little else. Yes, it was true that he'd been preeminent in his field, geology, and had specialized in riparian formations – that is, the structure of rivers – especially those that drained into the Danubian basin. The tributaries; the Drava, the Tisza, the Morava and the Mlava, and the mighty and magnificent Danube itself.

'But not the water,' he said. 'Don't ask me about the water. For that you would see my former colleague, Doktor Kubel, who remains in Vienna. If, on the other hand, you are interested in the *banks* of the rivers, then you've got the right fellow.'

What about, say, depth.

That would be Finkelheim. Seasonal flow, current, rock strata, all Finkelheim. Micro-organisms? Salinity? Fishes and eels? Kubel.

'Perfectly understood,' Marrano said. And he understood, as well, that research materials would be crucial to any study that the professor might agree to undertake. *However,* it just so happened that he was in possession of certain maps, good ones, that showed the rivers in detail. Would the professor, he wondered, be willing to review these maps, especially with regard to those characteristics that made navigation on the rivers possible?

Or, sometimes, impossible?

Oh yes.

Serebin played in the orchestra by going to Marseilles.

He stopped by the Gestapo office on the rue Montaigne to apply for the permit, was politely stalled, went again, then managed on the third try. They had finally, after some hesitation, accepted his *Reason for Travel,* as the form put it: an important émigré in distress – the name lifted from the files in the IRU office – a mission of mercy. He could have sought help from Helmut Bach, the Wehrmacht intellectual, but he sensed a turning point in his relations with Bach. The moment of truth – *the time has come for you to do a little favor for us* – was close at hand, and Serebin badly wanted to avoid the confrontation. In fact, they'd been uncomfortably polite to him at the rue Montaigne office. Fascism famously stomped around in jackboots, but it sometimes wore carpet slippers, padding about softly on the edges of one's life, and in a way that was worse. And, he thought, they knew it.

So it went. It was the 10th of February by the time he got on the train. Crossed into the Unoccupied Zone below Lyons at midday, reached Marseilles at night, and kept his appointment with the émigré, a senior civil servant in the Czar's last days. After ten years in France, his wife had abandoned him, taking the children with her, so he'd gambled all his money away, was thrown out of his apartment, and drank himself into the hospital. Otherwise, all went well.

This he explained to Serebin at some length, in a room in a boardinghouse in the Arab quarter. He'd never really liked the wife, the children were almost grown and he still saw them, money was money it came and it went, and, as for the vodka, he'd learned his lesson. 'From now on I will follow the French example,' he told Serebin, 'and drink wine.' A question of geography, he believed. In Russia, the weather, the air, the water, the very nature of life, was elementally antidotal to vodka, but, if you changed countries, you had to change drinks. 'As a journalist, Ilya Aleksandrovich, this might be useful to you.' Serebin tried to look intrigued, *an interesting idea.* In fact, the man was either completely unhinged or far too sane and, in the end, Serebin realized, it didn't matter. He gave him money, a copy of *The Harvest,* and all the sympathy and encouragement he could bear, then went off to a small hotel in the back streets of the city's Old Port.

The following morning, he was to see a Roumanian called Ferenczy, formerly a Danube river pilot. Polanyi had given him the details in the hotel room in Edirne. In the spring of 1939, when Hitler had taken the remainder of Czechoslovakia and war seemed inevitable, the French Service de Renseignements had tried to interrupt Germany's oil supply by bribing the Danube river pilots to leave the country. Some had, some hadn't, and the operation failed. Which left the French intelligence service with a number of Roumanian pilots scattered across Europe. In Ferenczy's case, they'd tried to help, restarting his life in Marseilles, where he'd become a trader; first in opium, then in pearls. The man's name, Polanyi said, indicated Hungarian descent. Which had likely, now and again, made life hard for him, so he was perhaps never all that loyal to the Roumanian state. 'A man with allegiance only to himself,' Polanyi suggested. 'If it was me, I'd start with that assumption, but, as usual, you'll have to make your own way.'

Using the Marchais alias, Serebin telephoned the pilot. He was, he said, 'a friend of your good friends in France.' Ferenczy, after some desultory sparring, accepted that explanation and agreed to see him in an hour.

Serebin was surprised to find himself invited to the man's apartment – a café would have been the traditional place to meet a stranger – but, as soon as the door opened, he understood why. Ferenczy meant him to behold the trappings of success. And so he did, pausing at the threshold of a parlor that virtually groaned with trappings. New and expensive furniture, shimmering fabrics, a splendid radio, a Victrola and a long shelf of records, a marble nymph, her hand reaching languorously for a crystal lamp. Ferenczy, in red velvet smoking jacket and emerald green ascot, beamed as Serebin took it all in and offered him a very old cognac, which he declined.

'Yes,' he told Serebin, answering an unasked question, 'fortune has smiled on me.'

'Clearly it has, even in the midst of war.'

'Business has never been better.'

'Still, the fall of France . . .'

'A catastrophe, but she will rise again, monsieur. She is indomitable.'

Serebin agreed.

'Always I admired this nation,' Ferenczy said. 'Then, by a stroke of luck, I was given a second chance at life. So I have, in effect, married my mistress.'

'Well, your mistress needs your help.'

Ferenczy's smile vanished, his expression now stern and patriotic.

'We are seeking information,' Serebin said. 'Firsthand information, the kind of thing known only to somebody with practical experience. You spent much of your life on the Danube, you know its habits, its peculiarities. That's what concerns us at the moment. Specifically, those stretches of the river where navigation is difficult, those areas where an accident, to a tug or a barge, would tend to disrupt the normal flow of commerce.'

'Commerce in petroleum.'

'Yes. As in '39.' Serebin produced a pencil and a notepad.

'It's a long river,' Ferenczy said, 'much of it broad and flat. From Vienna down to Budapest, all the way past Belgrade, the major hazard is flooding, and that depends on the spring rains. So, for your purposes, what you want is the Kazan Gorge, where the river passes through the

Carpathians. Using the common method of calculation, distance from the Roumanian delta on the Black Sea, that would be from kilometer 1060 down to 940. At that point, the river runs south, and forms the border between Yugoslavia and Roumania, and the section from Golubac, on the Yugoslavian side, down to Sip, turns into sixty-five miles of rapids, where the river sometimes narrows to a hundred and sixty yards. At the end of this stretch is the *Djerdap,* in Roumanian *Portile de Fier,* the Iron Gates. After that, the river widens, and runs on a flat plain to the sea, and there you can do very little.'

'And the depth?'

'God knows! In some places, fifteen hundred feet, in others, depending on the season, it can be as shallow as thirty feet, especially over what's called the Stenka ridge, where narrow channels are marked by buoys. You're actually *in* the mountains, you see, passing over sub-merged peaks and valleys. And it's dangerous – all shipping must take on a river pilot, that's the rule of the Danube Commission. Going downstream, the pilot boards at Moldova Veche, on the Roumanian shore across from Golubac. If you're headed the other way, the ship station is at Kladovo, but the Iron Gates, just north of there, are no longer the problem they used to be. After the Great War, Austrian engineers dug the Dezvrin ship canal, about two and a half kilometers in length, to bypass the rapids. But, even with the canal, the current is so strong that the engineers had to build a section of railway on the road above the canal, in order to use a towing engine that pulls traffic upstream by means of a cable.'

'So, then,' Serebin said, staring down at his notes, which made no sense at all.

Ferenczy rose abruptly, sat next to Serebin on the couch, and took his pad and pencil. 'Here is Golubac,' he said, writing *1046* next to the name. A specific kilometer? Of course. He probably knew it meter by meter. With some amazement, Serebin watched as a river pilot emerged from the persona of a middle-aged French fop. Ferenczy drew with a firm hand, using dashes down the center of the river to show the border, printing *Dunav* on the Serbian side, *Dunarea* on the Roumanian, for the river changed languages along with its depths and channels. The pilot drew teardrop-shaped rocks, an island, a road. 'Here is Babakai rock,' he said. 'In 1788, the Austrians stretched a chain across here to trap the Turkish navy. It's a red rock, you can't miss it.' At 1030, the Stenka ridge, three kilometers to 1027. In the middle, another rock. Next came *Klissura*. 'Greek word,' Ferenczy said. 'Means, ah, crevice. Very narrow, maybe too deep.' And down and down, here it curved, then curved back again, the river Czerna joined at 954, then the course twisted violently south, ten kilometers northwest of the Iron Gates. 'After this,' Ferenczy said, 'the ship canal.'

He handed the paper back to Serebin and returned to his chair.

'Can we do it?' Serebin said.

'Maybe.'

Serebin imagined the river at night, rushing water, dark cliffs above, a tugboat fighting the current as sailors hung off the side and tried to fix an iron hook on a sunken barge below the surface.

He ran his finger up the drawing and back down, pausing at the Babakai rock. 'The Austrian chain,' he said. 'Did it work?'

'No,' Ferenczy said. 'Betrayed,' he added. 'You have to remember where you are.'

Serebin returned to Paris the following day, arriving at the Winchester a little after five o'clock. There was a spectre standing in the doorway of the pharmacy next to the hotel. Some poor *clochard,* a shapeless figure in a ragged coat, just visible in the early evening light. The spectre stepped forward and called out to him in a stage whisper. *'Serebin.'*

Serebin squinted at the man as he approached. He looked, face starved and narrow and white, like a martyred saint in a Spanish painting – a saint with his beard shaved off. 'Kubalsky? Serge?'

It was. He nodded, sorrowfully, in reply, understanding all too well why Serebin wasn't sure.

They walked together through the lobby, the night clerk watching them from behind his desk. He might, Serebin thought, report what he'd seen, but that was the way things were, lately, and nothing to be done about it.

Climbing the stairs at Kubalsky's side, Serebin noticed that he now walked with a limp, and, the way Serebin put it to himself, *that he reeked of flight*. Of mold and mildew, of dried sweat. In the room, Kubalsky sat heavily in a chair by the desk, Serebin gave him a cigarette and lit it for him. He closed his eyes and inhaled deeply, exhaled long plumes of smoke that swirled and drifted about his face, a creature whose body ran on smoke instead of blood. And for that moment, Serebin thought, he became once again what he'd been all his life – The Journalist. For the gossip papers, the timber news, the mining gazette, writing a paragraph and counting the words, showing up at an office to see about his check.

After a long silence, Kubalsky said 'Christ,' quietly, almost to himself, then, 'Don't worry, Ilya, I can't stay here.'

'I'm not worried.'

'An hour, maybe. No more.'

Kubalsky started to go to sleep, cigarette still smoldering between his fingers. 'Serge,' Serebin said. 'Can you tell me where you've been?'

His eyes opened. 'Here and there,' he said. 'Down every rathole in the Balkans. It's crowded, I should warn you, in case you're thinking of trying it, you keep running into the same people.'

'You know, we thought you were . . .'

'Yes, I thought so too. In that alley behind the theatre. One of them got a hand on me, like a steel claw, but I hit him. Imagine that, but I did. He didn't like it, roared like a bull. Then shot at me as I ran away. I don't think either of us believed how hard I hit him. Nothing quite like fear, Ilya, really, nothing like it.'

'Organy?' It meant the men who worked for the organs of state security, the NKVD.

'They were.'

'Why, Serge?'

'Why not?'

That was, Serebin thought, glib, and ingenuous, but until a better two-word history of the USSR came along, it would do. Nonetheless, Serebin waited for the rest.

'All right,' Kubalsky sighed, resignation heavy in his voice. 'Sometime last year, June maybe, they showed up, one day, the way they do, and informed me that I had to talk to them. Or else. So, no choice – with these people you don't argue. All you can do is make sure you're never, ah, productive, so I wasn't. Still, there they were.

'Then, one day in November, they told me to call you and get you out of the IRU ceremony. They didn't say why, they don't, just 'Here's what we want.' But that evening, after the bombing, one of them came to my room. He wanted to know about the Turkish authorities – had they contacted me, had they contacted anyone else? Particularly, what *kind* of authority? The Istanbul police? The Emniyet? If the Emniyet, who? What rank? I didn't know a thing and I told him so. Well, he said, get in touch when it happens, because it will. Now, for some reason he was alone. It's never like that, you know, there's always two of them, they watch each other. But this one was alone, and he talked – the kind of talk that follows a triumph. He told me how the thing had been done; a man at the window, a signal when Goldbark went to look at his delivery, wasn't it all too clever for words.

'After he left, I began to suffer, there's no other word for it. I walked the streets for hours, drank up whatever money I had in my pocket, tried to calm down, but I couldn't. I was stuck midway between anguish and fury and I just couldn't get free. The next day, when it didn't go away, I understood that I had to *make* it go away. I mean, Goldbark had always been kind to me, to every-one, and then, I had to ask myself what came next – what else would they want? Then I realized that I had to talk to somebody, and the only person that made sense was you. Now, why they wanted you out of there I don't know, don't want to know – I surely don't believe it was because you were their special friend, I know you and them far too well for that. So, I tried to meet with you, secretly, and apparently I did something wrong, because they showed up at the movie theatre. Not the ones I usually saw, others, the big ones in the baggy suits.

'Anyhow, I got away, and I hid for a time in the city, but I figured I couldn't do that forever, so I sold what-ever I owned, maybe even a few things I didn't own, and I ran. Up into Bulgaria, Salonika, you name it. Finally, I had some luck, met an émigré Pole who worked on a train and got a ride to Paris in a freight car. I took a chance on the IRU office on the rue Daru, and found Boris Ulzhen, who told me where you were. I should add that he asked me no questions at all, whatever *that* means, just acted like it was all in a day's work. Which, come to think of it, it probably is, by now.'

Serebin went looking for his vodka. Maybe a third of a bottle left. He poured two glasses and gave one to Kubalsky.

'Thank you,' Kubalsky said. 'Of course I need money.'

For a moment, Serebin had a vision of his grandfather. He was laughing, which was typical of him, he did it all the time, though Serebin had been too young when he died to realize how much that meant. In this vision, he was laughing at his grandson. *Think it's a blessing? Yes? Ha, you'll see, my dear, you'll see.*

He saw. Rummaging in the top drawer of his bureau, then remembering to include what he had in his pocket. Still, it *was* a blessing, that night anyhow, to have something he could give Kubalsky. 'Could be more, tomorrow,' he said, handing over the money.

From Kubalsky, an indulgent smile. *No tomorrow.*

'And so, what next?'

'More of the same. I'll run around like a chicken with its head cut off, like half the people in Europe, while the other half tries to hide them, and the other half is looking for them.'

'Ah, Russian mathematics.'

'*Na zdorov'ye.*'

'You're very popular, this week,' Ulzhen said.

Serebin was at the IRU office to help with the newsletter – everything from correcting spelling to advice and sympathy for the tiny lady who tried to work the mimeograph machine. A small crowd stood around her as the blotchy purplish copies came through, all of them creased strangely at the upper right corner. 'Fucking *devil*,' Ulzhen said under his breath. The tiny lady had moist eyes, wore a cross around her neck, and was known to be devout.

'It's the feeder bar,' she said in despair. 'The tension!'

'Popular?' Serebin said to Ulzhen. Ulzhen was not precisely chilly, lately, something else. Wary, perhaps. Anyhow different, since the afternoon at the Brasserie Heininger. Well, add that to the list of things in the world he could not fix, a list that only seemed to grow.

Ulzhen took off his jacket and turned his cuffs up, a brawl with the mimeograph machine was guaranteed to be filthy business. Serebin's heart sped as he waited for an answer – he *knew* why Ulzhen had said that, and wondered only why Marie-Galante had chosen to make contact through the office.

'He called himself Jean Paul,' Ulzhen said.

'Who?'

'Jean Claude, is it? No, Jean Marc. There's a message in your mailbox.'

Serebin went over to the wooden frame divided into boxes, found a poem for *The Harvest,* an announcement for a meeting of the Stamp Club, and a sheet of stationery from the Hotel Bristol with a phone number and a message, asking him to telephone so that they could arrange to meet and signed *Jean Marc.*

For a moment, Serebin had no idea, then he recalled the balcony of the hotel in Switzerland, and Ivan Kostyka's *homme de confiance.* Disappointed, he headed for the IRU telephone.

Staying at the luxurious Bristol, Jean Marc had chosen a curious place for a meeting, a café in a small street in the 19th Arrondissement, by the St.-Martin canal – the abattoir district. Still, Serebin thought, watching unfamiliar Métro stops slide past, there wasn't a square foot of Paris that didn't have cachet for somebody. For those with a particularly elevated approach to their slumming, the onion-soup bistros over at the Halles markets had become passé, and, before the occupation had redrawn the social geography of the city, tuxedos and gowns had begun to appear at dawn in the neighborhood.

Serebin had a hard time finding it – even the streets liked to change their names up here. A common, local café, a bar, really, narrow and unlit, and virtually empty. Only two Arab men, drinking milky *pastis,* the propri-

etor, reading a newspaper by the cash register, and Jean
Marc, sitting at a corner table in the back. He was as
Serebin remembered him: young and handsome, tall,
with an aristocratic stoop, face cold and aloof. 'I hope
you don't mind this place,' he said, standing to greet
Serebin. 'It's private, and I'm meeting friends later on, at
Cochon d'Or. Good steaks from the district, and the
Germans haven't found it yet.'

When Serebin ordered a glass of wine, Jean Marc held
up a hand. 'They have scotch whiskey here, of course
you'll join me.'

'They do?'

'A good *marque* as it happens.' A sudden smile, all
warmth and charm, as he rested the hand on Serebin's
arm. 'A Parisian discovery, eh? Don't go telling the
world.'

'Two scotch?' the proprietor said.

'Oh, bring the bottle,' Jean Marc said.

A good idea for a February night, Serebin realized,
the taste dry and smoky, anything but sweet.

'Baron Kostyka sends his regards,' Jean Marc said.
'And hopes his, contacts in Roumania have turned out
to be worthwhile.'

'Some of them, certainly. He's in London?'

'He is. And delighted to be English, a new man. You'd
be surprised how much he's changed.'

Serebin had imagined, on getting Jean Marc's note,
that he'd been stationed on the continent, in charge of
Kostyka's European office. But, clearly, that wasn't the
case. 'You came here from London?' he said.

'Long way round. The only way to do it, these days.
Passenger steamer to Lisbon, then up from Spain. No
problem – as long as you don't get torpedoed. You do
have to have British connections to get a place on the
ship, and German connections to get into Paris, but, for
Kostyka, everything is possible. It's commerce, you

know, both sides need it, so, at least for the moment, business transcends war.'

Serebin was impressed. From his own experience, he knew what it took to move around Europe, but this was a level of freedom well beyond that.

'I'm here for a week,' Jean Marc said, 'then off to Geneva and Zurich – those meetings will go on for a while – and, eventually, back to London. What about you, will you stay in Paris?'

'For the time being.'

'Not so bad, is it?' Jean Marc refilled his glass, then Serebin's.

'Can be difficult – it seems to depend on how the Germans are doing. When they're content, when they think they're winning, life gets easier.'

That made sense to Jean Marc. 'But now, as I understand it, you're about to make them feel a great deal less content.'

Serebin shrugged. 'Oh, who knows,' he said.

'No, really,' Jean Marc said. 'If your operations in Roumania work out, they'll be in some considerable difficulty.'

'Well, it's not up to me,' Serebin said. He began to feel, for no particular reason, the first stirrings of some vague, intuitive resistance.

'I can't imagine why they'd call it off,' Jean Marc said, 'after all this time and effort. Germany runs on that oil. If I were in charge, I wouldn't stop until I'd done something about it.'

'Well,' Serebin said. It was all very complicated, wasn't it. 'Anyhow, the war goes on. Now there's something they call the Afrika Korps, to campaign in North Africa. That's been in the newspapers.'

'Yes, with Rommel in charge – which means they're serious.'

Again, time for more scotch. Had the bottle been full

when they started? It seemed that Jean Marc was in no hurry to meet his friends. Not a bad drinking companion, when all was said and done, the whiskey had a good effect on him, made him less guarded and distant. 'I grew up in this city,' he told Serebin. 'In the Seventh. A soft life, you would think, but not really.' What made it difficult, he explained, was that people envied privilege. And, in truth, why shouldn't they? They saw a fine house in Paris, a château in the countryside, a stable, a cellar of old vintages, aristocracy. 'Everything but money,' he said, 'which is why I work for Ivan Kostyka.' Still, nobody knew about that, and one had to keep up appearances, one had to play the part. Which meant you had to think before you spoke, you had to be conscious, always, of who you were and what that meant. Really, you couldn't trust people, that was the lesson learned by generations of nobility. People took advantage, didn't they. Once they thought you were rich and powerful, it was your obligation to help them out. Not only with money, with influence, connection. Suddenly, you were their best friend.

Now maybe it didn't matter so much, day by day, just something you learned to live with, and who really cared. But, when *women* were involved, well, then it was different, because the heart, the *heart,* had its own reasons.

Yes, they would drink to that. To women. To the heart.

What else, Jean Marc asked the world, made life worth living? What else mattered, compared to that? Yet even there, in that most private chamber – forgive the *double entendre* – even there, spontaneity, that wondrous, uncaring, ah, freedom, *abandon,* proved difficult to reach. So then, in those affairs, you paid for who you were, for what you were. For what you had to be. For example, Nicolette . . .

Serebin followed along. Yes, he understood. Yes, that was the way things were. Outside the café was Europe and all its sorrows, but Serebin tried not to think about it. After all, even with everything that went on out there, people still struggled with matters of the bed, matters of the heart.

Had he been in love with Nicolette? Jean Marc wasn't sure. Well, maybe, in a way. At what point did desire become something more? She wasn't the stableman's daughter, far from it. Still, they belonged to different worlds, different worlds, and it made anything beyond a *liaison* impossible. Yet that innocence, that carefree giving, had taken him prisoner. So many times they were together for the last time! What could he have done differently? What? And, the longer it went on, the harder it was to let go of it. Did Serebin see that? Did he understand?

The *homme de confiance* unburdened his heart, the scotch whiskey sank low in the bottle. Could it be stronger than vodka? Across the table, Jean Marc's face grew blurred and soft, and Serebin found himself slightly dizzy, leaning hard on the table. Jean Marc drank right along with him, but maybe he was used to it. And if Serebin got a little drunk, so what? *I am being murdered,* he thought.

What?

Where had *that* come from? Madness, no? *See what a life of secrecy does to you!*

He stood up, gestured toward the door at the back of the café. A visit to the *petit coin,* the little room.

Once there, he caught himself looking around for a window. His head swam – what was he going to do? Climb out into the alley? Run off into the night?

When he came back out, Jean Marc wasn't at the table. Serebin couldn't believe he'd simply left. At the bar, maybe. No. At, for whatever reason, another table? No. Only the two Arab men, now playing dominoes. Nothing unusual about them – heavy and dark, in the slightly mismatched coats and trousers they all wore. Serebin stared a moment too long – one of them glanced up at him, then looked away.

'Did my friend leave?' he asked the proprietor.

'He said he was late,' the man told him. 'To tell you he was sorry, but he had to be off.'

'Oh.'

'It's all paid for.'

Well, no point in staying there by himself. Serebin said good night to the proprietor, then went out the door. *Now where?* He remembered the trouble he'd had finding the place – a maze of unfamiliar streets, this one went off at an angle, that one cut across the other. He should have paid attention, on the way, but he hadn't. The Métro was this way? He wasn't sure. As he walked to the corner – maybe the name of the street would jog his memory – he heard a door close, somewhere behind him. When he turned around, he saw the two men standing in front of the café, talking. *Just two friends, out for the evening.*

He started walking. In Paris, you always found a boulevard, sooner or later. Follow the boulevard and you would eventually come to a Métro station. Or, he thought, ask somebody. But there was no one to ask. It was probably very busy here during the day – the men who worked at the abattoirs, the local people. But not now. Everybody had gone home.

The rue Mourette. All right, we'll take that.

The two men came along behind him. Headed for the Métro? Well, ask them. No. But they were walking a little faster than he was, not so much, just a little. So, give them time, let them catch up, and then he could ask them if they knew where the Métro was.

He'd seen knives, once or twice. One time in particular, in Madrid, during the civil war, he could never quite forget. It had been very sudden, when it happened, or he would have looked away. But, once you saw what you saw it was too late. The idea bothered him. Too easy to imagine, to imagine what went on, just at the moment, what it would feel like.

He could hear them, back there. Their steps. That's how quiet it was. *Run*.

Couldn't quite get himself to do that. Almost, but it seemed crazy, to take off down the street. Still, he could hear them. One of them talking, low and guttural. The other one laughed. At him? Because he'd speeded up? He came to a corner, now it was the rue Guzac. Ugly name. A bad street to die on. He looked up at the windows, but they were dark. Behind him, the conversation was louder.

He crossed the street, head down, hands in pockets, and headed back where he'd come from. Toward the café. Easy enough to see it, earlier in the evening. Even with blackout curtains over the windows, light showed around the edges. Where was it? Had he taken another street? No, there it was, but it was dark now. Closed. Somewhere behind him, the two men crossed the street and were now walking in the same direction he was.

The man in Madrid had screamed, he had really screamed, loud. But then it was cut off sharp, because of what happened next. Serebin took his hands out of his pockets, could feel his heart hammering inside him. Why was this going to happen to him? *Jean Marc*. He walked faster, but it didn't matter.

He turned a corner and started to run, then he saw a woman standing in the shadow of a doorway. Broad flat face, with lipstick and rouge, and stiff, curly hair. She wore a leather coat, had a bag on a shoulder strap. When their eyes met, she tilted her head slightly to one side, a question.

'*Bonsoir,*' he said.

'All alone, tonight?'

'Yes. Can we go somewhere?'

'It's fifty francs,' she said. 'Why are you breathing like that? Aren't sick, are you?'

'No.'

'Those your pals?'

The two men waited. Felt like standing in the street and talking to each other, nothing wrong with that.

'No, it's just me.'

'*Salops*,' she said. She didn't like the type.

'Your man around?'

'Across the street. Why?'

'Let's go see him.'

'Why? He won't like it.'

'Oh, he'll like it all right. Costs money, for me to get what I want.'

'What's that?'

'Maybe another girl. Maybe somebody watches it.'

'Oh.'

'All right?'

'Sure. Whatever you want, it's only money.'

'Three hundred francs, how does that sound?'

The woman gave a sharp whistle and her pimp stepped from a doorway. About eighteen, with a cap slanted over one eye and a smart little face.

That did it, the two men started to walk away. They were very casual, just out for an evening stroll. One of them looked back over his shoulder and grinned at Serebin. *We'll see you some other time.* Could they simply have intended to rob him?

The pimp was paid the three hundred francs, and all he had to watch was Serebin, disappearing down the stairway of a Métro station.

By post:

Zollweig Maschinenfabrik AG
Gründelstrasse 51
Regensburg

Deutsches Reich

28 February, 1941

Domnul Emil Gulian
Enterprise Marasz-Gulian
Strada Galati 10
Bucuresti
Roumania

Dear Sir:

We are pleased to accept your offer of Reichsmarks 40,000 for two Model XIV Rheinmetall turbine steam boilers. You may have complete confidence that these have been regularly inspected and maintained to a high order and we trust you will find them in perfect working condition.

On receipt of your draft in the above-named amount, we will ship, according to your instruction, by river barge, no later than 14 March, with arrival at the port of Belgrade expected by 17 March. All export permissions and licenses will be obtained by our office.

We wish you success in your new venture and, should you have further inquiries, please address them to me personally.

Most respectfully yours,

Albert Krempf
Managing Director
Zollweig Maschinenfabrik AG

A Vidocq/Lille steam turbine was available in Bratislava, manufactured in 1931, rated at 10,000 kilowatts of power delivered, 33 feet in length, 13 feet wide, 11 feet high, weighing 237,000 pounds. The Czech manager of the foundry guaranteed performance, documentation, and shipping. And well he should, Polanyi thought, at the price they were paying. Polanyi wondered how they would go about replacing it, with the war using up production capacity at an astonishing rate, but that wasn't his problem. Maybe it was a backup system, maybe this, maybe that – in the event, the opportunity was too good to pass up and no doubt they had something in mind.

As in Budapest, where agents for Marasz-Gulian located three turbine boilers, of similar dimension, with one old fellow, formerly the pride of the Esztergom Power Authority, weighing in at 'over four hundred thousand pounds.' They rather thought. And rescued, just in time, from the scrapyard.

'Let's see them haul that great fucker off the bottom,' Stephens said, at the restaurant overlooking the wharves. He handed Polanyi a page cut from an old Hungarian catalogue. A photograph of a giant turbine. A little man with a mustache, wearing a gray uniform, stood beside it, dwarfed by its size. 'From London, by diplomatic pouch,' Stephens explained. Then added, wistfully, 'Such strange and lovely things they have in London.'

Six turbines, then, with a seventh available in Belgrade, from a Serbian steel mill. 'Fourteen years old and no longer suitable to our needs, but perfectly reliable.' The decision to use steam turbines, a race of giants in the Land of Industry, had come after some consideration. Bagged cement would break loose from its load and tumble away in the current long before it turned to concrete, and there was no credible reason to ship concrete block to Roumania, where some of it, at least, was manufactured. Similarly, fire brick for blast furnaces, which weighed, as it happened, substantially less than common brick. 'And locomotives,' Stephens had said, 'are, alas, far too likely to be traveling by rail.' Scrap iron was currently in demand for German tanks, stone was quarried in Roumania. 'The world is lighter than one thinks,' Polanyi grumbled, poking at his aubergine.

And the cursed river could never really decide how deep it was, they found. Still, everyone, Herr Doktor Finkelheim, the Roumanian pilot, and specialists at universities in Birmingham and Leeds, agreed that the Stenka ridge was the place. Kilometer 1030. Dangerously shallow at the end of winter, before the spring rains left the river swollen and high in its banks. So, a barge with six feet of draft and six feet above the waterline, crowned with an eleven-foot-high turbine, would come to rest at twenty-three feet. A menace to navigation. Even if, in the course of the accident, one of the barges turned on its side – disaster! – they'd have six more down there, pulled under by the sinking tug. A great navigational mess, surely, but an expensive one to arrange.

'Don't worry about that,' Stephens said. The Special Operations Executive had a considerable imprest from Treasury, and he was, for the time being, their fair-haired boy.

It was Ibrahim who was sent to Bucharest to meet with Gulian. 'Stenka ridge,' he said. 'No question. An Austrian company dredges the ship canal and, in the present state of politics, now more than ever. They are always at it.' As for the appropriate cargo, Gulian shrugged and said, 'Well, a steam boiler.' He laughed. 'If what you want is sheer clumsiness, the most frustrating beast you could imagine, that's the steam boiler. Monsters, those things, ask your local industrialist.'

Bought new?

'No, impossible. They take months to order, to build, to deliver – a *cauchemar.*'

Then?

'In all commercé there are shadow markets, informal dealings between buyer and seller. In all products, machinery as much as any other. I can think of at least two agencies who work this area. And the war has made no difference to them – believe me, they prosper in war. They live on the margin, these men. Hang around your outer office, read the newspaper, discuss the day's events with your secretary. There used to be one – Brugger, was that it? Always with a toothpick in the mouth. He'd wait for me to go out for lunch. Hello, how are you, heard the one about the plumber and the midget? Want to buy something? Got anything you want to sell? Truth is, you don't need them, until you need them, and then you really need them.'

So then, who will actually buy the turbines?

'That's a problem. A paper company won't work, because the people who watch these things – import licenses and so forth – are not stupid. "XYZ," they'll say, "who's that?" Which means, if you don't have months to build up a shell business, you'll need the real thing. So, it's either me, or someone like me.'

And what happens after the 'accident'?

'Delay, temporize, misunderstand, deny, pull your hair out, declare bankruptcy, then run like hell. After all, what makes you think that what works in business won't work in war?'

Yes, but there's no history of Gulian, doing things like that.

True. 'But go see my enemies, they'll tell you they always knew it would come to that. So, finally, they'll be right.'

A lot of enemies, were there?

'I'm rich and successful,' Gulian said. 'You fill in the rest.'

So, through various banks, in Geneva and Lisbon, the money began to move.

28 February. At the IRU office, a quiet morning. On the radio, an endless suite and variations for guitar,

accompanied, now and then, by the rattle of a newspaper, and an occasional, mournful, ping from the tepid radiator, remembering better days. In the window, a lead-colored sky. Serebin dropped by that morning because he had nowhere else to go and nothing to do. This was called, in the parlance of the clandestine world, *waiting.* He needed urgently to speak with Polanyi – to tell him what had happened at the café by the abattoirs, to warn him, perhaps, of a dangerous change of heart, or to be scoffed at, gently, for seeing things that weren't there. But, short of an emergency wire to Helikon Trading, there was nothing he could do. He'd been left in Paris, awaiting assignment, dangling. Had the operation been, for whatever reason, canceled? Maybe. And the way he would be told about it was – silence. *No further contact.* Would Polanyi do that? Yes, that was precisely what he would do. That was, he suspected, the traditional, the classical, way it was done.

He considered the wire. Wrote and rewrote it in the Aesopian language they used, oblique and commonplace – *representative important principal currently unwilling to proceed.* In other words, *the bastard tried to kill me.* No, it wouldn't work. Or, worse, it would work, and stop everything cold for no good reason.

He spent the morning pretending to be busy, seated in front of a stack of problem papers – letters to be answered, forms to be filled out – that he shared with Boris Ulzhen, but mostly thinking about things that were bad for him to think about. Then the telephone rang, and a man called out, 'Ilya Aleksandrovich? A call for you.'

'Who is it?'

After a moment, the man said, 'Madame Orlov.'

The name meant nothing – *another lost soul.* Serebin hesitated, he was tired of the world, of people who wanted things. Finally, he lost the battle with his conscience and walked over to the desk. 'Yes?' he said. 'Madame Orlov?'

'Hello, *ours.*'

Four-thirty, she'd said.

But by five-thirty she still wasn't there. Serebin waited, looked at his watch and waited. Sometimes he stared out the window, at people passing by on the street in front of the hotel. Sometimes he tried to read, gave up, walked around the room, went back to the window. So she's late, he told himself, women do that in love affairs, it's nothing new. But this was an occupied city, and sometimes people didn't show up when they said they would. Sometimes, it turned out, they'd had to stand on line at a passport *contrôle,* and sometimes they were taken away to be questioned. And, sometimes, they just disappeared.

Then, after six, he heard footsteps in the hallway, almost running, and waited by the door until she knocked. She was breathless and cold, said she was sorry to be so late, put a chilled glove on his cheek and, eyes closed, lips apart, waited for him to kiss her. He started to, then didn't. Instead, from the curve between her neck and shoulder he inhaled a great, deep breath of her – perfume, plain soap, the scent of her skin, and, when he exhaled, it was audible; half growl, half sigh, a dog by a fire.

She knew what that meant. Held him tight for a moment, then said 'God, it's freezing in here,' and ran for the bed, shedding her coat and kicking her shoes off on the way, burrowing under the covers and pulling them up to her nose. He sat beside her, and she gave him her jacket and skirt, then her sweater and slip. A brief struggle beneath the blanket produced first an oath, then a stocking.

'How long?' he said.

She handed him a second stocking. 'The weekend. Labonniere's in Vichy, at the foreign ministry. So . . .'

'Are you . . . is it work? For us?'

She wriggled briefly beneath the covers and gave him a garter belt. 'No, love, it isn't.' She unhooked her bra, put it on his lap with everything else, then slid her panties off, reached out from her den and, turning them upside down, pulled them over his head.

'I dread going back there,' she said later. They were warm beneath the snarled covers, the room dark, the city silent. 'Awful place, the Trieste. One of those border towns where everybody's got it in for everybody else.'

'It's not forever,' he said.

'Mean and dreary, and it rains.'

'But' – he paused – 'you have to stay.'

She yawned and stretched, pulled the blankets around them. 'Don't tempt me, *ours*. Really, don't.' He had the BBC on the radio, tuned low for caution – it was against occupation law to listen to it – and a tiny symphony played away on the night table. 'I've convinced myself that it matters, what I do there.' She didn't sound convinced. 'Salon intelligence, so-called. Poor Madame X, how she pines for her *friend,* the Minister of Y, off in frigid Moscow for a week. Labonniere's pretty good at it.'

'You're careful, of course.'

'Oh yes, very. But . . .'

She didn't like talking about it, didn't want it in bed with them. She traced a finger down his back, began, lazily, to make love to him.

'Maybe better, in the spring.'

She put a finger to his lips.

'Sorry.'

She rolled delicately over on top of him so that her mouth was close to his ear and said, in a voice so quiet he could only just hear her, 'We will survive this, *ours,* and then we will go away together.'

Only when morning came and they were dressed could he bring himself to tell her what happened at the café. 'Strange,' she said.

'Yes.'

'I don't like saying this, but, if they'd really wanted to do something, they could have done it.'

'I know.'

'Maybe they were just trying to frighten you. A warning.'

'Maybe. Still, whatever it was, Polanyi should hear about it.'

'I can manage that,' she said, 'when I get back.' She put on her coat, they were going out for coffee. 'By now, you know, Polanyi and the people he works for, and the people *they* work for, have all got themselves committed to this.'

For a moment, they were silent.

'So,' she said, 'it's too late to stop.'

Very unwise to be seen together at the Gare de Lyon but he wouldn't let her leave him at the hotel. They looked for a taxi, but there was none to be found, so they leaned against each other on the Métro, then got off a stop before the station, found a café, held hands across the table, and said good-bye.

20 March. The parks still brown and dead, branches bare and dripping, rain cold, light gone in late afternoon, and hours and hours until the dawn. Yes, the last days of winter, the calendar didn't lie, but up here it died hard and took a long time doing it. On the Pont Royal, the émigré writer I. A. Serebin leaned on a balustrade and stared pensively down into the Seine.

Writing lines on a reluctant spring? Lines for a lover in a distant city? The river was flat, and low in its banks, it barely moved. Or was it, perhaps, just beginning to swell, just beginning to grow, from thawed fields and hillsides in the south? He couldn't tell, didn't know, was ignorant of water. All those years of idle staring at the stuff, the very essence of everything, and he knew nothing about it. Nonetheless, he studied the river and tried to read it because, if the spring tide had started to run here, it was running also at another river, south and east of here, at the Stenka ridge, at kilometer 1030. Certain individuals, in Istanbul and London, had to be gazing at their own rivers, he suspected. So then, where were they?

He needn't have worried.

When he left the bridge he walked over to the IRU office, then, eventually, back to the Winchester, and then, as was his custom, to a small restaurant in the quarter, where his ration coupons allowed him a bowl of thin stew, turnips and onions and a few shreds of meat, and a piece of mealy gray bread. Which he ate while reading a newspaper, folded by his bowl, to keep him company. He moved quickly past the political news – Hitler had issued an ultimatum to Prince Paul of Yugoslavia – to 'The Inquiring Reporter.' *Yesterday, our question was for men with long beards: Sir, do you sleep with your beard on top of the blanket, or beneath it?*

'Monsieur?'

Serebin looked up to see a woman in a black kerchief and coat. A plain soul, small and compact, unremarkable.

'All the tables are taken, would you mind terribly if I joined you?'

Why no, he didn't mind. All the tables were not taken, but why fret over details. She ordered a small flask of wine and the stew – there was nothing else on the blackboard – handing over her own coupons. And, when the waiter left, said, 'I believe we have a friend in common, in Istanbul.'

In the valley between winter and spring, old friends often reappeared. Maybe chance, or the stars, or ancient human something, but, whatever the reason, it was especially so that year. Helmut Bach, for instance, had left two messages at the IRU, the first week in March, and two more at Serebin's hotel, the second a brief note. Where was Serebin? Bach very much wanted to see him, they had some things to talk over. So, please get in touch. At this number, or at this one – the protocol office of the German administration – he was sure to get the message.

Des choses à discuter. A German writing in French to a Russian – what couldn't go wrong! But friends – even 'friends,' a cloaked term for a cloaked relationship – did not have 'things to talk over.' That was a threat. A warm little threat, maybe, but a threat nonetheless. Bach had invested time and concentration on him, now it had to pay off. The moment had come, was, likely, past due, for Serebin to give the occupation authority what it wanted – 'a talk,' or appearance at a cultural event, whatever might imply approval of the new German Europe.

That was to look on the bright side.

Because it did occur to Serebin that these affections from his German pal might have been provoked by the same source that had sent Jean Marc to buy him drinks. Not a direct denunciation to the Gestapo, merely a word with a diplomat or an urbane, sympathetic Abwehr officer. Because this wasn't force majeure, this was its close cousin, *pressure.* Which meant, to Serebin, that the unseen hand – mailed fist in a velvet glove – was, for some complex reason, working cautiously.

He thought.

Polanyi's courier had left him a perfect set of documents

for departure from Paris on 25 March. A new name – a Russian name, and a new job: director of the Paris office of a Roumanian company, Enterprise Marasz-Gulian, who was approved for travel to Belgrade, on business, via first-class *wagon-lit*. This meant two things: Serebin did not have to apply for permission to leave the occupied city – it crossed his mind that they might well be waiting for him, at that office – and, with his train leaving in four days, he could probably avoid responding to Helmut Bach.

Four days. And premonitions. He found himself taking inventory of his life at the Winchester, his life in Paris. Poking through notes and sketches for unwritten work, addresses and telephone numbers, books, letters. He'd known, when the Germans had marched into Paris nine months earlier, that he might not stay there forever. So he'd been rather Parisian about the occupation; try a day of it, see if you survive, then try another. Sooner or later, the French told each other, they'll go away, because they always did. And he'd imagined that, if it happened that he was the one who had to leave, he would be able to make a civilized exit.

But now he had a bad feeling. Clearly, Bach, which meant the Third Reich, was not going to leave him in peace, they were going to make him pay to live in their city. So, as the French put it, *fini*. That was that. He found himself anxious to see, one last time, certain places; streets he liked, gardens, alleys, a few secret corners of the city where its medieval heart still beat. It would be a long time before he saw them again.

Two sad days. The photograph of Annette, *Mai '38* scrawled on the back, taken in the garden of a house by the sea. A print dress, a pained smile – *why must you take my picture?* A letter from Warsaw, dated August of '39, mailed just before the invasion by a Polish friend from Odessa. A photograph of his father as a young man, hair like brushed wheat, standing stiffly beside an older, unknown, woman. The only picture of him that survived. *Put it all in a box and find a place to hide it.* He almost did that – he found a good box, from a stationery store, but he was too late.

When he entered the lobby of the Winchester, just after seven, box in hand, the clerk beckoned to him. This was the same clerk, an old man with white hair, who had watched as he'd led Kubalsky upstairs. Now, when Serebin reached the desk, he said, 'Ah monsieur, some good news for you.'

'Yes?'

The other clerk behind the desk, a heavy man with a dark, lustrous pompadour who kept the hotel books, looked up attentively, it was always interesting to hear about good news.

'Madame at the *crémerie* – in the rue Mabillon? Has a grand Cantal. If you go over there you can still get some.'

Serebin thanked him. Nothing like this had ever happened before, but the French character was dependably eccentric and sudden changes of weather were no surprise. He started to turn away from the desk, headed up to his room, when the man grabbed him by the wrist.

'Now, monsieur. Right away. For the Cantal.' The clerk's hand was gripping him so hard it trembled.

Serebin went cold. The envelope from the courier was in the inside pocket of his jacket. To carry two identities was a cardinal sin of clandestine practice, but Serebin had meant to hide the envelope at the IRU office.

'Now, please.' A glance and a nod at the ceiling – *they're up in your room.*

A few feet away, the bookkeeper put his hand on the telephone – the one used to call the rooms. The clerk saw him do it, turned toward him, and, for a long time, the two men stared at each other. This was nothing less than a struggle for Serebin's life, and Serebin knew it. A fierce, silent struggle, no sound in the lobby, not a word spoken out loud. Finally, the bookkeeper cleared his throat, a small self-conscious gesture, and took his hand off the phone.

'I'll show you where it is,' the clerk said. 'The *crémerie*.' He let go of Serebin's wrist and walked around the end of the desk. Turning to the bookkeeper, he said, 'Keep an eye on things, will you?' Then added, 'Monsieur Henri.' His first name, spoken in a normal tone of voice, dry and pleasant, but there was anathema in it, clear as a bell.

The clerk took Serebin by the elbow – he'd fought for this prize and he wasn't going to let it get away – and walked him to a door that led off the lobby and down a stairway to the cellar of the hotel. This was bravado, Serebin thought, profoundly French bravado. The old man knew the bookkeeper wouldn't pick up the phone once he'd left, and so virtually dared him to do it.

At the foot of the stairs, a dark passage, past ruined furniture and abandoned trunks, past carriage-horse harness and a rack of unlabeled wine bottles sealed with wax, the Winchester's private history. Another stairway led up to street level and a heavy door. The clerk took a ring of keys from his pocket, asked Serebin to light a match, finally found the right one, and opened the door.

Outside, an alley. Serebin could see a street at the far end.

'Take care, monsieur,' the clerk said to him.

'Who were they?'

A Gallic gesture – shoulders, face, hands. Meaning *who knows,* to begin with, but more than that: *they are who they always are.* 'Three of them, not in uniform. One in your room. Two nearby.'

'Well, thank you, my friend.'

Je vous en prie, monsieur. My pleasure.

He was at Anya Zak's apartment an hour later. He'd gone first to Ulzhen, but the concierge said they were out for the evening. 'So,' she said, when she opened the door, 'now you see the truth.' *The real Anya*. Who wore two heavy nightgowns, a pair of French army socks, and wool gloves, one green, the other gray.

Serebin sat on the couch, the empty box on his lap. Anya Zak stood over a hot plate and began to boil water for tea.

'I should tell you,' he said, 'that I am a fugitive.'

'You?'

'Yes.'

'Really. What have you done?'

'Nothing much.'

'Well, whatever it is, I hope it's very bad. Reprehensible.'

'Can I stay here, Anya?'

She nodded yes, and measured out tea from a canister as she waited for the water to boil. 'There are people, you know, who say you do things.'

'People are wrong.'

'Are they? Well, even so, I'm proud of you.'

He slept on the couch, under his overcoat — she insisted he take the blanket but he wouldn't. Neither of them really slept. They talked in the darkness, once the lights were out, about countries and cities, about what had happened to people they knew. Then he thought she'd fallen asleep. But he could see her shape beneath the covers, restless, moving around, turning over. At one point, when it was very late, she whispered, 'Are you asleep?' He almost answered, then didn't, and breathed as though he were.

THE
EMPRESS
OF SZEGED

26 March. Belgrade.

Or so the British cartographers called it. To the local residents it was Beograd, the White City, the capital of Serbia, as it had always been, and not of a place called Yugoslavia, a country which, in 1918, some diplomats made up for them to live in. Still, when that was done, the Serbs were in no shape to object to anything. They'd lost a million and a half people, siding with Britain and France in the Great War, and the Austro-Hungarian army had looted the city. Real, old-fashioned, neoclassical looting – none of this prissy filching of the national art and gold. They took *everything*. Everything that wasn't hidden and much that was. Local residents were seen in the street wearing curtains, and carpets. And, ten years later, some of them, going up to see friends in Budapest, were served dinner on their own plates.

Serebin's train arrived at dawn, a flock of crows rising to a pink sky from the station roof. His departure from Paris had turned into something quite like an escape – effected with the aid of Kacherin, of all people, the world's worst poet. Because Kacherin, who wrote saccharine verse about his mother, was also Kacherin the émigré taxi driver, and for Serebin, once he declared himself a fugitive, the Gare de Lyon was out of the question – *everybody* was arrested there. So he gave Anya Zak money to buy him a valise and some clothes to put in it, and Kacherin drove him all the way to Bourges – he'd only asked for Etampes – the demarcation line for the Unoccupied Zone. An unexpectedly useful accomplice, Kacherin, who eased them through checkpoint after checkpoint with a hesitant smile and a nervous laugh.

'Missed his train,' Kacherin told the Germans, making a bottle of his fist, thumb out, pinkie raised, and tilting it up to his mouth, while Serebin accommodated the fiction by holding his head in his hands. Oh those Russians.

Thus Kacherin did, in the end, turn out to have talent, it just wasn't what he wanted it to be. They talked all the way to Bourges – that was at least, Serebin speculated, part of the reason Kacherin agreed to take him. Talked and talked. About poetry, about history, stars, bugs, tarot, Roosevelt. The man had a passion for the minutiae of the world – should he perhaps consider writing about *that*? No, shut up and be nice, Serebin told himself, an admonition delivered in the voice of his own mother.

Not so good in Belgrade.

The bar at the Srbski Kralj – King of Serbia, *the* hotel in town – was throbbing, mobbed with every predator in the Balkans, anonymous men with their blondes mixed in among knots of foreign correspondents. Serebin counted four different languages, all in undertones of various volumes, on his way across the room.

'Ah, Serebin, *salut*.'

Here you are, at last. Marrano was glad, relieved, to see him. Introduced him to the two pale Serbs, in air force uniform, who shared his table, 'Captain Draza and Captain Jovan,' smoking feverishly and radiating conspiracy from every pore. Ranks and first names? This was either sinister or endearing, Serebin couldn't decide which. *Maybe both.* Russians and Serbs, Slavs who spoke Slavic languages, could understand each other, and Captain Draza asked him where he'd come from.

'Paris.'

'How can you live there?' They practically spit – living under German occupation was clearly outside their definition of manhood.

'Maybe I can't.'

'That cocksucker thinks he's coming down here,' Jovan said.

'He won't like it,' Draza said.

It was evening by the time Marrano and Serebin walked toward the docks, through mud streets lined by little shacks that served as cafés. Inside, fires glowed in open brick ovens, the patrons laughed, shouted, cursed, and somebody played a mandolin or a balalaika. Where the street curved downhill, Marrano stumbled over a pig on a rope, which gave a single, irritated snort, then went back to rooting in the dirt. Somewhere above them, a woman was singing. Serebin stopped to listen. 'Only the moon shines on the heights / And lights up the graves of the soldiers.'

Marrano asked him what it was.

'A Russian army song, "The Hills of Manchuria," from the 1905 war with Japan.'

'A lot of émigrés, here?'

'Thirty-five thousand. From Denikin's army, and Wrangel's. Cossacks and doctors and professors, you name it. There was a big IRU chapter in Belgrade but they broke away from the Paris organization. Our politics – you know how that goes.'

Now they could see the docks, where the river Sava met the Danube – lanterns fore and aft on barges and tugs, and their shimmering reflections in the water. A few flood lamps, where work went on at night, a shower of blue sparks from a welder's torch, red lights on buoys that marked a channel out in the river.

'Peaceful, isn't it,' Marrano said. 'Too bad it won't last.'

Serebin knew that was true. *Another city on fire.*

'The Balkans are a problem now, for Herr Hitler. Italian army pushed all the way up into Albania and the

Greeks not about to quit fighting. So, he's got to send a serious force, thirty divisions, say, to calm things down, and they've got to go through Yugoslavia to get where they're going. Which means the Belgrade government had better sign up with the Axis, or else. Right now, Hitler's at the edge of his patience; ultimatums, bribed ministers, a fifth column – Croatia, and what comes next is invasion. The Yugoslavs know it, and they'll give in, the government will, but the word at the Srbski Kralj is that the military, particularly the air force, won't stand for it.'

As they neared the harbor they had to wait while a man came and got his dog, some kind of immense Balkan mastiff, so black he was almost invisible, who stood his ground and growled to let them know they were not allowed to go down his street. 'A thousand pardons,' the man said, from the darkness.

'The two captains,' Serebin said. 'They're working for us?'

'For London, technically,' Marrano said. 'But the simple answer is yes. There is now a second operation, an alternative plan in case the barges don't work. In a way, it's a better idea, but it will require digging and drilling, will require overt cooperation from the Yugoslavs, and it took Hitler to press Belgrade very hard before we got the answer we wanted.'

'What will they do?'

'Take the cliff on the Yugoslav side of the river and drop it in the Danube.'

'By digging and drilling?'

'That's just to set explosive charges. Once we leave the freight business, we go into mining.'

They circled the harbor on an old wooden catwalk until Marrano found the dock he was looking for. At the far end, past river families cooking over charcoal braziers, past bargeloads of lumber and tar barrels and heavy rope, there was a small machine shop in a rusted tin shed. Inside, a workman at a bench was taking a carburetor apart, dipping each piece in a pan of gasoline to clean it. The shop smelled good to Serebin, oil and burnt iron, scents of the Odessa waterfront.

'Tell him we're Captain Draza's friends,' Marrano said.

Serebin translated, and the workman said, 'Then you're welcome here.'

'The magic formula,' Serebin said.

'In some places, yes. Others, I wouldn't try it.'

'Who are they?'

'Oh, Serbian nationalists. Ultranationalists? Fascists? Anyhow they're on our side, for the moment, so the name doesn't matter.'

Beyond politics, Serebin knew exactly who they were. They reminded him of a few of the men who'd served with him in the civil war, and in the Ukraine, during the war with Poland. When you needed somebody to go crawling around in the enemy camp, when you needed somebody to deal with the sniper in the bell tower, it was Draza and Jovan who went. And, not always but surprisingly often, did the job and came back alive. You saw it in their eyes, in the way they carried themselves. They were good at fighting, it was just that simple, and Serebin, the officer Serebin, had quickly learned to tell them apart from the others.

Marrano strolled out to the end of the wharf. 'Come and have a look.'

Serebin joined him. Roped to the dock were four barges, riding low in the filthy water, with tarpaulins tied down over high, bulky shapes. Serebin stepped over onto the first in line, put a hand on the canvas, and felt a round iron wall. All that time in Bucharest, this was what they got for it.

'There should be three more,' Marrano said. 'Two

from Germany, one here in Belgrade, but it looks like the German shipment isn't coming.'

'What happened?'

'According to Gulian, the honorable gentlemen at the Zollweig factory are having difficulties. They refer, in their wire, to 'an anomaly in the application for export license.''

'What does *that* mean?'

'I would say it means, in German commercial terminology, something akin to *fuck you.*'

'They were paid.'

'Oh yes.'

'So it's robbery. When all the nice language is peeled away, they stole the money.' He paused, then said, 'Or, if it isn't that, it is,' he looked for the right word, 'intervention.'

'That's a possibility. Very, *very* unappetizing, if true. Polanyi and I spent time on that, in Istanbul.'

'And?'

'Who knows.'

'Well then, four barges will just have to be enough.'

Marrano looked at his watch. 'Five, maybe. And, while we're waiting, let me tell you how we're going to do this.'

The workman finished his carburetor, drew a shutter down over the entry, snapped a padlock on it, and left for the evening. The weather was warm, it was almost a spring night in the harbor, so Marrano and Serebin sat on the wooden pier and leaned back against the metal shed. Marrano produced a page of typescript and gave Serebin a pad and pencil.

'Here in Belgrade, we're at kilometer 1170 of the river, which means we're a hundred and forty kilometers from the high ridge at 1030. The ridge runs for three kilometers, which should be enough – we don't know how much time it will take to sink these things, but with the weight they're carrying they'll go down in a hurry.

'The tug will have to stop at the Roumanian border post – that's at a village called Bazias, at kilometer 1072. If you leave here at one in the afternoon, figuring a speed of fifteen kilometers an hour, it gets you to Bazias by 7:30. Your papers are in order, and you should be through there in twenty minutes or so. Sometime after 9:45, you pass the pilot station at Moldova Veche, on the Roumanian shore. Supposedly, a pilot must be taken onboard for the passage through the Iron Gates. However, in real life, which is to say Roumanian life, all the big steamers do this, but only some, maybe half, of the tugboats. A pilot would complicate your life, but it isn't the end of the world, though it might have to be for the pilot if he decides not to be reasonable.

'By this calculation, you come to kilometer 1030 – there's a big granite rock protruding from the water at 1029, it probably has some sort of folkloric nickname – sometime after ten at night. So, when you sight the rock, that's it. The captain of the tugboat, discovering that one of his barges is sinking and taking the others down with it, now must cut the tow and, as soon as possible, alert the Danube authority.

'But by then, you'll be long gone. About forty minutes beyond the Stenka ridge, kilometer 1018, the river Berzasca enters the Danube from the north, coming down from the Alibeg mountains, part of the Carpathian range. There's a village where the rivers meet, and the tug will go a kilometer or so upstream, to a bridge over a logging road. On the bridge will be a Lancia, the Aprilia sedan, horribly dented and scratched, probably the color gray when first purchased or stolen, and it is not impossible that there was, at some point, a fire in the trunk. You may, if you're like me, spend an idle hour wondering how such a thing could possibly have happened, but cars don't live soft lives in this country and it remains a speedy and dependable machine. I'll be driving, and we'll take the Szechenyi road back to Belgrade. Then we stay here, see what develops on the river, and attend to our mining interests. Any questions?'

'The Szechenyi road?' Serebin knew it by reputation, a narrow track, hewn out of rock in the nineteenth century, at the direction of the Hungarian count who gave it his name.

'It works, I've tried it, just hope for dry weather. We use it also in the emergency plan, which has us bypassing Belgrade, crossing Yugoslavia by train – it is very difficult by car – or, in a real emergency, by plane, courtesy of our friends in the Royal Yugoslav Air Force, to a town called Zadar, between Split and Trieste on the Dalmatian coast. There we will be picked up by boat, probably the *Néréide* but with Polanyi you never know. The contact in Zadar is a florist, in a small street off the central square, called Amari. If you need to signal for help, no matter where you are, wire Helikon Trading with the message *Confirm receipt of your letter of 10 March*.

'Eventually, you can go back to Paris, or, if they've found out who you are and they're after you, Istanbul. I should add that when Polanyi was told of your meeting at the bar in Paris, it was his feeling that no matter what went on or didn't, your margin of safety has been compromised and you ought to get out.'

'He's right,' Serebin said.

'He often is. So then, Istanbul.'

Serebin began to describe his flight from Paris, but the ragged beat of a tugboat engine approached from the mouth of the harbor and he rose and followed Marrano out to the end of the pier. In the glow of the dock light he could read the boat's name, *Empress of Szeged*. So, a Hungarian boat. Which, when he thought about it, was no surprise at all. As the tug, towing a heavily loaded barge, slid cleverly up to the dock, Emil Gulian, looking exceptionally out of place in business hat, scarf, and overcoat, appeared at the stern, waved, then tossed Serebin a rope. 'Hello there,' he called out. 'Good to see you again.'

Serebin secured the line to a heavy bollard, then boarded the tugboat and walked forward to the pilot cabin. The *Empress* was manned by its owners, a young couple, both wearing the river sailor's uniform of dark blue shirt and trousers. Zolti, short for Zoltan, was Hungarian, lean and wiry, face weathered by life on the water. Erma, a Viennese, was a few inches taller, broad and fat, with an immense bosom, sleeves rolled back to reveal a pair of meaty arms, and a face that would stop a clock. A peasant face, broad and fleshy, with shrewd, beady eyes, a bulbous nose, and a wide slash of a mouth, anxious to laugh at a world that had laughed at her. All this crowned by ebony hair that had been chopped off with – Serebin thought about a hatchet, but, more likely, a scissors.

To Serebin the couple spoke German, Zolti very little, Erma chattering away, flushed and excited and, every few seconds, licking her lips. Maybe a nervous habit, or maybe, Serebin thought, she's beginning to feel it.

He certainly was. On the train down to Belgrade, it came to visit and stayed. Ticking away inside him, a knot in the chest, a dry mouth and, earlier that day, lighting a cigarette, he'd burned his palm with a flaring match.

'Are you going ashore?' he asked them.

'No, no,' Erma said. 'We stay here.' With a nod of her head she indicated the barges. 'On guard.' She picked up a short iron bar by the helmsman's wheel, gave it a comic shake and closed one eye, as though she were protecting a tray of cookies from naughty children.

Gulian and Marrano were waiting for him on the dock, both with hands thrust in the pockets of their coats. As Serebin descended the ladder, Marrano said, 'So?'

'They'll be fine.'

'Don't much care for the Nazis, those two,' Gulian said, shaking hands with Serebin. For the brief moment Serebin had seen him in Bucharest, at the Tic Tac Club, he'd been hesitant, retiring, the diffident escort of his nightclub singer girlfriend. Not now. He was younger than Serebin remembered, had a humorous face – a subtle, powerful smile that never went away, and the air of a man almost religiously unimpressed with himself, though that went for the world as well. He was also, Serebin thought, having a very good time – whatever leash he was off, a very good time.

'You'll be my guests for dinner,' he said.

The last thing Serebin wanted, but Gulian wasn't someone you said no to. They walked out of the harbor, found a café where Gulian made a telephone call – a nasty business, in Belgrade – then went off in a taxi to a small private house not far from the Srbski Kralj. For an elaborate dinner, served by two graceful young women, cooked by a man who kept opening the kitchen door a crack and peering out. Chicken-liver risotto, fillet of a fillet of pork, puree of roasted red peppers with garlic. Platters of it, which were tasted, then sent back to the kitchen, with Gulian calling out, 'Magnificent, Dusko!' each time, to spare the feelings of the chef. There were no other customers – they ate at a large table in the dining room – this wasn't precisely a restaurant, or it was a restaurant only when Gulian, or others like him, wanted it to be. For the finale, Dusko himself presented confitures of fruit doused with Maraschino.

Gulian hadn't actually intended to come to Belgrade. But, once 'those bastards over at the steel mill' began to procrastinate, he'd grabbed his checkbook and jumped on a train. 'They were paid what they asked for – that was my mistake,' Gulian said. 'When I didn't bargain, they said to each other, "Well, he really wants this thing, let's see how much."'

'What did you do?' Serebin asked.

'First of all I showed up. Second of all I yelled – in French, and a few words in German, but they got the idea. And last of all I paid. So . . .'

A very good host, Gulian; provident, and entertaining. He knew the country, knew its history, and liked to tell stories. 'Ever heard of Julius the Nephew, ruler of all Dalmatia?' No, actually, they hadn't. 'The last legitimately appointed Emperor of the West, designated by Rome in the middle of the fifth century. Despite, I should add, the plotting of one Orestes, former secretary to Attila the Hun.'

Well, it took Serebin's mind off what he had to do. And the stories were good, Gulian a sort of writer manqué, delighted by excess and eccentricity. 'When the Turkish vizier Kara Mustapha was defeated at Vienna,' he said, over a forkful of risotto, 'he could not bear to leave behind his most beloved treasures, especially the two most beautiful beings in his world. So, with tears of sorrow and regret, he had them beheaded, to make sure that the infidels would never possess them: the loveliest of all his wives, and an ostrich.'

After the dessert was taken away, Gulian called for brandy. 'To success, gentlemen. And, when all is said and done, death to tyrants.'

One-fifteen in the morning. Serebin back at the harbor, this time by himself. He alerted the tugboat crew to what he was doing, then settled down to wait, lighting Sobranies with cupped hands in the sharp spring breeze. The tied-up tugs and barges bumped against their moorings, and he could hear boat traffic out on the river, up from Roumania or down from Hungary, sometimes a horn, sometimes a bell. Overcast in Belgrade, as always, maybe one or two faint stars in the northern sky. 1:30. 1:45. *Serbian time.* Dogs barking, up on the hillside. A singing drunk, a car, whining as it worked its way up a long grade.

2:10. The sound he knew as a military engine; overpowered, untuned, and loud. He watched the headlights, bouncing up and down as the vehicle wound its way along the dirt track that served the harbor. It stopped briefly at the end of the dock, then drove onto it, and Serebin felt the pole-built structure sway and quiver as the old wooden boards took the weight. It was, he saw, an open command car, vintage maybe 1920. 'Greetings, Ivan,' a voice called out, Ivan being any Russian whose name you didn't know.

Captain Draza and Captain Jovan, drunk as owls and only an hour late. In light blue officers' uniforms, leather straps crossed over the tunics. They banged and rattled in their car, then hauled out a wooden crate, which they carried between them with a burlap sack on top.

'It's the armorers!' Jovan called out. Draza thought that was pretty funny. They dropped the crate at Serebin's feet. It landed hard, and Jovan said 'Oh shit!'

'No, no,' Draza said. 'No problem.' Then, to Serebin, 'How are you?'

'Good.'

'That's good.'

He rummaged around in the sack, found a screwdriver, and began prising boards off the top of the crate and tossing them over his shoulder into the water. When the crate was open, he lifted out a black iron cylinder with a ridged top and a shiny steel mechanism bolted into a recessed circle in the center, the whole thing maybe twenty-four inches in diameter, and tossed it to Serebin. The weight was a shock, and Serebin had to make a second grab before he got hold of it.

'Don't drop him, Ivan,' Draza said.

Better not to. Serebin knew a land mine when he saw

246

it but he'd never actually held one. 'Ahh, don't be like that,' Jovan said to Draza.

'He couldn't set it off if he wanted to,' Draza said. 'Here, give it to me.'

'It's all right,' Serebin said. He could live without whatever demonstration Draza had in mind. 'I've seen these before.'

'These?'

'Mines.'

'Oh, mines. Shit, not *these*. These are Italian. Dug up across the border a month ago, so, very up-to-date.'

'Where did you see mines?' Jovan asked.

'Galicia, Volhynia, Pripet Marshes, Madrid, river Ebro.' *We're all friends here but, if you have a minute, go fuck yourselves.*

'Oh, well, all right then.'

'To work,' Draza said, lighting a stubby cigarette.

They stepped onto the first barge, walked around the big turbine until they found a hatch with rope handles on the cover. Draza fought with it, finally broke it free, and handed it to Jovan. 'We'll need a bracket on that.'

Jovan peered into the sack, then groped around inside. 'It's in here?'

'Better be. I put it in.'

Jovan grunted, found a metal bracket with screws in the holes, and went to work.

'Down we go,' Draza said. He grasped the rim of the hatch opening and swung himself inside.

Jovan handed Serebin the sack. 'Forgot this,' he said.

Serebin followed Draza, who had turned on a flash-light in the pitch-black interior of the barge. The beam illuminated a few inches of oily water and at least one dead rat. 'Drill,' he said to Serebin. Serebin reached into the sack and took out a hand drill. Draza squatted, about twenty feet from the hatch opening, astride a wooden strut that spanned the sides and bottom of the hull, tried to bore vertically to the floor, scraped his knuckles, swore, then drilled in at an angle. 'Get me some wire,' he said.

With the cigarette in his lips, squinting through the smoke, he handed the flashlight to Serebin, took the mine in both hands, and lowered it carefully onto the strut. Unrolled a piece of wire, flexed it up and down until it broke, and wired the mine in place. Then, he pinched the steel bar in the center mechanism with thumb and index finger and tried to turn it. But it wouldn't move. He held his breath, applied pressure, then twisted with all his strength, fingers turning white where they gripped the bar. For long seconds nothing happened. Through clenched teeth he said, 'Fucking things,' and shut his eyes. Finally, the bar squeaked and gave him a quarter turn. He let his breath out, swore again, forced the bar around the first thread, unscrewed it the rest of the way and flipped it away into the darkness. Serebin heard the splash. Draza waited another moment, lost his patience, tucked his middle finger under his thumb and flicked it hard against the center of the mine. With a sharp metallic snap, the trigger popped up.

He swayed a little, adjusted his feet, and made himself a long piece of wire. Serebin moved the flashlight closer. 'Got a girlfriend?' Draza said.

'Yes.'

'Me too. You should see her.'

Draza wiggled his fingers like a pianist getting ready to perform, then began to wind the wire around and around the trigger. When he was done, he ran the wire down to the base, made one loop, pulled it tight, and handed the rest of the coil to Serebin. 'Do *not* pull on that,' he said.

He stood up, and wiped the sweat off his forehead with the back of his hand. He'd ripped the skin over his knuckles, and wiped the blood off on the side of his pant leg. 'Hey,' he called out to Jovan. 'You done?'

Jovan held the hatch cover a few inches above the opening. Draza reached up and wrapped the end of the wire around the bracket on the bottom, and Jovan moved the hatch cover just enough to allow Draza and Serebin to climb back up on the deck. The three of them knelt at the edge of the hatch and Draza fitted the cover back in place. 'Now,' he said, 'the next time you lift this up is the last time you lift this up. The firing device works by compression – you'll need a slow, steady pull to force it down. The tugboat captain knows about this?'

'He does.'

'No last-minute inspections, right?'

'I'll remind him.'

Draza hunted in his pockets, then said, 'You have a piece of paper?'

Serebin had the back of a matchbox.

'Write this. 67 Rajkovic, top floor left. Belongs to my cousin, but, if you need to find us . . .' Draza looked over Serebin's shoulder as he wrote. 'There, that's it.'

Jovan stepped onto the dock and took another mine from the crate.

'Back to work,' Draza said. 'Four more and we're done.'

4:10 A.M. He could hear the bar at the Srbski Kralj when the doorman let him into the lobby. A hundred people shouting, a fog of cigarette smoke, perhaps a stringed instrument of some kind, twanging desperately away in the middle of it. Serebin went to his room. On the table, a box wrapped in brown paper, and inside, a bottle of wine. Echézeaux – which he knew to be very good Burgundy. No written note required. *Good luck, Ilya Aleksandrovich,* it meant. Or however that went in Hungarian.

249

He took off his coat and stretched out on the bed and did not place a call to Trieste. Or, if he did, it was a private call, the kind where you don't use the telephone. It rained, a spring rain, very gentle and steady, through the last hour of the night, which should have put him to sleep, but it didn't. What he got instead was a daze – bits and pieces of worry, desire, pointless memory, a descent to the edge of dreams, and back round again.

The rain stopped at dawn, and the sun hung just below the horizon and set the sky on fire, rainclouds lit like dying embers, vast red streaks above the river.

27 March. *Pristinate Dunav.* An old sign, the paint faded and blistered. In the Serbian view, if you needed a sign to find the Danube harbor – as opposed to the one on the river Sava – you probably didn't deserve to be there.

One of the longest mornings he'd ever spent, not much to do but wait. He'd gone over to the outdoor market in Sremska street, bought a heavy sweater and corduroy pants and a canvas jacket lined with wool. Stopped at a café, read the papers, drank a coffee, went to work.

Almost didn't. The tugboat crew was ready and waiting. Zolti in a sailor's heavy jacket, Erma in what looked like an army coat – Greek? Albanian? – anyhow olive green, that fell to her ankles. She wore also a knitted cap, pulled down over her ears. The *Empress* was ready, she said. All warmed up. So, they shook hands, smiled brave smiles, talked about the weather, then Serebin said, 'Well, we might as well,' or something equally exalted, and Erma cast off from the dock. When she returned to the cabin, Zolti shoved the throttle forward, the engine hammered, the deck throbbed beneath Serebin's feet, and they went absolutely nowhere.

Erma looked at Zolti and said, *'Scheisse.'* A curse at

bad luck, but he was included. He rubbed the back of his neck, and tried again. The towlines snapped taut. And that was that.

'We need the current,' Zolti explained. 'Once we get out in the river.'

Serebin stood there, no idea what to do. *Hungarian spy dies of laughter in Istanbul.* Or, maybe, apoplexy. No, laughter.

Erma said a few sharp words, and Zolti took a wrench and left the cabin. They could hear him working, down below, and, after a while, he tapped the wrench against the hull and Erma rammed the throttle lever forward as far as it would go. Engine straining against the load, they pulled away from the dock an inch at a time, then made a long, slow, snail's journey across the harbor. Zolti reappeared, wiping oil off his hands with a rag. 'We need the current, ten kilometers an hour,' he said, apology in his voice.

'We could have left one of the barges behind,' Serebin said.

Erma wagged an index finger. Not the *Empress of Szeged.*

They turned southeast on the river. Gulls and gray sky. Serebin walked back to the stern, stared at the barges for a time, found a comfortable coil of heavy rope, and sat there, watching the river traffic. A passenger steamer, black-hulled, flying the swastika and moving slowly upstream. A Roumanian tug towing three barges with long, circular steel tanks bolted to their decks. Was this Ploesti oil, making its way up to Germany? He decided to believe it was. On the tug, a line ran from the roof of the pilothouse to a pole on the stern, holding shirts and underpants that flapped in the river wind.

There were fishermen in rowboats off the town of Smederevo. On the shore behind them, a ruined fortress, black and monstrous. Bigger than most, but otherwise the same; burnt stone, weeds in the fighting ports, they guarded every river in Europe and, if you spoke the language, somebody at the local café would tell you the name of the king. There was a dog sleeping at the end of a stone jetty, just past the entry of the river Morava, that woke up and watched Serebin as he went past. Then a motor launch caught up with them, flying the Yugoslav flag, and matched its speed to theirs as Zolti and the helmsman held a shouted conversation. They waved good-bye and the launch sped up, disappearing from view around a bend in the river.

Erma came walking back to the stern. 'They told us that they're checking cargo at Bazias,' she said. 'The Roumanian border post.'

'How do they know?'

'They have a radio – heard it from friends.'

Serebin wondered what it meant. 'Our papers are good,' he said. 'A commercial shipment to Giurgiu.'

Erma nodded.

'We'll just do the normal thing,' Serebin said.

After the village of Dubravica, the river began to narrow, and the banks were different. Not fields now, forest, bare willow and poplar, and flocks of small birds that left the branches and circled in the sky as the boat engines pounded past them. And, on both sides of the river, the land rose, not yet steep, just the first of the Carpathian foothills, the real mountains waiting downriver. Still, it was cold in their shadow and Serebin buttoned his jacket. 4:30. Bazias at 7:30. Erma took over at the wheel and sent Zolti back to the stern with a sandwich, fat sausage on black bread, and a cup of coffee. Serebin didn't really want it. 'She says you should eat something, because later . . .' He didn't bother to finish. Serebin drank the coffee.

The wind sharpened as night fell, and Serebin left the

open deck. The *Empress* had a searchlight mounted atop the pilot cabin, which threw a tight yellow circle on the water ahead of the boat. Maybe it kept them from running into the shore, he thought, but not much else – staying afloat more likely depended on a helmsman's knowledge of the shoals and sandbars. A wooden handle that operated the searchlight was set next to the wheel, and Erma reached over and swept the beam along the bank, turning trees into gray ghosts, and, then, revealing a stone kilometer marker with the number *1090* carved on it. Later on, Serebin watched a forest appear in the middle of the river – an island. Erma spun the wheel to the left and the *Empress* curved slowly around the shore, their wake breaking white against the tangled tree roots. 'Ostrovo island,' she said.

There was a bonfire onshore, sparks rising in the air to the height of the trees, and three men in silhouette who stood watching the flames.

Serebin asked if they were hunters.

'Who knows what they are.'

In the light, jagged granite rocks rose from the river. The boat passed within ten feet of one of them, which towered high above the cabin. Beyond the rocks, a fishing village, dark and silent, small boats tied up to a dock. Erma pointed an index finger at the ceiling, bobbing it up and down for emphasis. 'Hear that?' she said.

He had to listen for a moment before he heard it – soft at first, then growing, the low, steady drone of aircraft, a lot of them. He leaned forward and squinted through the cloudy glass of the cabin window, but there was nothing to see. The sound went on and on, rising and falling, for more than a minute. 'Luftwaffe,' Erma said. She had to raise her voice so he could hear her.

Was it? They were headed southwest, he thought, which meant Greece, or Yugoslavia – maybe even North Africa. If it was the Luftwaffe, they had to be flying from airfields in northern Roumania. To bomb who? British troops in Greece? 'Somebody's going to get it,' Erma said.

Sometimes the RAF flew over Paris at night, on their way to bomb targets in the Ruhr – steel mills, arms factories. People stopped talking when they heard the sound, and, in a silent café or shop, waited until it faded away. *Paris*. Sad, how doors closed behind you. He stared out at the river. Some people would wonder about him. Not Ulzhen, not Anya Zak, they knew, but others might. Or might not – it was no longer very interesting, when people went away. Marrano had told an odd story, over dinner, about Elsa Karp, Ivan Kostyka's mistress. She too was gone. Had left London, nobody knew why. There were rumors, Marrano said, as always. Stolen money? A secret lover? Connections with Moscow? Some people said that she'd left England by steamship, a freighter flying the flag of a neutral country. Serebin had wanted to hear more about it, but Gulian started to tell stories about Kostyka. 'We're not so different,' he said. Came from obscurity, both of them, no family, no money, on their own before they were sixteen. Serebin didn't think they were at all like each other, he knew them both, not well, but he'd . . .

'Up there,' Erma said.

Serebin could just see lights, shimmering in the haze that rose from rivers in the evening.

'Bazias,' Erma said.

First came a sign marking Roumanian territory – on the north bank of the river. Erma throttled the engine back to its slowest speed, barely making way, letting the tug and its barges drift to a stop, and Zolti threw a line to a Roumanian soldier who made them fast to a thick, wooden post. There were two boats docked on the upriver side of the canal – a Bulgarian tug hauling bargeloads of grain, maybe wheat, and a small river freighter, flying the Soviet flag, likely coming up from a Black Sea port. Two Russian sailors sat on the freighter's deck, dangling their legs over the side, smoking, and watching people go in and out of the customs post.

Not much more than a weathered board shack with a flag on a pole in the front yard. Erma said, 'You must bring all the papers with you.'

Serebin patted the envelope in the pocket of his coat.

It was warm inside the customs shack, a coal stove in one corner, and surprisingly busy. Serebin couldn't sort them all out – men from the tugboat and the freighter, two or three customs officials, an army officer, trying to make a telephone call – tapping the bar beneath the receiver and waiting for an operator.

One of the customs officials took his feet off a deal table, sat up straight, and beckoned to Serebin and the others. Zolti knew him – said something funny in Hungarian, obviously kidding him. The official grinned, looked at Erma, nodded toward Zolti, and shook his head. *Ahh, that guy.*

'Hello, Joszi,' Erma said. 'Busy night?'

'Who's your passenger?' the official said, stretching an open hand toward Serebin.

'Business type,' Erma said.

The official took Serebin's passport, wrote the nationality, name, and number in a ledger, opened a drawer in the table and stared down for a moment, then closed the drawer. 'Cargo documents, please,' he said to Serebin. Then, to Erma, 'Where you've been, darling?'

'Esztergom. Over to Bratislava, in December. Froze our you-know-whats off.'

The official nodded in sympathy as he went through the cargo documents, checking the signed approval stamps franked into the upper corners of each page. 'What are you doing with these things?' he said to Serebin.

'Mining iron ore, up near Brasov. There's a mill going in as well, and a foundry.'

'In Brasov?'

'Near there.'

'Where?'

'Sighisoara.'

'There's iron ore in Sighisoara?'

'Domnul Gulian is told there is.'

'Oh.' The official looked back down at the documents and found the Marasz-Gulian letterhead. Then he turned halfway around in his chair and called out to the officer trying to make a telephone call. 'Captain Visiu?'

The captain, young and rather smart looking, with a carefully clipped mustache, returned the telephone receiver to its cradle. He didn't slam it down, exactly, but used enough force to produce a single note from the bell.

Zolti, in Hungarian, asked the official a question.

The answer was brief.

'What is it?' Serebin said.

'The army's checking things, tonight,' Zolti said.

The captain presented himself to Serebin with a military half bow. He carried a large flashlight, and gestured toward the dock. 'Shall we go and take a look?' he said, in good French, then followed Serebin out the door.

Zolti undid the sailor's knot at one corner of the tarpaulin and raised it to reveal the iron wall of the turbine. The thing looked terrible, blistered paint, a savage dent, a large patch of rust shaped like a map of South America. The captain put a finger on it and a large flake fell off.

'We have to buy used,' Serebin said.

'Very old, isn't it?'

'Nothing our machinists can't fix.'

The captain paused, but decided not to comment. The three of them walked around the turbine, then, using the dock, moved to the second barge, which held the industrial monster late of the Esztergom Power Authority. Loaded at a dock in Budapest, it appeared to have been torn loose from its concrete base. The captain squatted and ran his flashlight underneath, looking for machine guns or Jews or whatever interested them in Bazias that night. Then he stood up and, when he moved back to let Zolti replace the tarpaulin, his heel landed on the hatch cover, which rocked beneath his weight. He looked down to see what it was, then stepped nimbly aside, as though he were afraid he'd damaged something. 'So now, the next,' he said.

He was quite thorough, Serebin thought. Even went up into the pilot cabin and had a look around. When he was done, the three of them returned to the customs post, where the official at the desk stamped their papers.

'Tell me, Joszi,' Erma said, 'what's the army doing up here?'

The official didn't answer with words, but his face wasn't hard to read. *Endless bullshit.* 'When you coming back, love?'

Erma thought it over. 'A week, maybe, if we can get a cargo in Giurgiu.'

'*If?*' The official laughed as he handed Serebin his passport. 'See you in a week,' he said. Across the room, the captain stood brooding over the telephone, tapping away.

With Zolti at the helm, they moved cautiously down the canal and out onto the river. 'How far now?' Serebin asked.

'Maybe forty kilometers,' Erma said. 'So, figure something under three hours. The Yugoslavs have a border post at Veliko Gradiste, about an hour from here, but we may not have to stop, we'll see. Basically, if you're leaving the country, the Serbs are glad to see you go.'

'Do we stop for a pilot?'

'Normally, we don't.'

'Good.' Serebin was relieved. 'Better not to deal with somebody like that if we don't have to.'

'We do what we want,' Zolti said. 'Pretty much they leave us alone – we've been at it for a long time.'

After that, it grew quiet in the cabin. The hills were tight to the shore now and the current ran fast and heavy under the keel, taking them downstream. When the boat swung around a broad shoal at midriver they could hear the rush of the water, churned to white foam by the gravel beneath it. 9:20. *Not long now.* They saw a single Roumanian tugboat, without a tow, working its way up to Bazias, a high wave riding the bow. 'Strong, tonight,' Zolti said, resettling his hands on the wheel, then glancing over his shoulder at the barges.

'. . . in the arms of Danubio,' Erma said. Her voice suggested the words of a song, recited by somebody who can't sing.

'Who's that?'

'The river god.'

An amusing idea – in daylight, on dry land. But this thing, this energy, beneath him deserved a god about as much as anything he'd ever experienced.

9:44. Kilometer 1050.

It was Erma who saw the searchlight.

Behind them somewhere, she said. Only a flicker, then it was gone – just in time for Serebin and Zolti to spin around and search the river astern and ask her if she was really sure about this. Because, when they looked, they couldn't see it. But there were rock walls for riverbanks now and a slight shift of direction would be enough to conceal anything.

Zolti looked once more, then again. 'Can't be,' he said.

But it was.

And in a little while they could all see it. A strong

white beam, growing slowly brighter as it caught up to them.

'How deep is it here?' Serebin asked.

'Here?'

'Yes.'

'Very deep.'

'Too deep?'

Zolti only now understood what he was getting at. 'Do you want to see the chart?'

No, he didn't need to see anything – these people knew the river. *Don't panic,* he told himself. It might be nothing.

It was not, however, nothing. It was, fifteen minutes later, a steel-hulled launch with *I77* painted on the bow, a Roumanian flag flying above the stern, and a pair of heavy machine guns, fitted with a curved shield, mounted just forward of the deckhouse. And, in addition, a siren, which wound up and down for a time, to be replaced by an officer with a loud-hailer – the amplified voice of authority intensified as it echoed between the cliffs above the river.

'Empress of Szeged,' it said.

That much Roumanian Serebin could understand, but for what came next he had to ask for translation.

'They're telling us to pull into the pilot station at Moldova Veche,' Erma said.

'Not for a pilot.'

'No.'

The patrol boat took up station off their stern quarter, which provided a clear field of fire through the gap, some thirty feet, between the tug and the first barge. Zolti pulled a cord fixed to the ceiling above his head, producing two bleats of the boat horn. 'That means we'll do what they want,' he said.

Using the side of her fist, Erma smacked the wooden skirting that ran below the wheel and a panel fell open, revealing a string bag nailed to its back. In the bag, a huge Mannlicher, the Mauser-style pistol of the Austro-Hungarian Empire – long barrel, ammunition magazine a box by the trigger guard – which gave off an oily shine in the glare of the searchlight. 'Just so you know,' she said to Serebin, pushing the panel back in place.

'What if,' Serebin said, 'we went aground. On the Yugoslav side of the river.'

'Aground?' Zolti said. Serebin saw what he meant – off the starboard bow, a granite wall rose from the water.

'And it wouldn't stop them,' Erma said.

Not much to say, after that. They chugged on through the night toward the pilot station. Inside Serebin, a mixture of rage and sorrow. *All that work.* And a memory of the river pilot, his red satin smoking jacket and his Marseilles apartment. *Betrayed,* he'd said. *You have to remember where you are.* 'I'm sorry,' Serebin said quietly.

Erma said 'Ach.' In a way that forgave him and damned the world for what it was and, in case he didn't understand all that, she dropped a rough hand on his shoulder.

The pilot station at Moldova Veche was set up like the customs post – a canal dug out of the bank beside the river, a dock, and a sagging one-story shack with a shed roof. Tied up at the far end of the canal were three or four small motor launches, clearly meant to ferry officials back and forth on the river. On the land side of the shack, a dirt path climbed a wooded hill, probably to the Szechenyi road.

There was a welcoming committee waiting for them on the dock: two Roumanian gendarmes, rural police, both with sidearms. Erma threw a line to one of them, and he secured the tug to an iron post. The barges drifted up behind the *Empress* and banged into the old tires lashed to the stern – even in the canal, the current on this part of the river was strong. The patrol boat docked behind the last barge, its engine running in neutral, thin smoke, heavy with the smell of gasoline, rising from its exhaust vents.

Inside, the pilot station was bare and functional, lit by two small desk lamps and a wood fire. A desk, a few wooden chairs, charts tacked to the wall, a coal stove. In one corner, staying well out of the way, an official in a simple uniform, probably the station supervisor. Well out of the way, perhaps, in deference to the two civilians in overcoats, one with briefcase, who rose to meet them. Clearly a chief and his assistant, the latter a well-barbered thug, stocky and powerful, a red and black swastika pin prominent on the lapel of his overcoat.

With a wave of the hand, the chief sent Zolti and Erma off to the custody of his assistant and led Serebin to a pair of chairs on the other side of the room. He was tall, with a fringe of gray hair, heavy rimmed glasses, and the face – the snout – of an anteater; long, curved and curious, built to probe. He wore a red, vee-necked sweater under his suit jacket, which served to temper his official demeanor. 'Shall we speak German?' he said courteously. He could speak Swahili, if it came to that, or whatever you liked. When Serebin nodded he said, 'So then, may I have your passport, please?'

Serebin handed it over, and the man took his time with it, touching his finger to his tongue to turn the pages, saying 'Hm,' and again 'Hm,' as he read. Followed the Paris representative of Marasz-Gulian on a series of logical business trips – Basel and Brussels, that kind of thing, had a look at the travel and work permits, slid them into the fold of the passport, slapped it against his palm a few times, then, not persuaded one way or the other, gave it back. 'Very good,' he said, meaning either *very good fake* or *everything is in order.* 'But we don't concern ourselves with documents, this evening.'

Serebin waited to see what came next. The man had

slid his chair to a position where he blocked Serebin's view of the other side of the room, but Serebin could hear Zolti's voice. Not precisely angry. Argumentative.

'We have here only some administrative difficulties. Not major, but they must be resolved.'

Across the room, Erma. He couldn't hear the words, but the tone was indignant.

The chief glanced over his shoulder, then returned to Serebin. 'My name is Schreiber, I am the second secretary at the legation in Bucharest, and I've come up here this evening to inform you that we must, regretfully, impound your shipment to Giurgiu. We will inform Herr Gulian of this action – we trust he will respect our decision. But, in any case, it's no longer your responsibility.'

'All right,' Serebin said.

'As for yourself, we will take you back to Bucharest, where all this can be worked out. A technicality – I shouldn't worry about it if I were you.'

'No?'

'No.'

'And the owners of the tugboat?'

From Schreiber, a dismissive shrug. Who cared?

Across the room, a certain metallic rattle, and an anguished cry from Erma. Schreiber grunted with irritation and looked around to see what all the fuss was about.

Serebin heard a pop and, instinctively, both he and Schreiber ducked their heads. Serebin stood up, could now see the assistant, thrashing and moaning on the floor. Beside him, a pair of handcuffs. Erma took two steps, leaned over the man and, with two more pops, put an end to the thrashing and moaning.

Schreiber leaped to his feet, arms flung wide, shouted, 'Oh for God's sake . . . ,' on his way to asking what somebody possibly thought they were *doing,* but he never got there. A small hole, the size of a coin, appeared in the back of his overcoat, where a shred of fabric now hung by a thread. He sank to his knees and coughed, hand politely over his mouth, then fell on his face, with a soft thud as his forehead hit the brick floor.

The room was dead still. Both gendarmes and the station supervisor were backed against the wall, hands high above their heads, eyes wide with terror. In the middle of it all stood Erma, small pistol in hand, trying to figure out what came next.

Serebin knew. He ran for the door, hit the dock in full stride. On the bow of the patrol boat, outlined in the glare of the searchlight, a Roumanian sailor was shouting at him. Had they heard the shots? Above the noise of their engines? Not possible. But, one of the people who'd been taken off the tugboat was now running back toward it. That couldn't be right. The sailor went for the holster at his belt and shouted an order, but he didn't quite have it right, because Serebin wasn't going back to the tugboat.

He dove over the low gunwale of the first barge he came to – the second from the end, *barge four,* the one with the Colossus of Esztergom, as luck would have it – and slithered on his stomach toward the hatch on the river side of the barge. The sailor – an officer, Serebin thought – fired at him twice, one round sliced the air above his head, the other hit the turbine and rang it like a bell. Serebin came around the corner, grabbed the rope handles of the hatch cover, and, with the recommended *slow, steady pull,* removed it.

The next thing he saw was the night sky. He'd been up in the air, he knew, but not for long. Because the *next* thing he saw was the Colossus, well, half of it anyhow, that had risen about ten feet off the barge and was now on its way back down, on end, still wearing its tarpaulin. It landed on its other half with a magnificent *clang,* then tilted over into the canal with a splash that sent a wave of water across the dock. Toward the pilot station. Which had lost a corner of itself and modestly lowered half its roof in case somebody tried to look inside.

Serb bastard — did you know? Not a land mine, an anti-tank mine.

He'd been lucky, he realized. By rights he should be somewhere up on the hill, but he was in business now and he didn't mean to leave it unfinished. He rolled over the edge of the next barge, barge three, and, using its cargo for cover, crawled to the hatch at the end nearest the tugboat. He took hold of the ropes, pulled, pulled harder, and the hatch cover came free in his hands. He swore, and peered into the depths of the barge's interior, saw the remnant of wire shining silver in the water, and came fairly close to going down there after it. Actually, very close.

On his way to barge two, he heard the patrol boat coming, engine wide open, searchlight beam moving down the canal. By now the crew had got its machine guns going, and began by raking the cabin of the *Empress,* splintering wood and shattering glass, the boat swinging on its tie line with the force of the heavy rounds. Serebin smelled burning and looked over his shoulder. The pilot station was on fire — had the blast wave blown the fireplace into the room? By the light of the dancing flames he saw a shadowy figure, running up the hillside through the trees. Zolti? Erma? He didn't know, but clearly this river was not, at the moment, the best place to be.

He was extremely careful with the hatch cover on barge two, visualizing the wire loop at the base of the mine's trigger, watching the wire as it depressed the lever, and, in the moment before the explosion, taking back what he'd called Captain Draza. Because the mine had been centered on the barge, the wire run far enough back so that the force of the blast was taken by the underside of the turbine.

And the hull. Because all that remained of the Colossus and its barge were bubbles. And the neighboring barges had been pulled halfway below the water by their towing links when the middle barge sank. He saw no more. Pressed his body between deck and gunwale as the mine went off, then covered his head with his arms as wood and metal rained down from above. He felt the barge begin to sink beneath him. Moved on to the first barge in line.

Somebody saw him.

He heard hunters' cries from the patrol boat, a long machine gun burst chewed up the deck a foot away, and he ran, then dove for shelter on the dock side of the turbine. Now he couldn't reach the hatch cover – on the river side of the barge, the large-calibre bullets tore the gunwale apart, and the patrol boat crept forward to try to get a firing angle for its gunner. They were excited, now that they knew where he was and what he was doing. As Serebin, on hands and knees, fled further into the defilade of the turbine, the light probed wildly and the gunner began to fire at the turbine itself, which pinged and rattled and echoed as it was hit, the occasional tracer ricochet sailing off into the night. And some of the rounds, hammered off with great enthusiasm but not all that much precision, ripped through the deck and, he hoped, down through the bottom.

The machine gun stopped abruptly – those long, indulgent bursts were soon enough, he knew, punished with a hiss of compressed air and a mad scramble by the server to feed in a new belt. Serebin looked at his watch, it had stopped at 11:08. Marrano was waiting for him downriver at Berzasca, but he couldn't move. One step away from the cover of the turbine, and that would be that. The pilot station was burning brighter now, he could hear the crackle of old wood, smoke drifted over the river, and the flames illuminated the dock with orange light. So, no darkness for him.

The officer on the patrol boat now came to his senses. Certainly he'd been on the radio, certainly other boats had been dispatched, and it had certainly occurred to him that he'd better win this little war before they showed up. So, all he needed to do was appoint a few volunteers to board the barge, use the turbine for cover, and attack from both ends. Serebin knew it would come to that and, soon enough, the sound of the patrol boat engine came toward him, as it maneuvered to position itself next to the barge. Now he had to do the one thing he most didn't want to do.

He turned, saw that the barge had been roped to a cleat, but, when he pushed against the edge of the dock, there was perhaps a foot of clearance. He lay prone on the gunwale, hesitated, finally slid one leg into the water. Bit his lip, then lowered himself the rest of the way. It was like being packed in ice, the cold gripped him so hard he could barely breathe. And then, the patrol boat's motion in the canal sent a gentle current toward the barge, which pressed against him, and began to squeeze his chest between the hull and the rough slab of timber that framed the dock. He fought it with both hands but it didn't give, so he had seconds to pull himself up on the gunwale. And into the light, into the view of the patrol boat. Still, better to die that way than to be crushed to death. As he started to climb, the barge moved. Only an inch, but enough. Using his hands, he slid himself along the timber to the edge of the hull, took a breath, went under.

Not more than a few feet to the tug, but cold and black as death. Finally a groping hand found the side of the boat and he hauled himself over the low freeboard and onto the deck. He was exhausted, finished. He lay still for a time, then began to work his hands, which had gone numb and stiff in the freezing water.

When he opened his eyes he saw that the patrol boat had maneuvered itself next to the barge, and, for a bare instant, there was a flicker of motion in the shadow of the turbine. Somebody on the boat began calling out to him – *you can surrender, we won't hurt you, there's custard for dessert.* It was all in Roumanian and he understood not a word of it but he got the general idea. In fact, it was whatever might keep him from hearing the armed sailors as they crawled around on the barge.

Not long until they figured out he wasn't there, so he slid forward as quickly as he could until he reached the foot of the steps that led up to the pilot cabin. Then he heard pistol shots, and he froze. Next came a shouted conversation between barge and patrol boat, and suddenly the searchlight swept over the water, the other barges, and finally the tugboat. Serebin lay completely still, pinned in the white beam, and waited for the machine gun.

It didn't come. The searchlight played on the cabin, then moved, slowly now, across the hill above the burning pilot station. Serebin scuttled up the steps and knelt at the foot of the helm. He made a fist and, imitating what Erma had done, hit the board skirting below the wheel. Nothing happened. He tried reaching behind the panel, but it was blocked by a board across the bottom. Again, he pounded. Nothing. *Christ, there's a trick to it.* Then he stood, turned his arm parallel to the skirting, and hit it with the side of his fist. And, by means of some fiendish carpenter's alchemy he could not imagine, it popped open.

The Mannlicher was nice and heavy, he knelt back down and curled around it, shivering, and, with thick, frozen fingers, managed to release the magazine. *Loaded.* He pushed it back in place with the heel of his hand, heard it lock in place with an emphatic click – the Austrians made good weapons – and worked the slide. The same fool's demon that had tried to trick him into blowing himself up now suggested it would be a perfectly fine idea to fire from the cabin. But, once again, he stopped just in time. Crawled back to the stern, got as low as he could, lined the barrel sight up with the center of the searchlight, and squeezed the trigger.

But the Austrians' good weapons didn't always send the bullets where the sight said they were going – low or high, left or right, he didn't know. However, all was not lost; the light remained undamaged but, as one of the sailors howled and swore like a man who's hit his thumb with a hammer, the beam shot straight up into the sky and stayed there. On the patrol boat, all hell broke loose – running shapes, shouted orders. Serebin waited, held his right wrist with his left hand and fought to keep the Mannlicher steady. When, a moment later, the light went back to work, it swung toward the stern of the tugboat. Had they seen the muzzle flare? He fired, shifted the gunsight, tried again, and once more. Then, with one brilliant, white, dazzling, final flash, the light exploded.

Serebin wasted no time. Blood pounding, head down, he sprinted for the bow, leapt onto the dock, and ran up the hill into the night.

It was damp and still in the forest, all wet leaves and bare trees. He climbed quickly, avoiding the path, and made it halfway up the slope when he realized he either had to sit down or fall down. He lowered himself to the ground, braced his back against a tree, wrapped his arms around himself and tried, by force of will, to stop shivering.

Looking through the woods below him, he watched the scene on the river. The roof of the pilot station had now collapsed into the burning walls, the second barge was gone and had taken the third barge down with it. The last barge in line was heeled over on its side, its turbine halfway into the canal. Sinking, he hoped. Why hadn't he thought to punch a few holes in the things? The patrol boat had tied up to the dock, but its search-light was still dark, and the officer hadn't, as far as he could see, sent crewmen up into the forest to look for him.

As the *Empress* was escorted toward the Moldova Veche station, he'd calculated the distance to the bridge on the Berzasca river as close to twenty-seven kilome-ters. It would take him all night – maybe well into the morning, to walk that far. Would Marrano still be there? Serebin wasn't sure. He would stay as long as he could, but the neighborhood wasn't going to get any friendlier as the night wore on and the Roumanians began to look for him. Still, there was no other choice, it was a long way back to Belgrade. And if Marrano, for whatever reason, was forced to abandon the meeting place, the only alternative left for Serebin was crossing the river into Yugoslavia.

He forced himself to his feet, found a tree-branch walking stick in a tangle of underbrush, and started climbing.

Count Szechenyi's theory of road building was simple enough: cut a right angle into a mountainside. This made for a winding ledge above steep canyons, shad-owed by Carpathian peaks that soared up into the night sky. Was the road in Transylvania? South of there, but not far. Maybe it didn't have bats, or coachmen driving black-plumed horses – yet, but it had everything else. Fog, that thickened by the hour, the steady wash of the river on the cliffs below, rocky outcrops that hung over-head, at least one owl – and something else he could only imagine, sometimes a deserted valley, and a wind that sighed in the trees, froze him to the bone, and now and then stirred the fog to reveal a crescent slice of pale and waning moon.

Enormous silence. And not a human soul to be seen.

For that much, he was grateful. At one point he stopped to rest, realized that the Mannlicher was getting heavier with every step, opened the magazine to find a single bullet, and threw the gun into the forest below. It did occur to him that an hour of sleep might actually speed him on his way, but he knew better than to do that. *Speed you on your way to heaven.* So he rose and trudged on, singing quietly to himself as he marched.

All through the hours of the night, he walked. Then, as light touched the eastern sky, he heard a creaking wheel, and the thud of hooves on stone, coming up behind him. He stepped off the road, half-ran, half-slid a little way down the hill, and hid behind a tree until he could see what it was. An oxcart, with high wheels built of thick planks, a man and a woman in the black clothing of Roumanian peasants sitting together on the driver's seat. Serebin decided to take a chance, and returned to the road.

When the man saw him he pulled on the reins, tipped his battered black hat, the woman beside him moved to make room, and Serebin climbed up next to them. In the cart, a small shape carefully sewn into a sheet. Serebin, in French, offered his sympathies, which, without understanding a word of it, the couple perfectly understood, and the woman thanked him in Roumanian.

This was better than walking, though not all that much faster. The ox plodded steadily along as the gray dawn – farm roosters at it in the distance – turned into a gray morning. The road grew wider as stone turned to dirt, and they passed through a series of mountain villages, sixteenth-century villages – mud, straw, and cow manure. In a narrow valley, a column of mounted soldiers approached from the other direction. Were they searching for fugitives? Serebin didn't let them get a look at his face, but when the officer at the head of the column saw what was in the cart he removed his hat, and inclined his head toward the couple.

Serebin rode on the oxcart until mid-morning, then they stopped by a path that wound through the fields – to a church, he thought, and a graveyard. Serebin thanked them, and continued on foot.

But not for long. When he saw, in the distance, a pair of bicycle riders, he rushed into the woods, tripped on a root and went sprawling. Then cursed himself for fleeing from phantoms – at the potential cost of a sprained ankle – until he saw that the young men on the bicycles wore the uniform of the national gendarmerie and had rifles slung on their backs. He waited until they passed, returned to the road, but was forced to hide three times in the next hour; first by a big sedan, then by a truck, and last by a band of singing German hikers. That did it. He found a cattle path and followed it to a village where he managed, by greeting an old woman over a stake fence, to buy an apple and a loaf of bread. Then decided not to test his luck any further and found himself a hideout in a willow grove, where he ate the apple and the bread, drank from a brook – the water so cold it made his teeth ache – and settled in to wait for dusk.

He woke suddenly, an hour later, had no idea where he was, returned to consciousness, and still didn't know where he was. He spent the rest of the day in the willow grove, sometimes dozing, sometimes watching the river, and was back on the road after sunset, now glad of the darkness and the gathering fog. The next village he came to was bigger than the others. It had a street – paved with quarried stone a long, long time ago, and a church – a cross mounted on the dome of an old Turkish mosque.

A small café was packed with men in dark suits, Serebin waited for one of them to leave, then tried to ask him the name of the village. It took some effort by both of them, but eventually the man saw the light and cried out, 'Ah, Berzasca. Berzasca!' Serebin kept walking. A few minutes later, he found the river, and an arched bridge built of stone block. Not the bridge he was looking for but, at least, the right river.

There was no path to the logging road – Serebin was supposed to have been on the *Empress,* having unloaded his cargo at the Stenka ridge – so he had to walk beside the river, forcing his way through the high reeds of a flooded marsh, with water above his knees. This took a long time, but he kept at it, and eventually saw a rickety bridge, moss-covered boards nailed across two logs. At the end of the bridge he found a pair of ruts that wound through the trees – probably the logging road and not the worst one he'd ever seen. But no sign of a car, and no sign of Marrano.

Serebin sat on the edge of the bridge and thought about what to do next. *Fishing boat down to Constanta? Oxcart, or car, up to Hungary? Try to cross the river?* Well, that was a problem. Because one thing they didn't have in this part of the world was bridges. Not where the river formed a border between nations, they didn't, and that was the Danube's fate once it left the plains of Hungary. Not that they hadn't built bridges, they had, at optimistic moments over the centuries, but then somebody always burned them, so why bother. And, in fact, for pretty much all the recorded history in this part of the world, most of the bridges had been built by conquerors – Romans after Dacian gold, Ottoman Turks, Austrian engineers – and had thereby earned themselves a bad reputation.

So then? He didn't know. He was tired, and sore, and cold, and that, just then, was all he knew. *God, send me a packet of dry Sobranies and a box of matches.* Something made him look up and there, at the other end of the bridge, a figure stood in the shadows at the edge of the forest. A sylvan deity, perhaps, but not the common sort – its hands hung casually at its sides, one of them holding a revolver, the other a briefcase. 'I was beginning to think you weren't coming,' Marrano said.

They had to follow the river back to Berzasca – the only other choice was to walk a long way east, where the logging road met the main road. Serebin told his story, Marrano listened thoughtfully, and now and then asked questions, most of which couldn't be answered. 'Certainly,' Serebin said, 'they knew we were coming.'

Marrano sighed. 'Well, at least we did something. Any idea what happened to the people on the tugboat?'

'They ran, with everyone else, when the first mine went off. They could've gone north, into Hungary, or maybe they stole a boat, somewhere downriver. With any luck at all, they got away.'

Pushing the tall reeds aside, they plodded on through the marsh until they reached the village street. 'Where's the car?' Serebin said.

'In an alley. I waited overnight, but when you didn't show up, I thought I'd better hide it.'

'So,' Serebin said, 'that's that. Now it's up to the Serbs.'

Marrano stopped for a moment, unbuckled his briefcase, and took out a newspaper. A Roumanian newspaper, from a nearby town, but the headline was easy enough to read, even in the darkness, because the print was quite large. COUP D'ETAT IN YUGOSLAVIA, it said.

'Who?'

'Us.'

'Will it last?'

'Not for long, the Fuehrer's chewing his carpet.'

'Too bad. What happened?'

'British agents kidnapped Stoyadinovich, Hitler's man in Belgrade. But then, forty-eight hours later, the government caved in anyhow and signed with the Axis. So, yesterday morning, the coup.'

'Back and forth.'

'Yes.'

'Was it the army?'

'Led by air force officers. Nominally, the country is now run by a seventeen-year-old king.'

They turned down a long alley. In a courtyard at the end, two boys were sitting on the hood of an Aprilia sedan, sharing a cigarette. Marrano spoke to them in Roumanian and gave them some money, clearly more than they expected. One of them asked a question, Marrano smiled and answered briefly.

'What was that about?' Serebin asked, sliding into the passenger seat.

'Could they drive it.'

Marrano started the car, eased back out of the alley, and drove through the village, back toward the Szechenyi road. 'We'll have to avoid the border post,' he said. 'By now, they've got themselves organized and they're certainly looking for you.'

The idea of cars, in 1805, did not occur to Count Szechenyi. On the dirt road, the speedometer needle quivered at thirty kilometers an hour but, once they reached the hewed rock, it stayed well below that. And they were soon enough in mountain weather; rising mist, like smoke, and a fine drizzle – the stone cliffs at the edge of the road shining wet and gray in the glow of the headlights. The road was, at least, empty. They worked their way past a single Gypsy wagon, and after that there was nobody.

'How far is it?' Serebin asked.

'To the border? About sixty kilometers.'

Serebin watched the speedometer. 'Five hours, maybe.'

'Could be.' Marrano glanced at his watch. 'It's after nine. We'll want to get rid of the car and take to the fields before dawn.'

They crept along at walking speed, water gathering on the windshield until it began to run in droplets and Marrano turned on the single wiper, producing a blurred semicircle above the dashboard and a rhythmic squeak.

Marrano peered into the darkness, then braked carefully and the car rolled to a stop.

'What is it?'

'A hole.'

Serebin got out of the car and inspected it. 'Not bad,' he called out. 'But sharp.' He motioned Marrano forward, used hand signals so that the wheels ran on either side of the hole, then took a step back, and another, to make room for the car. Glancing behind him, he saw that the cliff fell away down to the river, black water flecked with white foam.

The Aprilia drove past the hole, Serebin got back in, and they managed a few kilometers without incident, until a doe and her fawn appeared from the brush and the car slid a little as Marrano braked. The deer galloped away from them, then bounded off down the hillside.

1:20. A light in the distance, a suffused glow from somewhere below the road. Marrano turned out the headlights, drove slowly for a few hundred feet, than shut off the ignition and let the car roll to a silent stop. Even before they opened the doors, they could hear the sound of working engines as it rose from the river. They walked up the road and looked over the edge of the hill.

The Moldova Veche pilot station was floodlit by a giant river tug, with crane barges working at either end of the canal, and patrol boats anchored offshore. A few wisps of smoke still rose from the ruined structure, and two German officers stood on the dock, pointing as they talked. The last barge in line was nowhere to be seen, and the *Empress* had apparently been taken away.

'Turbines in the canal?' Marrano whispered.

Serebin nodded.

'Not so bad – they're working day and night.'

He was being decent about it, Serebin thought. 'Probably won't stop anybody from going anywhere.'

'No? Well, they've got the Germans in here, must mean something.'

They got back in the car. Marrano kept the lights off and drove close to the cliff wall, staying as far as he could from the sight line below them. When they were safely around a curve, he turned the lights back on. 'Is it getting narrower, here?'

'A little, maybe.'

The Aprilia climbed for a few minutes, the road swung away from the river, then descended, Marrano pumping the brakes as the sedan whined in first gear. In the sky ahead of them, a white flicker, followed by a zigzag flash against the clouds and a long, low roll of thunder as the rain intensified. 'Spring storm,' Marrano said. The wiper squeaked as it cycled back and forth. 'Must get that fixed,' he said.

2:00. 2:15. Hard work for Marrano, leaning over the wheel and squinting into the rain, shifting back and forth between second and third gears. The engine didn't seem to like either one and, as it labored, Serebin watched the needle on the temperature gauge.

'Road's not meant for cars,' Marrano said.

'Horse and carriage.'

'Yes. Make a note of that, would you. For next time.'

'I'll keep it in mind.'

A few minutes later, Marrano said, 'What was that?'

The road curved, hanging on the side of a mountain, and he'd seen a light, thought he had, somewhere ahead where, for a moment, a distant section of the road came into view.

'Some kind of light,' Serebin said.

'Another car?'

'Yes, maybe.' But on reflection he didn't think so. 'Was it fire?'

Marrano had to slow down as the road drifted to the left, then narrowed to the width of a single car. 'We're back on the river,' he said. Barely crawling, they approached a sharp corner to the right, then back to the left. On the other side, an army roadblock.

In the flickering light of pitch pine torches driven into crevices in the rock, a squad of soldiers, most of them trying to shelter in a hollow at the foot of the cliff, and a command car with a canvas top, parked against the cliff wall. Marrano managed to get the Aprilia around it with inches to spare, then stopped in front of a barrier – a pole laid across two x-shaped sawhorses made of cut logs.

Marrano unbuckled his briefcase, on the floor by the gearshift, and found what he was after just as an officer, water streaming down his rubber cape, stepped into the headlights and held up a hand.

Marrano rolled down the window. 'Yes, sir?'

The officer came around to the driver's window and peered into the car. He was young and vain and very pleased with himself, stared first at Marrano, then at Serebin, and said, 'Passports.'

Marrano took his passport from the inside pocket of his jacket and handed it to the officer. 'He doesn't have one,' he said casually, nodding at Serebin.

'Why not?'

'He's coming from the Bucovina. The Russians took it away.'

Serebin got just enough of this – the USSR had occupied the province a few months earlier.

Not an answer the officer expected. 'He'll have to wait, then. You can go ahead.'

'He can't wait, sir. It's his wife, she's giving birth in Belgrade.'

'Too bad.' He looked directly at Serebin and said, 'You. Get out of the car.'

'His wife, sir,' Marrano said. 'Please, she needs him by her side, she's not well.'

The officer's mouth grew sulky. 'Get out,' he said, flipping his rain cape aside and resting a hand on the flap of his holster.

Marrano held his fist just below the edge of the window, where only the officer could see it, paused a moment for effect, then uncurled his fingers. Four gold coins gleamed in the torchlight. The officer stared, transfixed. This was a fortune. He reached through the window, took the coins, and put them somewhere beneath his cape. Then he stood up straight. 'Now get out,' he said. 'Both of you.'

Serebin was watching Marrano's left foot, where it pressed the clutch pedal against the floorboard. It rose – quickly, but under control – as his other foot stepped on the gas. There was a soft thump – the officer sideswiped by the car, then Marrano drove full speed into the pole. Didn't work – the sawhorses slid backwards, so Marrano jammed the accelerator to the floor, the engine howled as the tires spun on wet rock, one of the sawhorses tipped on its back and the other disappeared over the edge of the road. The car leaped forward, bouncing over the pole, past a soldier's white face, his mouth open wide with surprise. Marrano hammered his hand against a knob on the dashboard and the lights went out. Something pinged against the trunk, something else made a spiderweb in the rear window.

Maybe Marrano could see ahead of them, Serebin couldn't. Only rain and the dark bulk of the cliff flying by on the right. Marrano speed-shifted, lost the road, and Serebin's side of the car went scraping along the rock. Marrano jerked the wheel, the car fishtailed and slid toward the outer edge of the road, then he took it back the other way, the right front fender caught the cliff, a headlight ring flew up in the air, and the car straightened out.

The road twisted, cornered, switched back on itself, rain streamed across the black windshield. Marrano, hands in a death grip on the wheel, powered through every turn, worked mostly in second gear, slammed his foot on the brake until the rear wheels began to slide, then accelerated out of the skid.

Then, on a long, even climb, the car lit up – a pair of headlights behind them, glaring yellow beams that sparkled on the fractured glass in the back window. Marrano ducked, grabbed Serebin by the shoulder of his jacket and pulled him down. A stone chip hit Serebin's door and he said, 'They're shooting at us.'

The car swerved violently, Marrano fought the wheel and said, 'Tire.' The headlights moved closer, the car wobbled on the flat tire, ground it off, then bounced along on the rim. 'It's over,' Marrano said. They were sideways for a moment, then off again as the back window blew in.

'Now,' Serebin said. 'Go ahead.'

Marrano said shit and turned left.

In the air, the silence went on for a long time. Serebin's mind was empty, or maybe just a name, as though it were the first word of an apology.

Then they hit some saplings, which bowed before

they broke, then brush, then earth; then a sudden drop that stood the car on its front end. It stayed there for a moment, canted over in slow motion, and came to rest upside down. Serebin wound up sprawled across the roof, facing the windshield, where two red impact marks pocked the glass. He felt the blood, seeping from his hairline, then smelled gasoline, kicked savagely at the door, which was already open, and slid himself out on the ground. He crawled around the car, found the driver's side door jammed shut, reached through the broken window, and cranked it up – with the car on its roof – until it was out of the way. Marrano's foot was caught in the steering wheel, Serebin got him loose, then hauled him out through the open window. This took some time, because only one hand worked, his wrist either broken or sprained.

He could see the lights of the command car, parked up on the road, and he could hear voices. Excited, he thought. Somebody had a flashlight, up there, and tried to find the sedan. 'Briefcase,' Marrano said.

'Can you walk?'

Marrano mumbled something he couldn't hear.

From the opposite shore, thunder, but not close, the storm moving west, the rain a light, steady beat on the river. Serebin leaned into the car and searched for the briefcase, finally found it pinned between the floor and the brake pedal, which had been bent on its side. He took out a small bag of gold coins and slid the revolver in his belt.

Some of the soldiers were now working their way down the hill – the flashlight, masked by a hand, was still clearly visible. Somebody fell, somebody swore, somebody whispered angrily. Serebin drew the revolver and thumbed the safety off. Turned around and took a good long look at the river, perhaps forty feet away. He put the safety back on, got his good hand under Marrano's arm, and began to drag him toward the water.

Plenty of driftwood logs on the shore, all sizes. Serebin got one of them launched, draped Marrano over it, held on and kicked, carefully keeping his feet well below the surface, until he felt the pull of the current. Back on the hillside, the search party was getting near the car. Serebin hung on to the log by looping his arm around it, kept his good hand on Marrano.

On shore, they'd apparently reached the car, and there was a loud conversation with somebody up on the road. *Search the woods.* Looking down the river, Serebin saw a low shape ahead of them, some kind of promontory jutting out from the shoreline. It took quite some time to get there, his legs numb and lifeless when he finally beached the log on the sand. Marrano was unconscious, Serebin pulled him a few feet up the slope, then fell. *Done.* No more he could do. He tried to force himself to get up, couldn't, passed out.

29 March.

'Good morning to you, sir.'

Logically, there was something in this Balkan opera of a city that could surprise the doorman at the Srbski Kralj but it sure as hell wasn't Serebin. With four days' growth of beard, wearing a sheepskin fisherman's vest one of his rescuers had given him, a bloody rag around his head, his left wrist bound to a stick with fishing line – just good old Mr. Thing in Room 74.

'Good morning,' Serebin said.

'Lovely day.'

'Yes, thank you, it is.'

'Need any help, sir?'

'No, thank you.'

Limping, he got himself up the stairs to the top floor, then down a long hallway. *Stained carpets, green walls, the aroma of yesterday's dinner;* all very appealing to Serebin, who was lucky to be alive and knew it. That went for Marrano as well. In the hospital for a day or two but he would live to fight again.

He stopped in front of the door numbered 74. He'd had a key to this door, once upon a time, but it was long gone. Or was it this door? Because, if this was his room, why was somebody laughing inside? Tentatively, he knocked. Then knocked louder and Captain Draza, wearing only undershirt and underpants, threw the door open and gazed at him with surprise and delight. 'Say, look at you!'

A fine party, it must have been. Or, perhaps, still was. Captain Jovan, in underpants only but wearing a uniform cap, was sleeping in the room's easy chair, a bottle between his thighs. The air was thick with black tobacco and White Gardenia, the bed occupied by three young women, one very young, all of them striking, but striking in different ways. *Mysterious, Milkmaid,* and *Ballerina,* he named them. Mysterious and Ballerina sound asleep, Milkmaid sitting propped up on pillows, reading the book of Anya Zak's poetry she'd given him for the train. 'Hello,' she said, rather formally, and, an afterthought, pulled the sheet up over her bare breasts.

'Ah, Natalya,' Draza said. What way is that to greet a guest?

Jovan was suddenly awake. 'Welcome home,' he said. 'We've been waiting for you.'

The room had been – sifted. Nothing was broken, but everything had been picked up and put down somewhere else. This apparently made it hard for Captain Draza to find what he was looking for but, eventually, beneath a pile of women's clothes, tunics, and a holstered pistol on a belt, a newspaper was discovered. 'Famous guy,' Draza said, handing him the paper and pointing to a headline at the bottom of the first page:

BRITISH SABOTEURS ATTACK RIVER TARGETS

They had put the Moldova Veche pilot station out of commission for ten days to two weeks. Burned down the office, destroying valuable charts and records. And severely damaged a repair ship, when a booby trap blew up while a sunken barge was being craned to the surface.

Draza took the newspaper and read his favorite part aloud. '"The Axis has been put on notice that the British Lion will strike anywhere, at any time, to disrupt the supply lines of its enemies."'

Jovan liked hearing that. 'To victory,' he said, and drank to it.

'You don't mind we're here, do you?' Draza said. 'We were waiting for you to come back, so, we thought, what better place to wait?'

'You're welcome here,' Serebin said. 'But I'm going to wash, and then I need to sleep.'

Jovan stumbled out of his chair, caught himself, then stood upright, swaying. 'Right here,' he said. 'It's very comfortable.'

'And we'll be quiet,' Draza said, quietly.

The following morning he stopped at a barbershop for a shave, bought a new jacket, and, feeling better than he had for some time — the cut on his head was healing nicely — went to see Marrano in the hospital. When Serebin showed him the newspaper he laughed, holding his side. 'So, success,' he said, 'and you'll notice what it doesn't say. About German diplomats.'

Serebin had noticed, had become, over the years, something of an expert on what newspapers didn't say. 'Any chance the Yugoslavs will blow up the river?'

'Not now. They're mobilizing — they've had their

coup, and they'll pay for it soon enough. All the foreign journalists are getting out, legations shutting down, arms dealers – that whole crowd, going back wherever they came from. As for us, you'd better get out right away, I'll follow in a day or two. Our friends in the air force will know the details.'

'Then I'll see you in Istanbul,' Serebin said.

'Well, somewhere.'

Serebin was glad to go home, wherever that was. He'd slept in the chair, after drinking much of the night with the captains. And their girlfriends. Just looking at them, blithely immodest as they strutted about, smoked cigars, drank and laughed and teased, had done his heart immense good. And before Draza passed out, he'd found it necessary to tell Serebin how sweet these girls were. 'Patriots,' he'd said, pretty much the last word before Serebin and Jovan put him to bed.

That was one word for it, but then, early in the morning on the day after he said good-bye to Marrano, it made a lot more sense. Out on a field – an airfield because there were planes parked on the weedy grass, but pasture was what it was – a line of biplanes. 'The Yugoslav air force,' Draza said.

Hawker Harts, and Furies, Bristol Bulldogs – with their wings on struts above and below the pilot cockpit, armed with a single machine gun, they were the aircraft of the early 1930s but they looked like they belonged to an earlier time – descendants of the Spads and De Havillands of the 1914 war – and Serebin doubted they could stay long in the air with German Messerschmitts.

'You have others?' Serebin said.

'No. This is what the British sold us, but they're faster than you think.'

He sent a mechanic off to get Serebin a flying jacket and goggles – he would fly in the cockpit, for gunner or bombardier, behind the pilot.

'You have to fight with what you have,' Draza said. 'Anyhow, the same Englishman that sold us the planes helped us with the coup. So, I leave the judgments to others, but that's the way the world is, right?'

Serebin put on his flying gear and climbed up into the gunner cockpit behind Draza, who turned and handed him a road map of Yugoslavia and Macedonia. 'Change of plan,' he said, 'you're going to Thassos.'

'In Greece?'

'Sort of. An island, smugglers' paradise. The Adriatic's no good now – too much fighting; Luftwaffe, RAF, Italian navy. It's crowded.'

The mechanic pulled the blocks from the wheels, then spun the single propeller, which produced coughs and smoke and backfires and, eventually, ignition. The Hawker bumped across the rutted field, lifted with a roar, flew over the Srbski Kralj and waggled its wings, then, bouncing up through the thermals, climbed to five thousand feet and turned south. In a bright blue sky, above fields and forests, sometimes a village. Captain Draza turned halfway around in his seat, shouted 'Mobilization,' and pointed off to the east. Extraordinary, to see it from above. At least a thousand carts, drawn by plodding teams of oxen, long columns of infantry, field guns on caissons. Draza turned round again, and, with a broad grin, made the victory sign.

3 April. London. It was a long ride by tube to Drake's club, on Grosvenor Square, so Josef the waiter always left home early to make sure he wasn't late to work. Now and then, when his line had been hit the night before, he had to walk, and sometimes, going home after work, he had to make his way through the blackout, or wait in an air raid shelter until the all clear sounded.

Still, he didn't mind. A cheerful soul, with a game leg

and merry eyes, who'd lost his hair in his twenties – 'from worrying,' he liked to say – he'd snuck out of Prague in April of '39, after the Germans marched into the city, and, with wife and baby, somehow made his way to London. The young men who'd worked at the Drake had gone to war, so new service staff had to be hired, but the management was more than pleased with Josef.

Josef with a hard *J*, to the spruce types who stopped at their club for drinks or dinner. He worked hard at being a good waiter – he'd been a good teacher of mathematics – doing his best meant something to Josef and the club stewards knew it. Now that his wife was pregnant again they let him do all the work he wanted, and often sent him home with a little something extra in a napkin. Life wasn't easy, with rationing, for a family man.

So they let him work private dinners, which got him home after midnight, but every little bit helped. The private dinner on that April night was given in honor of Sir Ivan Kostyka, and went pretty much like they all did. A dozen gentlemen, and rather elegant, even for Drake's – Lord this and Colonel that, another known as Pebbles. Josef overheard what was said without really listening to it. Two or three speeches, one of them in a distinctly foreign accent, with words like 'appreciation' and 'gratitude.' For? Well, Josef didn't know – the speakers didn't precisely say, and his English wasn't all that good anyhow.

He did, however, notice that, like the man with the foreign accent, some of the men were not native to Britain; one with a white goatee, another with a vast stomach and a rumbling laugh. Foreigners like him. Well, not much like him.

Josef had cleared the dessert, and was preparing to serve the port, when Sir Ivan stood and thanked the men at the table for honoring him. He was sincere in this, Josef could see, even moved. One of the men said

'Hear, hear,' then they all rose, as if to propose a toast. Josef waited patiently, but it wasn't exactly a toast. What happened next was unusual, but, he thought, *well done,* as the spruce types had said more than once during the dinner. Well done because it was from the heart, and they all had the sort of self-confidence that allows men to sing without fussing overmuch about carrying a tune. It was, anyhow, an easy tune to carry:

> *For he's a jolly good fellow,*
> *for he's a jolly good fellow,*
> *for he's a jolly good fell-ow,*
> *which nobody can deny.*
> *Which nobody can deny,*
> *which nobody can deny,*
> *for he's a jolly good fell-ell-ow . . .*
> *which nobody can deny!*

29 July.

Serebin woke up long after midnight, tried to go back to sleep, then gave up and climbed out of bed. No point tossing and turning – especially on a hot summer night. Summer nights were famously hot in Istanbul but it was more than that. It wasn't the heat that woke him, he thought, it was a cricket on the terrace, the soft air, the sense of a summer night of life going by.

The floorboards creaked as he walked down the hall to the white room. Plenty of paper and pencils there. He'd never told Marie-Galante that Tamara had meant the room as a writer's cell, but it had taken her about ten minutes to figure it out. 'We'll put you in here,' she'd said. So, mornings, there he was. It was hard, with war everywhere, to figure out what he ought to say, or who might want to hear it. Still, he kept at it, because he always had.

As for her, she'd done exactly what she said she

would, and so they *ran away together.* Not far, only to Besiktas and the little house above the sea, but, nothing wrong with that. She'd bought new towels and sheets and tablecloths, marshaled the Ukrainian sisters in a magnificent French campaign of waxing and polishing, so that now everything smelled like honey and glowed like gold.

Out on the Bosphorus, a dark ship with a long, white wake, headed up toward the Black Sea. Maybe to Bulgaria or Roumania, he thought, but not much farther, unless it was a supply ship – German, Italian, or neutral. One place it wasn't going was Odessa. They were fighting there now, the city besieged by Roumanian armies, the defenders wildly outnumbered, but holding on, refusing to surrender. Stories of heroism every day in the newspapers, which they clipped, at the IRU office, and pinned to the bulletin board. Serebin went in from time to time, offering to help out, to do whatever he could. So, a new *Harvest,* but the émigré writers here weren't as good as the ones in Paris. Patriotic now – it was Russia fighting, not the USSR, Stalin had said that and everybody believed him. On the Danube, the oil barges moved upriver to Germany, day and night.

They followed the war, Serebin and Marie-Galante, in the newspapers with their morning coffee, on the radio when they had afternoon drinks, and with people they sometimes saw in the evenings. Marie-Galante could not be in the world without invitations. The precise nature of the social chemistry eluded him, but somehow people knew she was there and invited her places, and sometimes she accepted, and so they went.

They had one that evening – he thought it was that evening, he'd have to make sure. Some kind of dinner at the yacht club, a beautiful invitation, on thick, cream-colored stock with an elaborate crest on top. Given by people he'd never heard of, for, apparently, some couple connected with the Norwegian royal family, now in exile in London. What were they doing in Istanbul? Well, what was anybody doing. Waiting, mostly.

In the same post there'd been a note from Polanyi. He hoped they were well, perhaps he would see them at the royal dinner. 'Someone I want you to meet,' he'd said. Marie-Galante had stood the invitation on the mantelpiece above the fireplace, which was what she did when something appealed to her, so, clearly, they were going. It was – something to do. Not that they were bored, or anything like that.

He opened the drawer of the table, found a Sobranie and lit it. Turn the light on? Work for a while? No, he wanted only to watch this summer night as it went by. The ship was almost out of sight now, so he stared at the dark water, finished his cigarette, and walked back to the bedroom.

Too warm for a sheet or a blanket. He watched her for a moment as she slept, then lay down carefully on the bed. *Wouldn't want to wake her up.* But she slid back against him, her skin silky and cool, even on a hot summer night.

'Where were you?' she said, not really awake.

'Just walking around.'

'Oh *ours, mon ours,*' she sighed. 'What is to become of us.'

Silence, only the beat of waves at the foot of the cliff.

'No, no,' she said. '*Beside* that.'